HIS CURVY FRUSTRATION

A SMALL TOWN CURVY GIRL ROMANCE

BOOK BOYFRIENDS WANTED
BOOK FOUR

MARY E THOMPSON

BOOK BOYFRIENDS WANTED

Hi friend! Grab a slice of cake and a drink. It's always nice to have you visit. We know you don't want to miss anything, so sign up to keep in touch.

Romancing the Curves comes with subscriber exclusive freebies, sneak peeks, and a first look at everything Mary has to offer. Be the first to know about new releases and sales and all the curves ahead!

SUBSCRIBE NOW AT MARYETHOMPSON.COM

Happy reading!

To Mary, who is always there for me with encouragement, understanding, and a kick in the butt when I need it!

JAMES

I sipped my beer and took in the crowd around me. It was a quiet night at O'Kelley's, and I could drink in peace. I needed it. Everything in my life felt upside down lately. I didn't know what it was, but having a new partner to work with was not going to help the situation.

"Hey," a woman's voice said next to me.

I looked up and forced a smile. She was pretty, but I wasn't interested. "Hey."

"Want to get out of here?" she asked.

I looked more closely at her and finally recognized her. We'd slept together before, so a preamble wasn't necessary. It was good, but I was only out for a drink. I wasn't looking for a woman to take home.

"Sorry, but I can't," I told her. I couldn't even remember her name. What kind of person had I become?

"Are you sure? Because I can wait if you need to finish your drink or something?"

I shook my head. "Nah, it's okay. You should go."

She narrowed her eyes and stared at me for another

minute. I waited for her to do something like toss a drink in my face, but she just walked away.

"Everything okay?" Hudson Grant, the owner and bartender of O'Kelley's, asked me.

I nodded. "Just great. Give me another. I'll be right back."

Hudson nodded and replaced my empty beer with a full one as I slid off the stool and headed for the bathrooms.

I was not the kind of man who hid from people in the bathroom, but that was exactly what I was doing. I didn't know who I'd become over the last year, but I did not like the man I was.

I washed my hands and walked out of the bathroom, only to have someone push me into the wall. My instinct was to shove them back and pin them, but her scent tickled my nose a second before she thrust her tongue into my mouth.

A part of me responded and kissed her back. I had no idea who she was, but it didn't matter. She was a woman and she was willing. It had been a while since I'd let myself just enjoy life, women, anything. I was playing the good samaritan thing a little too well through the summer, walking women home and leaving them on their doorstep without going inside.

I was ready to get inside this one.

But there was a little part inside my head that said I shouldn't. And that part won out.

I grabbed her shoulders and pried her off of me. It was the same woman who sat next to me at the bar. Her mouth was still open from trying to swallow me whole, and her lipstick was smeared on her lips. It took her a second to open her eyes.

"Why are you stopping? Want to just go into the bathroom?"

I blanched and wondered how big of an ass I really was. "No, sorry. Not tonight."

"But you looked at me before you came back here. You gave me the signal. I'm all ready for you." She pressed herself against me, rubbing her body on mine. My cock tried to get a rise out of her, but it was no better than watching a sappy movie. I was just not into it.

"I'm sorry, but I didn't mean to give you any sort of signal. I'm…not tonight."

"Are you meeting someone else?"

It sounded good. "Sure, yeah. I am."

"Oh," the woman finally said. She took a step back. "I didn't realize. I'm sorry."

I nodded and stepped around her. Women were nuts.

I walked back toward the bar, wiping my face to remove the lipstick I was sure was all over, and caught Hudson's eye. He smirked knowingly and walked away.

Another woman was sitting on the stool next to mine. She was stunning from behind. Perfect, round ass. Narrower through the waist. Curves for days. Even her hair was curly, tight black ringlets my fingers itched to run through.

But the last thing I needed was to have to fight off another woman. It didn't matter that one glance had my dick twitching, I was there for a night off.

With a sigh, I reclaimed my stool. She turned to look at me, a smile already curling her lips up.

Until she saw who I was.

"What the hell are you doing?" she blurted.

My night just got worse. I should go back to the woman who tried to accost me in the hallway. It would have been a better spend of my time than trying to play nice with Trinity Mayer. "Well, I was trying to enjoy my evening. I guess that's done now."

"Go sit over there," she snarled, nodding across the bar.

I picked up the glass in front of her and sniffed it, drawing back at the sweet scent. I set it down and lifted my glass, the one Hudson refilled before I went to the bathroom, and took a sip.

"I was here first," I said, flashing her a grin.

Trinity Mayer was the last person I needed to see. We butted heads since the day she arrived in MacKellar Cove. I was on duty when I saw her trying to break into a car on Riverview Road. It was parked in front of the new Waterfront Villas. Anyone would have assumed she was trying to steal something. The fact that it was daylight didn't mean people didn't do bad things.

She didn't see it that way. She thought I was profiling her and took offense to the fact that I tried to arrest her. Tried because the building manager saw us talking and vouched for her. Then he let her into her unit.

Trinity never let me forget that I made a mistake. I tried to talk to her about it when my friends became her friends, but she was less than interested. So instead, I tried to irritate the hell out of her every time we spoke.

She stood and picked up her drink, putting space between us. The way her shorts tugged at her ass had my cock pressing against my zipper.

"Are you running out on your check? Because I could arrest you for that," I said, wanting her to stay.

She glared at me over her shoulder, and I grinned. I loved that fire in her eyes. The fire that said she was the kind of woman who would be fun in the bedroom.

I hadn't had sex in a while, and great sex was definitely not happening. That had to be why I was thinking about sex with Trinity. She hated me, and I wasn't a big fan of hers. We were not going to get together, even for a night.

"I'm not leaving, just moving to another seat. One that isn't near you," she spat.

I couldn't stop my lips from lifting at her sassy words.

She walked away without another word. I watched her

head for a table for two in the corner. She could see the whole place from there and no one could sneak up behind her. Smart woman.

Hudson walked over and leaned against the bar in front of me. "You survived the bathroom?"

I rolled my eyes at him. "I think that woman is a sucker fish or something. She tried to leech onto me."

"You didn't have a problem with that a few months ago," Hudson said.

I shook my head. "I'm too old. I feel like I should be doing something different."

"We are not old," Hudson said firmly. "And should is a stupid word. Do what makes you happy. And if it's her, get the hell out of my bar."

I was about to ask who when Hudson walked away. Almost immediately, the same woman wrapped herself around me. "Did your date not show up?"

I fought the urge to groan and forced a smile for her. "Not a date."

"Oh, then you are free."

"No, I'm not," I said firmly, forcing her off of me. "I am not interested tonight. I don't think I can get much more clear than that. Please, leave me alone."

She glared at me like she couldn't believe I was rejecting her. I really didn't know what she expected, but she wasn't about to get it from me.

She huffed and stomped away. She gestured to her girl-friends who all turned and glared at me. One of them flipped me off. I rolled my eyes and looked away.

Hudson carried a plate of food out of the back. The smell of fried food and charred meat made my stomach growl. I wanted to ask him who ordered it but he didn't pause long enough. I watched as he headed for Trinity and set the plate in front of her.

Maybe if I played nice, she would share.

Before I reached her, another guy sat down. I pivoted to an empty stool, pretending that was my plan all along.

"Hey," the guy said. "How are ya?"

Really? That was his opening line?

"Who are you?" Trinity asked.

I glanced behind me at them. The guy grinned. I rolled my eyes. He had to be a decade younger than Trinity. But I had no idea what kind of guys she went for so maybe he was her type.

"I'm your next boyfriend," he said.

I snorted. He did not just say that.

Trinity leaned back and crossed her arms over her chest. "Oh, really? What makes you say that?"

He shrugged. "Well, you're hot and I saw you looking at me."

She nodded. There was no way she was buying his crap.

"Those are pretty low standards. What if I have a horrible personality? Or I talk while I eat?" she asked.

He grinned and leaned in. "You won't be able to say anything with me in your mouth."

I was up off my stool and grabbing the guy by the neck before she had time to respond. "Okay, time to go," I told the guy.

"What the hell, dude?" Trinity's next boyfriend shouted. "I was talking to her."

I shook my head at the man-child. "And she's here with me, son." I flashed my badge. "I hear you saying things like that to another woman, you'll be talking to a few bars all night, and not the kind you can walk out of when you choose."

I crossed my arms and blocked the guy from looking at Trinity. I was sure she could handle herself, but a guy like that needed to know he couldn't talk to any woman that way, not just Trinity.

"Whatever. She's not that hot anyway," the douche snarled before he walked away.

I glared after him for a second then turned to check on Trinity. She flipped me off.

"Really? Are you threatening an officer?"

She breathed a laugh and shook her head. "No, sir. That wasn't meant for you."

My cock ached at the sound of *sir* on her lips. I glanced toward where the guy went then sat down in the chair opposite her to hide my erection. "Why were you talking to him?" I asked a little more harshly than I intended.

She rolled her head back and stared up at the ceiling.

"He's just trying to screw you. He isn't really interested," I added.

"How do you know that isn't why I came here tonight?" she asked. One brow went up, daring me to argue with her.

I pulled back and studied her. My gaze slid down her curvy figure. She was stunning, if I was being honest. She usually wore low-cut tops that showed off her perfect breasts and tight bottoms that accented her hourglass figure. But she sat across from me in a fitted tee and long cotton shorts. She was not there to hook up. Not in those clothes.

"You aren't here for that. You'd be in one of your outfits that leaves nothing to the imagination if you were."

"Maybe I'm branching out. Looking for the kind of guy who wants a little mystery."

I raised an eyebrow and considered her for a long moment. "Why would you want a guy like that?"

"A guy like what?"

"A guy who just wants sex and has no intention of anything more? You know what that says about you, right?" I asked, hating her just a little for wanting to screw some random guy.

"Do you really think you're the only one who's allowed to go home with someone and it's okay? Are you really sitting here telling me I'm not allowed to sleep with whomever I want? Because last I checked, you have zero claim over my time or me, Officer," she spat.

Her chest heaved with her angry words. Her breath came out in pants. She was furious, and so was I. She was seriously telling me she was going to go home with some random guy. Didn't she know how dangerous and stupid that was?

"And here I thought you were smarter than that."

She opened her mouth, probably to yell at me again, but Hudson interrupted us and asked, "You two okay?"

"Yep," I said, getting up. "We're great." I walked into the crowd wondering why in the hell I cared anyway.

I SULKED on my barstool and ignored the rest of the bar. I refused to look in Trinity's direction again, telling myself it didn't matter what she did with her night. If she wanted to take home half the bar, that was her business.

Hudson gave me space for the next hour or so, refilling my glass but not saying a word. Only when I asked for my fifth, or was it my sixth, beer of the night did he stop in front of me.

"What the hell was that?" he said.

I glared at him. We'd been friends for years. We played baseball together in high school. Hudson went on to play in college, but I wasn't good enough for that. I barely scraped together enough loans to pay for two years of community college before I transferred to a state school to finish my criminal justice degree. I applied to the police academy as soon as I finished college, and by then, Hudson had moved back to MacKellar Cove with a wife and bought O'Kelley's. I always planned to get the hell out of town and never look back, but life had other plans for me.

"Nothing," I said knowing I'd never be able to explain it.

"Want to try again?"

I shook my head. "Want to give me another beer?"

"Am I giving you a ride home?"

"You already have my keys."

Hudson nodded. "Yeah, but I wasn't sure if you were going to walk or stay here or if you wanted to go home."

"I need to go home. I should have gone home with that other chick. The one who actually wanted me."

Hudson's brows went up but he didn't make a comment.

"I don't get her. She said she was here to find some guy to take home but she didn't look like she was all that interested. And that guy? I mean, really? Not him. He was like twelve."

Hudson nodded so I kept going.

"And she's not like that. Right? She flirts a lot, well, not with me, but with everyone else. But she was brushing the guy off. I didn't ruin anything. She wasn't really going to go home with him. Was she?"

Hudson just stared at me.

"I don't know. It doesn't matter. She's too good for me. I'm just the poor kid who thought she was a bad person. I'm the bad person. I didn't give her a chance to explain. I should have listened to her, but I saw what she was doing and assumed she was taking advantage of someone leaving their keys in the car. I screwed up."

"Piper," Hudson called out.

"Yeah?" Piper said, walking over. She smiled at me and turned to Hudson.

"I need to take him home before he embarrasses himself more. Can you handle things for a little while?"

Piper nodded. "Of course. Take your time."

"Don't leave alone. Wait for me to get back," Hudson said.

She smiled. "I will. And Steven is still here, too. We'll all stick around."

Hudson nodded and walked around the end of the bar. "Let's go," he told me, helping me to my feet.

Hudson got me into my truck and pulled out onto the street. I slumped against the door, letting the cool feel of the air conditioning sink into me.

Hudson didn't say anything on the drive. When he pulled into my driveway, he parked in my usual spot and went to the door, leaving me to get myself out of the truck.

I hadn't had that much to drink in a while, and I was feeling it as I worked my way to the door. Hudson waited for me to get inside and followed me in, putting my keys on the table by the door and waving as I staggered toward my room.

The front door closed quietly as I flopped onto my bed, thoughts of Trinity mixing with visions of her with someone else.

Yep, I was going to be sick.

2

TRINITY

*H*ome sweet home. I took a breath of the fresh air streaming through my open sliding glass door and sighed. Moving to MacKellar Cove over a year ago was a risk, but it felt like home. My condo felt like home. And I really couldn't imagine leaving and going anywhere else.

Especially for a guy.

I rolled my eyes. I couldn't help it. My friend, Karissa, made a dating app. Since I was definitely single, I signed up. I'd met a few decent guys, but none were really right for me. But the latest one...he seemed perfect. Until he admitted he lived almost two hours away.

Not happening.

He thought since I grew up in Syracuse I would just turn my life around for him because I lived there already and it was easy for me to go back.

Ha! He didn't know me.

I looked around my messy apartment and shook my head. Not even Officer James Rucker managed to run me out of town yet. If he hadn't gotten me to leave, neither was a man

I'd never actually met. No matter how great he was through the app.

I buried myself in work over the next few hours, letting the rhythm of stringing beads for a long necklace distract me from everything else.

I lost track of time and nearly dropped the piece I was working on when someone knocked on my door. I finished what I was doing and hurried to answer it.

Karissa Thomas hugged me and breathed a sigh of relief when I let her in. I shared a birthday with her mom, the woman who convinced me to take a chance and move to MacKellar Cove in the first place. Ms. Georgia died before I made the move, but Karissa and the rest of her group of friends welcomed me in and made me feel like I was always a part of them.

"Hey," Karissa said after a second. She was on her phone, which meant she was returning emails or answering questions or doing something for her business. She was a powerhouse and a woman who feared nothing.

"Hey," I answered, surprised it was already lunch time. "Sorry. I didn't realize what time it was."

Karissa waved a hand. "I never know what time it is. If I didn't set alarms for everything, I'd never leave the computer. My mom always said I would die of starvation right there in front of the screen if I didn't set reminders to stop for food once in a while."

"What are you working on now?" I asked, moving into my kitchen. All the condos were set up in a similar way with the kitchen near the front door. A breakfast bar divided it from the dining space and the living room. To the side were two bedrooms with a large shared bathroom in between, complete with a laundry closet in the bathroom. Karissa and Finley lived downstairs from me, so their condo was the same except the living space on the right instead of the left.

"Actually," Karissa said, pausing until I looked at her, "I've been developing an app for you."

"What? Why?"

Karissa shrugged and handed me her phone. "I wanted to show you what I could do. I figured part of your hesitation was not knowing what it would look like, but if I went ahead and created it, then you could get a feel for it."

I took the phone and my mouth fell open. It was stunning. Classy and elegant but simple. I didn't know it could be all that. "Karissa, this is too much. I mean, I don't know if I can pay you what you probably should have charged me for this."

Karissa waved her hand. "Don't think about that right now. I had fun with it. Book Boyfriends Wanted was my baby for so long, but now that it's out there, I needed a new passion project. This was exciting and different for me. And honestly, it was crazy simple by comparison."

I scrolled through the pages she had set up and found one after another examples of my work. She obviously pulled them from my website, but the way she displayed each page was perfect. You could search by style or color or what the item was, and on each item page, she added other selections that would coordinate.

"Wow. I love it."

"Good. Then we can activate it and put a link on your website."

I stared at the screen another minute then finally handed over her phone. "I don't know if I'm ready for this."

"For what? An app?"

I sighed and searched for the words that would explain what I meant. "It feels like a lot more than just an app. It feels like I'm pushing things to a new level. I love what I do, but it's hard to explain."

"You want more?" Karissa supplied.

I chewed on my lip and nodded. "I do. I want to give back in some way. I've been making videos of how to do certain things that beginners could do."

"Really?"

"Yeah. I learned how to do all this from my grandma, but if she hadn't been around to help me learn, I would have ended up doing something else. I want to give other women a chance to learn something like this and maybe change their lives a little."

"Wow. That's awesome. It makes me feel totally selfish for wanting to develop an app so I have enough money for a double mastectomy."

"What?" I asked her, my eyes automatically dropping to her chest. "Why?"

Karissa shrugged and for the first time looked less than sure of herself. "My mom died of breast cancer. She caught it really late. I have the gene, which means I have a good chance I'll develop the same. But if I get a double mastectomy, my chances are dramatically less. It could save my life."

"Oh, wow, Rissa. I had no idea you were thinking about all that."

She nodded. "I've been trying to decide what to do for a while. I think I've finally decided I want to do it."

"Insurance won't cover it?"

"I have private insurance since I'm self employed. They don't cover the whole thing."

"Wow," I said again, at a loss. "I think we need a drink."

Karissa laughed. "A toast to my boobs."

I snorted a laugh. "To your boobs." I poured us glasses of wine and grabbed the salad and sandwiches I made for our lunch. We toasted and dished out lunch and sat on the balcony overlooking the cove.

"I'll make you a deal," Karissa said, turning to me.

"What deal?"

"If you give the app a chance, I'll help you get your videos loaded and create a page on the app for them."

"How is that a deal?" I asked.

Karissa shrugged. "It'll help me to focus on something other than cutting off a part of my body."

I reached over and grabbed her hand. "Fine. Since you need the distraction."

Karissa grinned. "Good. Now, tell me all about the guy who hit on you last night and James coming to your rescue."

I groaned and shook my head. Life in a small town.

I wasn't sure if I was ready to talk to a new guy, but after spending the afternoon with Karissa, I decided to see if I had any new matches. There were things I liked about Karissa's app, but it was intimidating to say yes or no to someone when you had no clue what they looked like.

That was the whole point of it, but it was something I was still getting used to. I hated to think of myself as being shallow, but the reality was, I was a little. I'd been judged enough by men for my top-heavy, hourglass figure, but I still judged a man by his appearance. I was no better than them.

I found a new match. His profile was funny, and his pic was a lobster, which made me laugh. I liked a guy with a sense of humor. It was one of the many things missing in my last relationship.

I took the plunge before I thought twice about it and sent the guy a message asking where he lived. Best to get that out of the way off the bat.

JAYPO

It's not a good idea to tell a stranger where you live.

DIAMONDGIRL

True, but I don't want to start talking to someone who lives hours from me and expects me to uproot my life.

JAYPO

Valid point. I'm within 10 minutes of A-Bay.

DIAMONDGIRL

Okay, good. That works. Anything else you can tell me?

JAYPO

I don't play games. And I don't stick around if you start.

DIAMONDGIRL

I agree.

JAYPO

I've never done online dating before.

DIAMONDGIRL

Well, I'm happy to be your first.

JAYPO

Well…

I laughed and shook my head.

DIAMONDGIRL

Not like that! I just meant the first person you're talking to. Unless you're talking to other women.

JAYPO

Nope, just you. I'm a one woman kind of guy.

I sighed.

DIAMONDGIRL

My favorite kind of guy.

JAYPO

LOL. Sorry I have to cut this short, but I'm working right now. Can I message you later?

DIAMONDGIRL

I'd like that.

JAYPO

Good. Talk soon.

It wasn't the kind of talk that lit a fire in me, but I didn't need fire off the bat. He was nice and flirty, but not the creepy kind of flirty where you felt like you needed to shower.

I made my plans for the next day and laid out the supplies I would need so I could jump into the video I wanted to shoot. I was starting to really enjoy doing something new and different but still creating beautiful pieces.

By the time the sun was drifting low over the river, I wanted to get outside. I tried to force myself to go for a walk at least once every day, even if the walk was just up the street for food.

The smell of the river and the fresh air outside sent me straight to the Riverwalk on the back side of my condo. The path led from just past my building along the cove to Catherine Park in the center of town and then beyond to the north side. It was peaceful. Benches were spaced along the walking path for people who wanted to sit and relax, but the wide path was easy for just about anyone to walk.

My phone buzzed in my purse, and I stopped to check the message. I smiled when I saw a picture from my grandma of a new bracelet she made. I told her about working with resin and she wanted to try it out. It was getting harder for her to hold beads in her hands, but the resin was less of a challenge for her.

Looks great. You're already a pro.

I hit send and was about to slip my phone back into my purse when it tugged on my arm.

Then harder, a yank. I felt like I was operating in slow motion. I grabbed the bag, but there was a man holding onto the strap.

"That's mine. What the hell?"

"Give it to me," he growled. His voice was deep but sounded young. I could see a little bit of his face but not much with his hoodie pulled low. We were between street lights, which made it even harder to make out any of his features.

He pulled again, harder. I tugged back, not ready to let go of my stuff. I had my phone in my hand, but my purse had everything else. My keys, my wallet, my favorite pair of sunglasses.

He wrapped the strap around his hand and yanked my purse away from me. Since I was pulling back, I smacked myself in the face when I let go. I fell to the ground, landing hard on the pavers. A jolt of pain burst through me.

The guy ran away. His fast steps echoed off the buildings around me as he disappeared into the night.

It took me a minute to process what just happened. Someone walked by and asked if I was okay. I shook my head.

"Can I help you?" the man asked.

I recoiled. He was another stranger. Someone I didn't know. Was he going to kick me while I was down?

"How about I go get someone?" he asked, understanding my fear. "Did you see who did this?"

"I…"

"I'll go get someone," he said, turning to walk away.

"No," I said firmly. "I'm okay. Thank you."

I struggled to stand but managed to get up on my own. My face hurt and my hip was sore, but otherwise I was fairly sure I was okay. Or I would be. Eventually.

I thought about going back home, but I had no way to get into my apartment. Tears built behind my eyes as fear sank in. The person who took my purse had my address from my license and keys to my home. I couldn't go back home. I had nowhere to go.

"Are you sure you're okay?" the man asked.

I'd forgotten he was there. I had to get off the Riverwalk. I needed to figure out what I was going to do. My entire body trembled with fear and adrenaline. I finally nodded at the man and told myself the same thing I said before I called the police when my mother was abused by her ex.

I was not weak. I was strong. And I was smart. I did all the things you should do. He caught me off guard.

Thankfully, I was close to O'Kelley's and Hudson was there. He took one look at me when I walked in the door and ushered me back to his office. He stood guard while I used his private bathroom.

I finally worked up the nerve to check out my reflection in the mirror. Better than I expected. My hair had something in it, and my lip was bleeding and already starting to bruise. All of it could be fixed. Later. I knew the drill.

I heard murmured voices outside the door and knew the cops were there. Hudson asked before I went in if I wanted him to call. I hated the thought, but I was not going to let that guy get away with it.

I flushed the toilet and debated not washing my hands in case there was evidence on them, but that was going too far. I didn't touch the man who stole my purse. I washed them and snarled at the substance in my hair. It was going to be a pain to wash it out. I'd just washed my hair that morning, but I needed to do it again when I got home.

I took a breath and told myself I was strong. The cop was there to help. I didn't do anything wrong. I could tell him what happened and then go on my way.

I opened the door and the voices stopped. Hudson was right there in front of me. I'd never seen him look so concerned. "Are you okay?"

I nodded. "I'm fine. Shaken up, but I'll survive."

"Good," the other man said. "Then maybe you can explain to me what the hell you were thinking?"

Officer James Rucker. The bane of my existence. He'd been a thorn in my side for a year, and the look on his face said he wasn't done.

He also wasn't in uniform, which made me wonder why he was there at all.

"I thought you were going to call the cops," I said to Hudson with a growl.

"I am the cops," James replied. "I was on my way here and heard the call. I'm a cop, which you know."

I gave him my sweetest smile and said, "Well, if you're not on duty, then why don't you go on about your night and I can talk to someone who isn't going to immediately assume I'm a criminal."

He growled and took a breath. I glared at him, waiting for him to give in. Then he pulled out his phone and dialed a number.

"Officer Rucker, badge number 2857. I'm at O'Kelley's with the call that just came in. Will you send Hughes out here?" He paused. "Yeah. Okay, thanks."

He hung up the phone and looked at me. "A female officer is on the way. You can speak to her and tell her everything that happened. Until she gets here, I'd like to ask you a few questions, if that's okay."

"I don't need to talk to a female cop. The guy yanked my purse off my shoulder and..." I broke off, emotion and fear mingling inside me. I stared up at the ceiling and tried to stop the tears that I knew were coming.

The office door opened and closed, and when I looked, James and I were alone.

"Trinity, I'm sorry this happened to you. I should have started with are you okay?"

That did it. That was all he had to say, and I lost it. I crumbled. I sank to the floor where I stood and put my head in my hands. Tears poured down my face. Fear overwhelmed me.

Then he sat down next to me and held me while I cried.

3

JAMES

I hated when women cried. My mom was a crier. She told me it was how some women, some people, released the extra energy inside. That it was like screaming or laughing, but when an emotion was so intense that they couldn't hold it in.

My mom cried when she was happy, but more often, she cried when she was scared. When she worried about paying the bills or losing her job. When my brother or I got into trouble for doing something stupid when she was at work. When the latest man left and took something that mattered to her.

Holding Trinity while she cried reminded me of that kind of crying. Scared. Her world was shattered. She might have grown up in a city where crime was a regular occurrence, but in MacKellar Cove, crime was almost laughable. Crime was kids stealing street signs and public intoxication. It wasn't theft or assault. Not usually.

I wanted to hold Trinity and tell her there was nothing to worry about, but I couldn't make her that promise. Her lip was bleeding and her cheek was bruised. She looked shaken. And that was what did me in. I lit into her because I'd never seen her look anything other than determined. She was strong. A part of me figured I'd walk into the office with Hudson and have to hold her back from going after whoever did this. Instead, I was the one ready to find the person and pummel him.

No one was going to hurt her and get away with it. Not while I was around.

A knock on the door brought Trinity's head up. I caught a whiff of her hair, then froze when her eyes locked on mine. She was close. Close enough that it wouldn't take much for me to lean in and claim her lips. Claim all of her.

Then the knock came again, louder, with her name added to it in a female's voice.

Trinity scurried away from me and scrambled to stand. Unfortunately for me, she stuck her perfect ass in my face when she stood. Holding her was bad enough, being teased by her curves was torture.

"Come in," Trinity said loudly.

The door opened just enough for Officer Hughes to stick her head in. She smiled and kept her gaze focused on Trinity instead of letting it linger to where I sat on the floor, even though she knew I was there.

"Hi, Trinity. I'm Officer Jessica Hughes. Can I come in?"

Trinity nodded.

Jess opened the door and stepped inside. She closed it behind her and asked the question I couldn't choke out when I first saw her. "Are you okay?"

Trinity's lip trembled but she caught it between her teeth and nodded.

"Why don't we talk about what happened. Would you like Officer Rucker to leave?"

Trinity drew in a shaky breath and glanced at me. There was gratitude there, but she still didn't like me. Not that I could blame her. I wasn't her biggest fan either. She breezed into my town and turned me upside down, and then acted like I was dirt on the bottom of her shoe. Nope, I didn't need that.

I stood and smiled. "I'll let you two talk." I stopped next to Jessica and quietly said, "I'm not leaving so call me if you need me."

Jessica nodded but never took her gaze off Trinity. I didn't want to, but I had no choice. I let myself out of the office as Jessica invited Trinity to sit.

Hudson was back behind the bar when I made it out there. I took a seat at the end, close to the hallway, so I could watch for Trinity.

"She okay?" Hudson asked.

I shrugged. "I don't know. I guess so."

"You okay?"

I glared at Hudson, but it was clear he saw right through me. We'd been friends for far too long. He knew my tells, but he rarely called me out for shit I didn't want to admit. I shook my head.

"You'll get whoever did this." Hudson set a bottle in front of me and walked away, leaving me to think about Trinity.

My gaze lingered on the hallway, waiting for Trinity to walk in. I vibrated with tension, needing to go back in there and see what was going on. I wanted to be out looking for whoever did this. But I didn't have a description and I didn't have a right.

"Where is she?" Karissa and Finley asked from right next to me.

I hadn't even noticed them walk up, but both were right there. "She's talking to the police."

"Aren't you the police?" Finley asked.

I nodded. "She didn't want to talk to me. I called for a female officer."

"A female officer? Was she...?" Karissa let the unasked question linger in the air.

I shook my head. "I don't think so. She didn't tell me anything, though."

"Oh, God," Finley breathed. "She has to be so scared. Who would do this? This is MacKellar Cove. It's safe."

"Usually, yes," I said, not telling her I had the same questions.

"Can we go talk to her?" Karissa asked.

"Let's give her a few more minutes with Officer Hughes. I want her to have a chance to go through everything first," I told them.

They nodded and took the seats next to me, both of them hovering on the edge.

"How did you know what happened?" I asked them after a minute of all three of us staring at the hallway.

"Hudson called. He figured she wouldn't want to walk home alone."

I nodded absently, not willing to admit I'd been looking forward to walking Trinity home and making sure she was okay myself. It wasn't my place. And she wouldn't have wanted me to do it anyway.

I sipped my beer and watched for her. Hudson asked if Finley and Karissa wanted anything but both shook their heads. We didn't speak, just waited, until Trinity walked out with Officer Hughes.

Finley and Karissa were out of their seats and surrounding her in a heartbeat. Trinity nodded and smiled and accepted their hugs. I stared, knowing I wouldn't be welcome.

Officer Hughes took the seat next to me. "She's okay. Shaken up, but okay."

"Any idea who did this?"

She shook her head. "Unfortunately, no. She's going to sit down tomorrow with someone, but she said she didn't get a good look at his face."

"Thank you for coming down here. I know you don't usually make this trip," I told her.

She nodded. "We all have to work together. Listen, the guy took her purse. Including her license and her keys. She's shaken because he knows where she lives and can get in."

"I'll take care of it," I said without hesitation. I'd changed the locks for my mom more times than I could count and knew how to do it in my sleep.

"I figured," Jessica said with a smirk.

I sipped my beer and ignored her. We'd known each other a few years and only worked together a handful of times, but she was someone I considered a friend. All the towns in our area shared resources as much as possible, including covering for each other and helping each other out when needed. Jessica worked in Morristown, about thirty minutes north. I'd been up there and she came down here on occasion. She tried to set me up with her sister-in-law once, but it was comical how bad we were for each other.

"You should come up for dinner sometime. Greg would love to see you," she said.

I nodded. "I'm sure that's why you're inviting me."

She grinned. "It's as good an excuse to find out what's going on with you and our victim as any."

"Then you don't need to worry because the short answer is nothing. The long answer is not a damn thing."

"Uh huh. If that's what you say. Listen, I'll type up this report and send it down to you. Let me know if you need anything else." She stood and straightened her shirt.

"Thanks, Jess. I appreciate it."

She smiled. "Any time. See you soon, Ruck."

I nodded as she walked away. When I turned back to Trinity, she was huddled at a table with Finley and Karissa, an untouched pitcher of beer in the middle. I debated walking over to talk to her, but it was for the best that I just stayed away.

"Another?" Hudson asked, nodding to my nearly empty beer.

I shook my head. "Nah. I've got work to do."

He narrowed his gaze, but I shook my head and left a twenty on the bar then walked out.

It was one of those nights when everything felt off. The air was still around me, but inside I was unsettled and off kilter. I turned toward Waterfront Villas and pulled out my phone. I made it my business to know the local business owners and Richie was no exception.

"Officer Rucker? What can I do for you?"

"Sorry to call so late, Richie. I was just at O'Kelley's and one of your residents was there. Her purse was stolen. It had her license and keys in it. I was wondering if I could stop by and change her locks so she feels safe going home when she's ready."

"Yes, sir. Of course. I can take care of it, too."

"Nah," I said, knowing I wouldn't rest until I knew she was safe. "I'm almost there. But if you can meet me up there with a spare set of keys and a new lock, that would help. Apartment 3C."

"I'm on my way," Richie said solemnly.

I took the stairs up to Trinity's apartment, needing the exercise to burn off some of the tension still racing through me. It gutted me to see her so upset, and then to have her turn and need someone else and not want me around. It was for the best, though.

Richie was outside Trinity's apartment when I walked out of the stairway. He flashed me a tense smile. "Is Trinity okay?"

I nodded. "She's with Karissa and Finley. I imagine she'll stay with them tonight, but I wanted to take care of this for her."

"Of course. Thanks for letting me know, Officer."

I nodded and got to work. Richie stayed next to me the entire time, handing me tools and helping me secure and test the new lock. When we were done, he snapped his black toolbox closed and held out the keys to Trinity's apartment.

"Will you see her again tonight?"

I shook my head. "It's best if she doesn't know I was here. Why don't you call her and say you heard what happened and changed her locks. Ask if it's okay to leave the keys at Karissa and Finley's or something like that."

Richie nodded. "Okay."

"Thanks, Richie. I appreciate the help."

"Any time, Officer. Thank you for letting me know. If I see anything suspicious, I'll call you."

I nodded and rubbed my jaw. "Thanks."

I took my time walking back down the stairs then back to my truck. I thought about stopping in O'Kelley's to have that second beer, but I wasn't sure I could see Trinity again and not make her come home with me.

I drove home thinking about my mom. It had been a few weeks since I made an effort to see her. She was always working, but I kept coming up with excuses why I couldn't go to her place for dinner. She didn't understand why I wanted her to move out of the apartment I grew up in. She said she raised my brother and I there and loved it. I said it was a hellhole that reminded me of how little we had growing up. Even that was being kind.

I sighed as I pulled into my driveway. My own home wasn't fancy or special, but it was a vast improvement from where I grew up. It was clean and simple, and it was almost all mine. Six more years and I'd have it paid off and I would finally be able to breathe at night knowing no one would come and take it from me.

The outside lights lit up the butter yellow clapboard siding. The inside wasn't nearly as bright with gray walls in almost every room. My mom kept trying to get me to paint, but neutral was best for value. It meant more people could see themselves there. Not that I was selling, but if something happened and I had to, it would be less work for me.

I tossed my keys on the entry table and went straight to my safe to lock up my gun. Once it was secure, I went back to the kitchen and grabbed the plate of leftovers I put in there the night before. Food, sports, and a quiet night alone. I guess it worked.

I was in a shitty mood when I got to work the next morning. My new partner was arriving that day, and I was not looking forward to it.

That and I barely slept all night worrying about Trinity and if she was okay.

I forced myself to put Trinity out of my mind and tried to concentrate on work. I grabbed a cup of coffee from the breakroom and went to my desk to see what happened overnight.

As usual, it was a quiet night. All except Trinity's incident. Jess's report was in my inbox and I read through it, getting more and more annoyed with each word. The guy grabbed her purse and yanked, but he didn't touch her. That was the only thing that kept me from losing it when someone said my name.

"What?" I barked. Almost kept me from losing it.

"Hey. I'm your new partner. I'm Rowan Masterson."

I looked up at the guy and glared. He definitely didn't have cop written all over him. The edge of a tattoo peeked out of his uniform collar. His hair and full beard were both short and neat. He looked uncomfortable in uniform, but he was wearing it. His hand was extended, waiting for me to shake it.

He didn't let it fall until I reached over and shook his hand. He nodded once and took the guest chair next to my desk. "What are we working on today?"

"How long have you been a cop?"

"Five years," he answered without hesitation.

"Why did you move here?"

He shrugged. "Needed a change of scenery."

"What the hell does that mean?"

"It means I was sick of wondering how many people were going to die every night and I wanted to go somewhere with a little less action."

"Cops are supposed to like action."

He shook his head. "No, we're supposed to protect and serve. We're supposed to help people. Too many don't do that. I had enough."

I narrowed my gaze at him and wondered what the hell he was talking about. At the moment, it didn't matter. I could look into the guy later.

"So, is there anything I should be working on?"

I shook my head and stood. "No. We need to go."

"Where are we going?"

"To look at the site of a robbery last night. Check the area. See if anything was left behind. Protect and serve, right?"

Masterson nodded once and stood. I was not impressed with him even though I knew his resume wasn't bad. He had an air of distrust and cockiness that said he was going to be a pain in the ass to work with.

We parked near Catherine Park and headed down the

Riverwalk toward O'Kelley's where Trinity was the night before. Officer Hughes' report said she checked out the spot where Trinity was robbed, but in the darkness, she couldn't see anything that made her think there was a reason to restrict traffic in the area. I wanted to double check in the daylight.

Masterson followed me down the walkway, hands on his hips the whole time. He looked like he was about to shoot someone at any minute. People gave us a wide berth, not that I could blame them.

When I made it to the area where Trinity was, just beyond O'Kelley's but not quite to Waterfront Villas, I stopped and looked around. The path was dirty but nothing stood out to me. There was a spot that could have been where Trinity fell, but it also could have been someone who dragged their feet. No blood was on the ground, and no items were left behind. It was a complete bust.

I turned and walked back toward Catherine Park, ignoring Masterson as he followed behind me. I turned at the corner and went in the front of Cracked hoping to find Blake.

She was pouring coffee for a customer and smiled when I walked in. She nodded to a table, understanding that if I was there, it wasn't just for breakfast.

When Blake was done with her customer, she brought two mugs over and set one in front of each of us. "Morning, gentlemen. Breakfast or information?"

"Breakfast," Masterson said the same time I said, "Information."

Blake raised her brows and turned her focus on Masterson. "Hi, I'm Blake. You must be new to town."

He blanched ever so slightly before nodding. "Just moved here over the weekend. I'm Rowan."

"Nice to meet you. What can I get you for breakfast?"

He grabbed a menu and Blake ignored me while he looked. I cleared my throat but she continued to ignore me. He finally looked up and said, "Western omelet, bacon, and sourdough toast."

"Coming right up." She finally turned to me. "And for you?"

"How's Trinity?"

"She's shaken up. She stayed with Fin and Rissa last night. She said she's afraid to go home."

"Have you seen her?"

Blake shook her head. "Not yet. It was late when Fin texted us to tell us what happened. Ian wanted to walk me here this morning. It's really messed with people's heads."

"There's nothing to worry about. This is the same place it was yesterday," I told her calmly.

"Yeah, except our friend had her purse stolen," Blake said with a shudder. "It's a little scary. I actually drove here today instead of walked."

"MacKellar Cove is still safe, Blake. I'll find whoever did this."

Blake smiled and nodded. "I know. And thanks. Breakfast?"

I rolled my eyes and nodded. "Well, I am here."

Blake grinned and left to put in our order.

"You can't promise things like that," my new partner said as soon as Blake was gone.

"Like what?"

"That you'll find the guy who did this. If her friend was robbed, she should be scared. And you saying you'll find whoever did this is not going to make it better. You'll make it worse when you can't solve it."

"Listen, this is your first day. I've been here for more than fifteen years. I know how this town works. We will find whoever did this. We don't have a lot of crime, and we always solve our cases."

Masterson glared at me and sipped his coffee. The feeling was mutual, and I wasn't upset when he didn't speak to me the rest of breakfast.

Fucking partners.

4

TRINITY

Sleeping on the couch was getting to me. I really appreciated Finley and Karissa letting me stay with them, but I was anxious to be home. Three nights away felt like hiding instead of healing.

The building manager, Richie, told me he changed the locks on my condo right away, but I still worried about being there alone. Finley went with me to get some clothes, but every second I was in there I felt like something was off. But I couldn't hide forever. And I couldn't sleep on a couch forever.

"What do you want to do today?" Karissa asked, handing me a cup of coffee and sitting on the chair opposite the couch.

She and Finley had been awesome. Fin's work schedule made it so she wasn't home as much as Rissa, but neither of them made me feel like I was being ridiculous for staying with them. They never asked how long I wanted to stay or if I was ready to go home. They just let it be normal that I was sleeping on their couch instead of two floors above them in my own condo.

"I think I need to go home," I admitted, taking a sip of the rich, dark coffee. They had better coffee than me, but even that didn't make me want to stay.

"Whenever you're ready, but you know you can stay here as long as you'd like," Karissa said.

I nodded. "Thanks. I just feel like I need to be home again. I'm so used to being alone all the time, and to be honest, I'm kind of missing it."

Karissa chuckled and crossed one leg over the other. "Trust me, I get it. I'm the same way. I'm big and loud a lot of the time, but that's because I'm alone so much and have been for so long that I almost go overboard when I'm around other people."

I sighed. "I'm never around other people. I am just home alone."

"You're with us. When we all go out," Karissa said, her dark brows pulling together.

I shrugged. "I know, but I guess I mean other people. Strangers. Not dangerous ones, but in general. I think there's a part of me that's afraid to put myself out there."

"What do you mean?"

I sipped my coffee and considered my words. "I was matched with someone. He sounds great. Funny and clever and kind. He lives close which is better than the last one who lived in Syracuse and didn't tell me. But I'm afraid to meet up with this guy."

"And that means you're afraid to date?"

"I never knew my grandfather. He died a long time ago. And my dad died when I was thirteen. My mom dated after that, but it wasn't always great, as you know. I just wonder if maybe dating is more trouble than it's worth."

Karissa huffed a laugh. "I have been on a handful of dates in the last two years. A few were nice guys, but none of them were men who really made me want more than a few nights out. I've had men who were nothing more than sex and men who were nothing more than friends who kissed me at the end of the night. I'm jaded after my mom died. I see the world as deadly and dangerous. Even silently, it can kill you. And I'm thinking about cutting off my boobs, one of the things that makes me attractive to men. My dating life is going to go from barely surviving to dead as a doornail. And I'm totally okay with that because I feel the same as you. I don't know if dating is really worth it."

"Says the woman who built a dating app," I said with a smirk.

"I know, right?" Karissa laughed. "I think if there was a way to know the other person was going to make you as happy as Ian makes Blake or Ramsey and Melody or Colin and Elise, that would be different. I would love to create something that really found you another person who would be it, who would end your dating life forever, that would be awesome."

"You know, that sounded creepy. End your dating life forever," I repeated in a deep movie trailer voice.

Karissa and I laughed.

"But yeah," I agreed, "I'm with you. This guy I'm matched with, he could be great or he could be a total ass. And I won't know until I give him a chance and get to know him."

"I could look him up for you," Karissa offered.

I shook my head. "Thanks, but no. I'm not going to support your habit."

Karissa scowled at me. When she launched her app, she looked up everyone we were paired with. She knew Blake and Ian were paired together even though Blake didn't, and it created a few issues. She promised she would be better, but I wasn't taking any chances.

I laughed. "Maybe I should just not message him anymore. Just let it die out and not worry about him."

"I think you should message him because life is too short to die alone."

"Do you think that's going to happen?" I asked her, hearing the pain and fear in her voice.

Karissa shrugged. "I think I studied romance and relationships for years when I was building Book Boyfriends Wanted. I searched for reasons to explain why people fall in love, and why they fall out of love. I read more about relationships than I knew existed. And at the end of it, there are so many things that you can't quantify, so many pieces of the puzzle that have to fit together perfectly, and so many times they don't, that I have very little hope left for me. I have hope for everyone else, because your hope hasn't been shattered, but mine is almost gone. Especially if I go through with the surgery."

"Then you need to find a man who is going to want you more than he wants your boobs," I told her.

Karissa chuckled. "If one exists. Maybe I should add that to the questionnaire. If your significant other lost a piece of their anatomy to save their lives, would you still want to be with them?"

I grinned. "Anyone who answers no to that question should be deleted from the site."

Karissa laughed and nodded. "Absolutely."

Karissa stood next to me while I unlocked my front door. The key stuck a little going in, causing a hint of panic to flare up. Did the person who took my purse damage it by trying to use the old key? The key went in all the way and turned, unlocking my door with a soft click.

I took the key out and sucked in a breath, then pushed my door open. Everything looked the same as the last time I was there. My coffee maker lid was flipped up, waiting for a new pot to be brewed. My clean dishes were in the drying rack. A stack of mail I hadn't gotten to yet was slumped over on the edge of the counter. A pair of flip flops was next to the wall, waiting for me to trip over them.

Farther inside, the rest of the condo hadn't changed either. The living room was dark from the drawn curtains, but nothing was out of place. As far as I could tell, it was the same mess I left it in. Paperbacks on the coffee table, my iPad on the couch. A sweatshirt was on the floor in front and the blanket was hanging off the arm.

My bedroom looked the same. Unmade bed with the sheets halfway to the floor. Laundry littered all over my bedroom. The towel I used last was on the edge of the bed from where I forgot to hang it up, as always.

My office, the closest thing to organized in my condo, was picked up and perfect. Nothing was off anywhere.

But I still had that creeped out feeling.

"What do you think?" Karissa asked softly.

I took a breath and spun to look at her. She was standing next to my kitchen peninsula, watching me. "I think everything is where I left it, but…"

"It just feels different," she supplied.

I nodded. "It does. Like someone might have been in here, but left no trace."

"Richie said he changed the locks right away, right? I mean, he was done before we even left O'Kelley's. Smart calling him so fast."

I narrowed my eyes and shook my head. "I didn't call him at all. I assumed you guys did."

Karissa shook her head and glanced around again. "I didn't. And I don't remember Finley calling him either. I was with her the whole time."

"Then how the hell did he know?" I whispered.

"Let me check with Fin," Karissa said, digging her phone out and texting Finley.

I chewed my nail and watched Karissa, wondering how in the world Richie could have found out I was robbed if Fin—

"She didn't tell him," Karissa said. "You need to call him. Right now."

I nodded and pulled up his number. I paced as I waited for him to pick up the call. He didn't normally work Saturdays, but he always answered.

"Yellow?" he said, his over-excited accent changing the word.

"Richie, hi. It's Trinity Mayer."

"Hi, Trinity. How are you? Any problems with the new lock?"

"No, it's fine. I just got here. But, um, how did you know it needed to be changed? I thought Karissa or Finley called you, but they said they didn't. And they thought I called you, but I didn't. And I don't know how you knew—"

"Officer Rucker," Richie said, cutting off my panicked tirade.

"James?" I blurted, looking at Karissa. She nodded as if that made sense to her. "He called you?"

"Yeah, well, Officer Rucker is a friend to everyone in the community. He's the kind of guy who likes to make sure people are safe and know they're safe. He's actually the one who changed the lock, but I let him borrow my tools and provided the lock so I can get in if needed."

"Why would he do that?"

"He said your keys and wallet were stolen. He wanted you to feel safe. But he, uh, he actually asked me not to tell you, so maybe you could keep this between us?"

"Um, yeah, sure. I, um, yeah," I stammered, trying to understand.

"Thanks, Trinity. Hey, let me know if you need anything else."

I nodded. "Yeah, okay. Thanks, Richie."

"Any time. See you soon, Trinity."

"Bye," I said absently. I stared at my phone, wondering what in the world just happened.

"James is friends with everyone. It makes sense he would have called Richie to make sure everything was okay. I don't know why I didn't think of that. Or why you didn't. You talked to him that night."

I nodded, barely paying attention to Karissa.

"Have you talked to him since?"

I shook my head.

"He didn't tell you he was going to change your locks?"

I shook my head again.

"Well, like I said, that's just who he is. He's just one of those guys who's nice to everyone, you know?"

I scoffed. Too late I tried to cover it with a cough, but Karissa wasn't fooled.

"What was that for? You don't think he's a good guy?"

"He's not to me. He doesn't like me. He treats me like crap all the time. The first day I moved here he acted like I was a common criminal. I almost left." I held Karissa's gaze, knowing she would understand.

Karissa shook her head. "No, James isn't like that. He's never…no. What did he do?"

"He tried to arrest me! I locked my car keys in here, and my condo keys in my car, and I was trying to get into my car to get them."

Karissa raised an eyebrow and dropped her chin. "Seriously? Trin, I would have thought you were a criminal if I saw you. You were breaking into your car?"

"I know it looked bad, but he didn't let me explain. He just lost it."

"And you what? Stayed calm and explained you weren't trying to break into a random person's car but that it was your car?"

"Well, I…Fine, I yelled back. Feel better?" I scowled.

Karissa twisted her lips as she fought her grin. And lost. She burst out laughing. "You do realize he was doing his job, right? And you were breaking into a car. In a town so small that he knows basically everyone. Trust me, I understand profiling, but that's just not James. Haven't you two talked since then? He's been out with us a ton."

"And we don't talk. He was at O'Kelley's the other night when I was there and he accused me of being a slut because some guy was being an ass and hitting on me."

"That still baffles me," Karissa said. "James Rucker? Are we talking about the same person here?"

I nodded and gave her a humorless grin. "One and the same."

"I've never seen him like this. You're seriously blowing my mind right now."

"I guess I just bring out the worst in him."

"Yeah, well, he changed your locks, so he still wants you safe."

I looked around and took a breath. "Yeah, I guess."

Karissa rolled her eyes and snickered. "Maybe he has a thing for you and doesn't know how to say it."

"Ha! That's a good one."

She shrugged. "You never know."

I shook my head. "I'm pretty sure I do. He's an adult. If you think he doesn't know how to tell a woman he likes her, then you haven't been paying attention. He goes home with a new woman almost every weekend."

"Maybe he's not the one with the crush." She smirked.

I laughed. "Yeah, because I really want to date a man who accused me of being a thief with his first words to me, accuses me of being a slut, then accuses me of it being my fault when I get robbed. Yep, he's a real catch."

Karissa snorted. "Okay, fine. I have to agree with that one. But really, he's not like that. He's a good guy."

"Uh huh. Sure. I'll take your word for it."

Karissa chuckled. "Okay, fine. I'm going to head out if you're good. I have some work to finish. Let me know when you want to turn your app on. I can set it up any time! And we had a deal, remember? You agreed."

I shook my head. "I'm still thinking about it," I admitted.

Karissa hugged me and said, "No pressure. Let us know if you need anything. Any time. Middle of the night, whatever. We're here."

"Thanks, Riss."

She nodded and waved as she walked toward the door.

The door closed behind her, and I took a breath. After a second, I went and locked the door, then turned to my condo again.

"Officer James Rucker," I said to myself with a laugh. I never would have thought he'd be the one to make me feel safe. Especially not twice in one week.

I SPENT the afternoon getting work done. I hated that I didn't feel comfortable opening the slider out to my balcony. Fear was a funny thing, and it was in my head. Logic told me whoever stole my purse could not climb the side of my building and get into the sliding glass door, even if it was open, but logic didn't have a place where fear lived.

When my stomach started to growl, I finished up the necklace I was working on and pulled a drape over it to protect the pieces. I learned the hard way that if I didn't do that, I would inevitably bump my table or knock something off and would have to start over.

Since I hadn't been home in three days, I didn't have a lot of food in my house. I considered ordering in for about three seconds, then decided I could eat a can of soup and some crackers I found in the back of the pantry.

The crackers were stale and the soup was just okay, but it was food. I curled up on the couch with the remote and turned on a rom-com Finley and Karissa were talking about the night before.

The movie was half over when my phone buzzed with a new alert. I picked it up while watching the screen as the main characters kissed for the first time. I sighed, letting their happiness fill me.

My heart jumped. It was another notice from my newest match.

JAYPO

If we were together right now, what would we be doing?

I snickered. Interesting question.

DIAMONDGIRL

Well, I'm watching a movie, so maybe that?

JAYPO

Is that a question or an answer?

DIAMONDGIRL

LOL! Both?

JAYPO

Well, it's good to know we'd be laughing.
How was your day?

DIAMONDGIRL

Weird, actually.

JAYPO

Not the answer I expected. What was weird?

DIAMONDGIRL

I found out someone I don't really like did a favor for me.

JAYPO

Why don't you like this person?

DIAMONDGIRL

He just has this air of superiority. He's one of those people who thinks he's better than everyone else, and I don't handle people like him very well.

JAYPO

I know exactly what you mean.

DIAMONDGIRL

Sorry. It sucks, doesn't it?

JAYPO

Yep, but I've learned we can't change people. They are going to be who they are. We have to either choose to accept them or choose not to allow them into our lives.

DIAMONDGIRL

That's very profound and insightful.

JAYPO

Two things most people would not associate with me.

I laughed again. He was funny, and talking to him was even better than the movie. It had definitely been a long time since that was the case. And even though I was feeling a little down on relationships, it was nice to flirt with someone and know he wasn't judging me for the sweats I had on or the wrap around my hair or the situations I ended up in through no fault of my own.

But it was not a night to think about James Rucker. I had JayPo to talk to. And he was so much better.

5

Karissa and Finley offered to meet me in the lobby to walk to girls' night together, but both of them were already out and it felt ridiculous to ask my friends to walk me through our small town.

Then I stepped outside alone and realized I was terrified. I'd been in either Karissa and Finley's condo or mine, and being outside, and alone, was a little overwhelming. I hadn't been out of the building since the night I was robbed. A police officer even came to me to try to get a sketch of the guy. Not that I was helpful.

The afternoon sun was still bright, giving me a sassy glow and telling me I was being stupid. I wanted to flip the sun the bird, and yes, I knew I sounded nuts. I took a deep breath and focused on everything around me. People were walking up and down the street. I wasn't alone. I was okay.

I looked straight ahead and made my way to Book Boyfriends Unlimited, Finley's bookstore. We always had girls' night there, and it had definitely become a place I was comfortable. It was impossible not to be comfortable when surrounded by books. Books about people falling in love and finding their happily ever after. I wanted that, but it wasn't a guarantee. Not everyone got a happily ever after.

I knocked on the door to Book Boyfriends Unlimited and waited for Finley to let me in. She closed earlier on Sundays so we could meet in the back of her store and not be interrupted by customers.

"Hey," Finley said as she opened the door. "How are you?"

I smiled and hugged her. "I'm okay."

"Yeah?"

I nodded. "Yeah. And I won't break."

Finley grinned. "Good. For what it's worth, you're brave. I've never been scared like that here. I always thought of MacKellar Cove as small and safe, you know?"

I did know. It was one of the many reasons I decided to move there. Growing up in Syracuse wasn't bad. I felt safe for the most part. Even moving to the other side of town, away from my mom and grandma, I didn't live in fear. I was alone without them around, but I wasn't constantly worried about my personal safety. The few times I was in the wrong place at the wrong time, it worked out. I was scared, but never hurt. Moving to MacKellar Cove, I thought that wouldn't happen again. That there were no wrong places. Being faced with reality felt like a slap.

"I know," I admitted.

Finley locked the door behind me and wrapped her arm around my shoulder. She led me to the back where everyone except Laura and Melody were already sitting.

"Hey," they all said, their faces matching looks of concern.

"How are you?" Blake asked.

I shrugged. "I'm okay. This is the first I've been out, and it feels a little surreal. I should be totally fine, but walking here was a bit stressful."

"Last night was also her first night home," Karissa told the others. "Did you get any sleep?"

I shook my head. "Not really. Every little noise had me jumping. I tried to nap on my couch this afternoon, but even that wasn't possible."

"Want me to stay with you?" Karissa asked.

I shook my head again. "No, but thanks. I need to figure out how to feel safe again."

"It won't be easy," Elise said with a kind smile.

A knock on the door startled me and made me jump. Finley got up to answer it. Everyone else studiously avoided saying anything to me, letting me have my panic moment without judgement.

I took a deep breath and tried to calm my racing heart.

"You okay?" Karissa asked.

I nodded and gave her a weak smile.

Finley returned with Melody, Laura, and Piper. Piper was a server at O'Kelley's and someone I thought was sweet, but I didn't know her well.

"Piper was on her way out when I was leaving O'Kelley's, so I invited her along," Laura said. "She was complaining about going home alone. I figured she could use some company."

We all agreed and welcomed Piper. She looked like she felt a bit out of place, but Blake cut her a slice of pound cake and handed over the strawberries and whipped cream. Piper grinned widely.

"You guys do this every week?" she asked.

We nodded.

"Damn. I need to be off more Sunday nights."

"You should be. We talk about men and books and eat cake," Finley said.

"Sounds like a perfect night," Piper said, adding whipped cream to her cake. "Thanks for letting me crash."

"You're always welcome," Finley said.

Piper grinned. Her gaze landed on me and her smile fell

away. "How are you? Hudson has been going nuts since you were attacked. He won't let me leave the building unless he's with me. Any of us. We all have to walk out together. We were always careful, but he's taken it to a whole new level."

"I'm okay. Hopefully Hudson is overreacting," I said with a forced grin.

"James seems concerned," Blake said. "Ian said he's scowling more than usual lately."

"I wonder if it has anything to do with his new partner," Melody said. "He just moved here and I don't think they're getting along yet."

"Colin was over there this week," Elise said. "He met the guy. Rowan something. Said he seemed a bit rough, like he was pissed off at the world."

"Maybe that's why he and James aren't getting along. Too much frustration in one partnership." Laura laughed.

We all laughed with Laura.

"James is still a good guy, though," Karissa said. "To most of us, at least." She gave me a pointed look that no one missed.

"What happened with you and James?" Blake asked.

"Nothing," I answered too quickly. "It doesn't matter."

"He tried to arrest her because she was trying to break into her own car. The day she moved here. And she never told any of us," Karissa supplied.

"Really?"

"Why were you breaking into your car?

"Why didn't you tell us?"

"It was forever ago," I said. "And I didn't know any of you then. Plus, once I realized who he was and that you all knew him, I couldn't tell you guys that I thought he was a jerk."

"I would have," Elise said. "But I can't say anything bad about James. I always thought he was really sweet, even if he's really dumb when it comes to women. We almost hooked up once. A long time ago."

"You never told us that!" Blake said.

Elise shrugged, and I tried to push down the sick feeling in my stomach picturing them together.

"It was forever ago. I knew who he was, but I didn't know him well. We were both at O'Kelley's the one night and were playing darts and flirting. He ended up having to break up a fight and left. We never mentioned it to each other, and it never happened again. We didn't kiss or anything. Just some brushes against each other and sexy talk," Elise said.

"Does Colin know?" Laura asked.

Elise shook her head. "No, but it wasn't anything. And it was before I met Colin. Years ago."

"Don't you think you should tell him?" I blurted.

Elise turned at my harsh tone and raised an eyebrow. She smirked at me and said, "Nope. Because there's nothing to tell. You, on the other hand, you look like it bothers you a lot."

I scoffed. "Not even a little. He makes me crazy. And not in a good way."

"You and James?" Piper said. "Yeah, I can totally see it."

"Um, no," I argued. "He hates me, and the feeling is mutual."

"I don't think he hates you," Piper said, tilting her head to the side. "He watches you when he's at O'Kelley's. He almost seems intrigued by you. Like he's trying to figure you out."

I shook my head. "Trying to figure out how he can run me out of town more likely."

"I kind of see it, too," Karissa said. "He changed your locks without telling you and asked Richie not to let you know. He was there when Hudson called in and sat with you until that other cop showed up. He was watching out for you. I don't think he hates you like you say he does."

I rolled my eyes. "No. Officer James Rucker is not my friend. He's not watching out for me. He's not anything. We have mutual friends, but the only times we ever talk to each other, we fight."

"I thought you said Pride and Prejudice was your favorite romance ever," Finley said.

I shrugged. "Yeah, so?"

She smirked. "You really don't see it?"

"See what?"

"Oh, my God, you're right," Blake said. "I couldn't see it either. Not when it was me."

"The rest of us could," Elise said.

"Yeah, but I don't think I wanted to. I wanted to believe I was smarter or something," Blake said.

"And how did that turn out?" Laura asked with a snicker.

"Will you guys tell me what you're talking about?" I asked.

"You're Elizabeth, and James is Darcy. You bicker constantly, pretend you can't stand each other, but really, you're both secretly waiting for the other to pay attention and say something first," Finley said.

I snorted and looked at them, waiting for them to laugh at their joke.

They didn't.

"No. Not even a little bit. Elizabeth and Darcy were romantic and sweet. They were snarky and protective. It was so different. That is not us at all." I shook my head and crossed my arms over my chest. They were out of their minds.

"Except it totally is. It's exactly like you are. I mean, I didn't realize it until you started talking about how you don't like him and he's not the same person with you that he is with everyone else, but I definitely see it. And with Piper saying he watches you...definitely," Karissa said with a satisfied grin.

I rolled my eyes and shook my head. "You guys read too many romances if you think James and I could ever have anything other than animosity between us."

"Angry sex can be really hot," Melody said. "Sometimes I pick fights with Ramsey just so he'll go a little crazy."

"Ooh, he does that, too? For Ian it's getting jealous. We saw William at the store the other day with his new wife, and Ian got so mad when I hugged him. I thought he was going to lose it right there in the parking lot. He pressed me against the side of the car and kissed me until I was panting." Blake closed her eyes and hummed.

"Colin is so even tempered that I don't think I could rile him up if I tried, but he gets this dark look in his eyes that says he can't wait another second. When I see that, I run from him, and he stalks me. That is hot as hell," Elise said with her own salacious grin.

"Make up sex is definitely the best kind of sex," Finley agreed. "But angry sex can be fun."

"I like when it's followed up by that sweet, slow, sexy sex. Like you can't rush another second and have to enjoy each other. Sometimes angry sex leaves me unsatisfied, but making love is always good," Karissa said.

"You have to have it all," Blake said. "With William, it was always the same. I could have predicted everything down to what he would say and when. It was boring. Sex was boring. That should never be the case. Even if it's good sex, if it is always the same, it gets boring. That's what I love about sex with Ian. It's different. I don't know how, but every single time it's different."

Melody leaned forward and nodded, pushing her brown hair back. "I agree. Especially now. For so long, we were dancing around each other. We were afraid to say or do the wrong thing, but now, we just remember every time we're together how close we were to losing each other. I've cried a few times."

"During sex?" Finley asked.

Melody nodded. "Yeah. Ramsey totally understood, though."

"I've done that, too," Elise admitted. "To have someone in my life who loves me so much and makes me feel like I can be and say and do anything is overwhelming at times."

"Exactly," Melody said.

"I want that," Finley said with a scowl. "I've never had that. None of my exes were anything like that. Of course, that's why they're all exes."

"I thought I had that once," Piper admitted. "He really made me feel special."

"What happened?" Laura asked.

Piper gave us a sad smile. "It just didn't work out. We wanted different things. We grew up together, but when it came down to our futures, we just didn't match. I think about him sometimes, but I know I'm better off with someone else. Someone who really wants the same things I do."

"Have you ever looked him up to see where he is?" I asked.

Piper shook her head. "Nope. I don't know if I want to know. I like to imagine he's happy. Our differences weren't things we could overcome. I hope he's found what he was looking for and is happy."

"Are you on Karissa's app?" Blake asked. "Book Boyfriends Wanted?"

"Of course," Piper said with a grin. "I've met a few decent guys through there. None that stuck, though. Maybe one day."

"Trinity had a new match last week," Karissa said, bringing me back into the conversation.

"I did," I admitted. "He's funny and sweet."

"That sounds promising," Finley said.

I nodded. "I think so, too. I wasn't sure about giving him a shot, but I'm going to try."

"And if that doesn't work, you can always have some angry sex with Officer James Rucker," Laura said with a smirk.

I groaned and rolled my eyes while they all laughed at me. He was the last man I wanted to have sex with, angry or not.

WE FINISHED the pound cake and polished off the whipped cream and strawberries. I stayed behind with Karissa and Finley to clean up. It had become my habit, so I told myself it wasn't because I was afraid to walk home alone in the dark.

No one had to know the truth.

"Sorry we harassed you about James," Karissa said. "I really do think you two would be good together."

I shook my head. "And I think you're all insane."

Karissa chuckled. "You never know. How's your week this week? I was thinking of working in the park a day or two if you have anything you can do outside."

I thought through my plans. I didn't have too much going on, and a day in the park sounded like it might be just what I needed. "That works for me. Any particular day?"

Karissa shook her head. "Not really. We'll check the weather and make sure we won't get rained on."

"Sounds good."

Finley vacuumed the sitting area while Karissa and I straightened the shelves where we'd knocked books over. I read the back cover of one that caught my eye. A pastel pink sunset highlighted a couple in each other's arms, seconds from a kiss.

"That's really good," Finley said when she turned off the vacuum. "I read it the other day."

"Set it aside for me and I'll come pick it up this week," I told her.

Finley nodded and slid the book under the counter. She gave us a discount a lot of the time, but we all refused to let her give us books for free.

"All set?" Karissa asked.

Finley looked around and nodded. "Yeah, we're good. Let's go home."

We walked outside and waited for Finley to lock the door then turned toward our building. My eyes scanned the immediate area for anyone I didn't recognize or who gave me a bad feeling. The only people around were couples and another group of friends.

"Piper seems nice," I said, wondering what they thought of her.

"Yeah, I love Piper. She puts Hudson in his place. She doesn't take crap from anyone," Finley said.

"Are they together?" I asked.

"Oh, God, no. It's more like a brother / sister kind of relationship. Piper started working there years ago. She's had a few different jobs in the area, at MacKellar Cove Inn, at Cove Bakery, and even at Island Designs. She came up here one summer and never left," Finley explained.

"I can understand why," I said with a smile.

"No kidding," Karissa agreed. "I never thought to invite Piper. I kind of feel badly that we didn't before."

Finley shrugged. "We all sort of came together through your mom. We met Piper through O'Kelley's mostly. She's awesome, but it never crossed my mind. I don't think she was bothered by anything, though."

Karissa shook her head. "No, she's pretty easygoing. You have to be to work with Hudson and his mood sometimes."

"His wife died, right?" I asked.

Finley nodded. "Years ago. He hasn't really gotten over her. I don't know how you do."

"My mom will never get over my dad. It's not easy."

"I think when you really love someone, a part of you never gets over losing them," Karissa said, pausing to open the door to our building.

Finley and I walked in ahead. "Has he signed up for Book Boyfriends Wanted?"

Karissa laughed. "Not likely. I don't know for sure but I doubt it."

"We should set him up with someone," I said.

Finley and Karissa exchanged a glance and shook their heads. "Not a good idea," Finley said. "I love Hudson, but he has to be ready to date. Otherwise, he'll break someone's heart without meaning to. He's not ready yet."

"Good point," I admitted. We got to their floor, and Finley and Karissa moved away from the stairs.

"You okay to go up alone?" Karissa asked.

I smiled and nodded. "I'm good. Hopefully tonight is a better night. I'll see you guys soon."

"Night."

"Good night."

I climbed the next two flights of stairs and took my new keys out of my pocket. I hadn't decided if I was going to carry a purse again or just keep what I needed on me. For now, I was content not to have something someone could grab and take from me.

I turned the corner to my condo and saw a figure in front of my door. I was about to scream when he stood and turned to face me.

"What the hell are you doing here?" I blurted.

Officer James Rucker.

6

JAMES

I had hoped to be gone by the time she got home. I intended to be. Honestly, I wasn't even sure why I was there in the first place. I wanted to check on her. To make sure she was okay. Then I realized she wasn't home and sat there for a minute. Just being outside her door made me feel better. Like anyone who dared to threaten her could sense I'd been there.

I was definitely losing it.

I hadn't heard her climb the stairs. I was sure I would have, but I didn't hear anything until her keys jangled in her hand when she turned into the hallway. By then, it was too late to disappear without her seeing me.

"I wanted to check on you," I admitted to her. "Make sure you weren't doing anything that would invite danger into your world again."

I didn't know why I said that. No, that wasn't true. I knew exactly why I said it. And I got what I wanted. That flash in her rich, brown eyes, that fire that said she wanted to slap me. That anger that turned me on. I hadn't felt passion like that ever in my life. I had girlfriends and fuck buddies and one night stands, but none had made me feel like I couldn't breathe without a glimpse past her defenses. Not until I met Trinity.

"You're a first class asshole," she spat, walking toward me. Her eyes were narrowed, glaring a hole right through me. A hint of red rose on her brown cheeks, whether from anger or embarrassment, I wasn't entirely sure.

"So I've been told."

She scoffed. "Not nearly enough. How dare you say it was my fault that he stole my purse. I did nothing wrong. Would you have accused me of being to blame if he forced himself on me, too?"

Fire licked through me, anger hot and fast. I stepped closer to her, knowing she would look up at me when I did. Her gaze locked on mine and widened when she saw my eyes. "No woman deserves any of that. No person. You should be able to go where you want and do what you want. Don't ever blame yourself."

She rolled her eyes and turned back to her door. "Says the man who keeps accusing me of inviting danger in."

"I just want to piss you off," I confessed, the words escaping without a thought.

"And why the hell would you want to do that?" she asked, her voice confused as the lock clicked open.

"Because I love the spark in your eyes when you are."

She turned back to me and looked up. I didn't realize how petite she was until she was right there in front of me, her gaze locked on mine. Her eyes slid down my body, tightening every inch of it until I throbbed with need. She licked her lips and met my gaze again. The anger was still there, but it was mixed with desire. "Screw you, James," she whispered.

I stepped closer to her. She backed up, her back hitting her closed door. Her breath mingled with mine, both of us breathing heavy, our chests nearly touching with each ragged inhale. "Say the word, Trinity."

I'd barely gotten her name out when she went up on her toes and smashed her lips to mine. I didn't have time to be shocked by the move. My hands went to her hips and hauled her against my body, both of us fighting for control of the kiss.

She groaned and pulled back. She turned the knob and yanked me inside her apartment, then locked the door. I didn't wait to press her against the door and lean into her, letting her feel exactly how much I wanted her.

She moaned and pulled at my shirt. When she got her hands under it, she splayed her fingers wide then curled them and ran her short nails down my chest.

I groaned, the bite of her nails just the right touch to take my cock from throbbing to ready to blow. I needed to be inside her, and it needed to happen soon.

"Clothes off. Now," I commanded her, not letting her move from the door.

"Then back the hell off," she spat at me, shoving my shoulder. "You better have a condom."

"Always," I growled. I needed her to think this was something I did all the time. That she wasn't special. She hated me, and admitting to her that I'd been fantasizing about her for months was not going to happen.

She kicked off her shoes and tugged off her shirt. Her light pink bra made my mouth go dry. She was stunning. I wanted to drop to my knees and feast on her, but she was still stripping.

"What the hell are you doing?" she asked, stopping her movements.

"Nothing," I stammered. "Nothing." I shook my head and made quick work of my clothes. When I was done, she was standing in front of me naked, a beautiful brown goddess. I was fucking done for. She was the most stunning woman I'd ever seen.

Then she turned her back to me and bent at the waist, putting her hands on the front door.

"You're not going to let me kiss you?" I asked, knowing as soon as the words were out it was a mistake.

She snorted. "We don't like each other. This is sex. Sex doesn't need to involve anything other than you sliding in and out of me until we're both satisfied."

I didn't like it, but I wasn't going to argue when I was given an opportunity to be with her. I rolled on the condom and pulsed when I looked at her. She was on display, her perfect body ready for me. I could see her skin glistening between her thighs. Again, I wanted to drop to my knees and lick and suck and devour her, but she made it clear she wasn't up for that.

I positioned myself behind her and lined up to her entrance. I teased her a little with my cock, loving the fact that she groaned at the sensation. When her back sagged, I thrust into her hard, stealing her breath and making her moan. Her body locked down on my cock, and I nearly lost it right then.

"You should not feel this good," she said. "It's not fair."

"Agreed," I said before sliding out and thrusting in again.

She moaned and arched her back then met my next stroke with a thrust of her own. My hands went to her hips, digging into her plump flesh. I held her there while we worked together to set a rhythm that had my eyes rolling back.

I'd never been a selfish lover, but being with Trinity made me want to take from her. I wasn't going to last long with her, my cock already begging for a release. She fucked me back, but her body wasn't ready to let go yet. I needed to feel her, to have her tighten around me and scream my name.

I slid one hand up her back, letting the delicate touch confuse her senses, and the other around her hip and between her thighs. I pressed my front to her back so I could reach and groaned when I rubbed over her clit.

"Oh, God," she whispered.

"Close, but not quite," I said, kissing her shoulder. "Come for me, Trinity."

She grunted and bucked against my hand, almost like she was trying to push me off but it felt too good to resist. I didn't let up, pinching her clit between my finger and thumb.

Her movements became more erratic, and her channel tightened down on me. I licked her spine and pressed down hard on her clit, rubbing fast over it, and she splintered.

"Yes! Oh, God, yes! Oh, oh, oh! Yes!" she shouted as she came.

I grunted, the feel of her coming on me enough to send me into overdrive. I grabbed her hips again and pumped myself into her, spilling inside her as she panted and moaned and twitched around me.

My knees threatened to give out as my cock swelled and burst, but I held Trinity, taking my strength from hers. We stood like that, her hands on her door, my hands on her body, until we both could breathe normally.

She made a move to stand. I backed up and groaned at the feel of sliding out of her. I stepped away, conscious of the fact that she hadn't looked at me since she took her clothes off.

"Thanks," she mumbled before picking up her clothes and making a move toward the rest of the apartment.

"Shouldn't we talk about this?" I asked.

"Nope," she said, continuing to walk away.

I stared after her, wanting to nibble and lick my way up and down her spine. She turned and a door closed, eliminating her from my view.

I closed my eyes and shook my head. She was done with me.

I went into her kitchen and wrapped the used condom in a paper towel then buried it in her trash. I picked up my clothes and put them back on slowly, hoping she would come back out and have a conversation. When I'd stalled as long as I could, I called out to her.

"I'm leaving now. Lock your door."

"I will," she called back, her voice closer than I expected. She was standing on the other side of her bedroom door, listening for me to leave.

I sighed and walked out, wondering what in the hell I'd been thinking.

I WAS STILL BEATING myself up on Wednesday when I got to work. The last thing I wanted was to have to talk to my new partner all day, but I didn't get a choice. Masterson was there waiting for me when I walked in, ready to go.

He questioned my every move all morning until I was about to lose my fucking mind on him. He wanted to know why I let Mrs. Gregoire go without giving her a ticket. He asked why we didn't pull over the car that swerved in front of the school. He questioned my decision to issue a warning to Mr. Albert instead of taking him in when he had ten parking tickets in the system. Masterson did not understand life in a small town.

"So, do we just drive around all day and waste taxpayer money, or do we actually do things that help out? Writing a few tickets gives us income. Is that so hard?"

I took a deep breath and reminded myself I'd lose my job and my house and probably go to jail if I throat punched the guy. Instead of choosing that option, I decided to check in with Richie and see if he'd heard or seen anything.

"Stay here," I told my partner, not wanting or needing him to follow me inside the building.

"Why? What is this place? I'm not going to watch the car while you go have a quickie," he growled.

I spun back around and glared at him. "I'll be back in five fucking minutes."

He snorted. "Poor woman. You should treat her better than that."

I growled. The asshole was definitely getting a throat punch. One day.

I walked away, leaving him to cackle like an old lady on the sidewalk. The lobby was empty and quiet, like I expected. I was hoping to not run into Trinity, or Karissa and Finley for that matter.

Richie's office was on the ground floor near the back of the building. His door was open and music filtered into the hallway as I got closer. I knocked on the frame and walked in when he looked up and grinned.

"Afternoon, Officer. How are you?" Richie asked, standing and offering his hand.

"Good, Richie. Any news?" I'd told him many times to call me James, but he refused. Said it was a sign of respect.

"No, sir. I wish. I've been on the lookout for someone who might come by and try something, but I haven't seen a thing. Do you think we'll find whoever scared Trinity? It's been a week."

I nodded. "The longer it is, the less likely, but I'm not giving up. Have you talked to her?"

"Trinity?" I nodded again. "No, I haven't seen her. But that's not unusual. She's pretty quiet, keeps to herself. She's probably home if you want to go up and speak to her."

My cock twitched at the thought. Her soft moans filled

my ears and clouded my brain. I ached to touch and kiss her again, but she was done with me.

"I'm good. I'll just head out. Let me know if anything happens."

"I will, Officer. Thanks for checking in."

I nodded and walked out of the office. I was still thinking about how soft Trinity's skin was and how much I wanted to run up the stairs and have that quickie my asshole partner thought I was having when I walked into the lobby.

A kid, no older than fifteen, was standing near the mailboxes. He glanced back when I walked in. His eyes widened. He held a purse in his hand, one he looked like he was about to set on the table in front of the mailboxes. He snatched it back.

"Excuse me," I said to him.

Just that fast, he wrapped his arms around the purse and took off. His open backpack bounced as he slung it over his shoulder and ran. He slammed out the front door, racing away.

I rushed after him, calling out as soon as the fresh air hit my face. "Hey! Stop!"

The kid was ahead of me, a good distance away. He looked back to see how close I was, and my partner stepped into the kid's path.

He slammed into Masterson, bouncing off the man's chest and stumbling backward. Masterson had his gun out, pointing at the kid, before he turned to see what he ran into.

I hurried over, making it to their sides in a few seconds.

"Please, sir," the kid begged. "I'm sorry. I know I shouldn't have done it. My mom…I can't go to jail."

"What did you do?" Masterson demanded of the kid.

His bottom lip trembled and tears filled his hazel eyes. His shirt had a stain near the shoulder, and his jeans were torn in a way that was clearly from wear and not fashion. His clothes were a few sizes too big. His hair was brushed but in need of a cut, not just a trim. The dirt streaked across his cheek said he had more issues than just holding a purse that didn't belong to him.

"I stole this from a lady last week. She was walking on the Riverwalk, and I grabbed it from her. I think she got hurt, but my mom…we don't have any food. She works two jobs, but my little brother and I only get one meal a day. My mom gets less. All her money goes to paying for the room we rent and the debt my worthless dad left her with. I didn't mean to hurt that other lady. I didn't know she would fight me, but she looked like she had money. I didn't want her stuff. I know it was wrong, but—"

"Turn around. Put your hands behind your head," Masterson barked at the boy.

He dropped his head and sighed, then lowered the purse and his backpack to the ground. He turned and put his hands behind his head, meeting my gaze for the first time since he was inside the building.

I knew the pain in his eyes. I'd seen that despair in the mirror more times than I could count. A tear streaked down his cheek as Masterson read him his Miranda rights and snapped cuffs on his wrists.

I bent and picked up the purse. I knew what I would find before I opened it, but I had to know. I found her wallet without much trouble and sighed heavily when Trinity's face smiled up at me from her license photo.

"Who's your mom, kid?" I asked him without looking up.

"Anna Charlotte," the kid said with a hiccup.

I sighed again. I knew Anna. She grew up not far from me in Oak Hill. If there was such a thing as government housing in MacKellar Cove, it was where we lived. A small community of apartment type buildings with low rent. If you were lucky, you got a place with one bedroom, but most were efficiencies. They didn't care how many people stayed in one unit, as long as the rent was paid on time.

Anna was a year or two younger than me in school. She was smart, but she hung out with people who praised different skills. She married her high school sweetheart when she got pregnant, but he was the kind of guy who thought women were disposable. After Anna's second son was born, her husband took off. She tried to help her parents and gave them money to get out of Oak Hill, but they took the money and ran off, leaving Anna alone with two young boys and no support.

My mom still lived there and knew Anna, so she told me the whole story. The husband was still the husband because she couldn't find him to get a divorce, which meant Anna was responsible for his debts.

She couldn't handle one more thing.

"In the car," Masterson said, opening the back door for the kid to get in.

Anna's son did as he was told, not fighting at all. He was defeated, and he knew it. I'd been there. I'd been the kid who stole something and ended up on my way to jail. But I had a cop who looked out for me. Someone who took time to help me. Someone who changed my entire life.

It was time I paid it forward.

7

"Hold up a minute," I said to my new partner before he climbed in the car.

"Yeah?" he said, clearly low on patience.

"We're not taking him to the station."

"Are you kidding me? Why the fuck not?"

"Because he's a kid."

Masterson shrugged. "And?"

"He deserves a second chance."

"He deserves to go to jail. His mom will bail him out and he'll be home soon."

"His mom doesn't have the money to bail him out."

Masterson huffed and shook his head. "So, we just let him go? Isn't this the guy you've been looking for? The one who stole the purse? You changed the woman's locks and you're all up on her, and you found the guy, but now you don't want to throw everything at him."

Countless questions raced to the tip of my tongue, but I wasn't about to give my new partner the satisfaction of knowing he'd figured out more than I'd told him about Trinity. Instead, I shook my head.

"No, I don't want to throw everything at him. He's a kid. He was trying to help his family. He made a mistake, and he was here to try to make up for it a little. He's not a bad kid."

"You know him?"

I shook my head. "I know his mom."

"Dad?"

"No dad. Skipped out on them. Left Mom with a bunch of debt."

"Asshole."

I nodded, knowing no other words would help. That one said it all.

"I don't like it," Masterson said. "But I get it."

I nodded once and took the win. We both got in the car and I swung around to head out of town. None of us spoke as I drove toward Highway 12 then turned north. When I pulled into the neighborhood where I grew up, my palms dampened and my throat closed up.

I hated being there. I tried to get my mom to leave, but she refused. Always said it was home. Not for me. As soon as I could, I got the hell out of there. I was happy to never set foot in that neighborhood again. But as a cop, I had no choice.

"Why are we here?" Joey asked.

The fear in the kid's voice made me wonder if there was something else going on. "I thought you lived here, Joey."

"I do, but my mom's going to kill me. You can't ask her for money right now. She doesn't have any. She's trying her hardest. Just take me to jail. She's going to have to pay someone to watch my little brother, but it'll be cheaper than getting me out."

The kid's voice shook. A tiny hiccup said he was crying in the back.

"We're not asking your mom for money," Masterson said. "We're letting you go home."

"What? Why would you do that? I stole from that lady."

"Are you going to do it again?" I asked.

"No. Never. I'm sorry. I shouldn't have done it. My brother hadn't eaten and my mom almost passed out. I just wanted to help them."

I parked in front of his building and got out of the car. I opened his door and helped him out, then unlocked the cuffs that bound his wrists together. I spun him to face me. "Look at me, Joey."

He took in a shaky breath and met my gaze. His jaw was set and strong. He looked like his father, like the man I had vague memories of from high school. Light brown hair and blue-green eyes. Tall and thin but strong. My guess was Joey was around fifteen when I saw him at Trinity's, but standing there with fear and determination in his gaze he looked much younger.

When I was the one crawling out of the back of a police car, I was only thirteen. My brother was seven. I stole cans of beans from the grocery store and got caught with them in my pockets. My brother would cry on the weekends because we didn't have food to eat. My mom did the best she could, but school provided most of our meals. Over the weekend, we were lucky if we had one good meal a day. Beans were a staple for us since they were cheap and lasted a while, but even beans were too expensive sometimes.

People who had never struggled with something basic like having food couldn't usually understand how frightening it was to not know if you would eat again soon. Because it was never just the food. At Joey's age, he'd figured out that if his mom couldn't buy food, she also might not be able to afford rent. Their heat or water could be turned off. It was a tough situation, to say the least.

"I've been in your shoes." I pointed to the building next to his. "I grew up in that building. Do you know Ms. Amelia?"

Joey nodded.

"She's my mother. We are going to help you and your family. But the only way I can do that is if you stay out of trouble. You got me?"

Joey nodded again, relief flooding his gaze.

Masterson stayed at the car while I walked Joey up to the door. The lock on the outside was broken, so we walked right into the building. I followed Joey up the stairs to the second floor. The place smelled of urine and BO. Voices shouted to each other from behind closed doors that were too thin to allow for privacy. A baby cried in one unit.

Joey walked up to the door with a nine on it and opened the unlocked door. I looked at it as I stepped inside and saw that the knob was barely hanging on. It had a lock, but a good push would knock the door off the hinges.

"I'll get my mom," Joey said softly, hanging his head as he walked toward the only bedroom.

They were lucky to have a bedroom. The kitchen was to the left, with a small table crammed in the tiny space. The faded yellow walls and once tan countertops slapped me in the face with familiarity. All the units were designed the same, and it was like being in my mom's place, the memories of being that kid in trouble rising up.

"Oh, God," a small voice breathed.

I turned and looked at her and almost didn't recognize Anna. She was tall, like her son, but she had curves where he was thin. Her eyes had heavy bags beneath them, dark and purple like she hadn't slept well in forever. Her hair was greasy and stringy.

"Hey, Anna," I said with a smile I hoped reassured her.

"What can I do for you, Officer?" she asked, crossing her arms over her chest.

"Let me help you, Anna."

She scoffed. "You ran out of here so fast you'd have thought your ass was on fire."

I nodded. "I wasn't the only one."

She scowled. "Yeah, well, you didn't come back."

"Why didn't you tell me things were so bad?"

"Don't fool yourself into thinking we're friends, Officer. I don't know you and you don't know me."

I sighed. She was right. "But you know my mom."

A hint of a smile curled her lips up. "I do. And Amelia is a lifesaver, but I can't have her save me."

"Do you know why I'm here?" I asked, changing the conversation in a way I hoped would encourage her to listen.

She looked at Joey and shook her head. "I'm guessing to arrest him."

I shook my head. "Not today. He's promised me he won't steal again."

She spun on her son and got up in his face. He was a half a head shorter than her, which made me think he was younger than I'd assumed. Especially when his lower lip trembled.

"You stole something? What were you thinking? You could have been hurt. Why would you take something that didn't belong to you? I've told you so many times that I will take care of everything."

"Matty was hungry, Mom. He was crying. And you're always working. You were sick. I know you work hard, but we don't have enough food. We never do."

Anna glanced at me and closed her eyes when she saw me watching, taking in every word they said. After a moment, she turned back to me, but grabbed Joey's hand.

"Matty is my ten year old. Joey here is only fourteen. He watches his brother after school so I can work. I'm doing the best I can. I didn't know."

"I'm not here to judge you, Anna. I want to help. But we both know the only way I can help you is if you let me."

"What? Do you want to be our knight? Come on, James, we both know you have no interest in being here. You're cringing just standing in this place. You've likely been breathing through your mouth since you set foot in this building. If I could do anything to get my boys out of here, I would. But I don't have a degree, I barely graduated from high school, and I'm already working two full time jobs to try to make ends meet. There's not enough with the debt my husband put in my name."

"Have you filed for bankruptcy?"

She scoffed. "And ensure these boys never get out of here? No thank you."

"What can I do?" I asked her. She knew what she needed, but she was also going to have to accept help.

"Nothing. There's nothing you can do. You made your life better. I just keep screwing up mine. I'll figure it out. I always do."

"Anna—"

"Please. Don't," she said, her eyes begging me to let it go. She didn't want help. Not yet. She was scared and alone and she'd reached the place every person in Oak Hill got to at some point. She had to decide what she was going to do. If she was going to fight or if she was going to give up.

Anna didn't want help, but she was a fighter. She would find a way, and if I had anything to say about it, she wouldn't have to do it alone.

As I WALKED out of Anna's, I thought about reaching out to my mom. She was the director at the community center in charge of youth programs. There was a fee, but they offered scholarships if there was a need. Usually they filled up quickly, but if they had any openings, it could help Anna out, or make it possible for Joey to get a job.

I was overdue for a visit with my mom, so I decided not to call and just to go see her later. A move that was definitely warranted when I caught sight of the scowl on my new partner's face.

"Is there anyone in this town you'll actually arrest?"

I sighed. "You don't understand how this town works. You can't haul in everyone who does something."

"I think you're the one who doesn't understand how this job works. You're supposed to bring people in. It's not our job to judge them, it's our job to turn them in and let their peers judge them."

I scrubbed a hand down my face and sighed. "Joey is fourteen. He has a brother who is ten. He stole Trinity's purse because his brother had no food. Joey isn't a malicious kid with evil intentions. He was trying to feed his little brother."

"And you think that makes it okay?"

I shook my head. "No, but I also know the position he's in isn't an easy one."

"What are you going to tell the woman who had her purse stolen? That it wasn't a big deal because it was a kid?"

I drew in a breath and held it. I thought about Trinity for a second and all the breath rushed out of me. I could still smell her scent if I closed my eyes. Taste her kiss. Feel her body tight around mine. The image of her bent over in front of me, her curvy body slick and ready for me, had me swelling behind my zipper.

I shifted in my seat and pictured her scowling at me. That was an easy one since she usually was. But that shifted to tears. The fear in her eyes the night Joey grabbed her purse was real. And to walk in and tell her that it was a kid and I let him go...I wasn't sure how that would go over.

"I'll deal with Trinity."

"And the captain?"

"Him, too."

Masterson rolled his eyes. "I should just ride in the back."

"Why?"

"Because you have me handcuffed, too. I can't do my job if you aren't going to actually take anyone to jail or write a damn ticket."

I huffed and backed out of the parking spot we were in. The idea of handcuffing my partner and tossing him in the back of the car held some real appeal, but I was pretty sure that was one thing I couldn't get out of if I did it.

WHEN MY SHIFT WAS OVER, I headed to O'Kelley's. I was in serious need of a beer, and maybe a word or two of advice. Hudson always had both.

I parked at a stool on the end, like usual, and nodded when Piper set a beer in front of me.

"Alone tonight?" she asked.

I nodded. "Yep."

"Long day?"

I nodded again. "Definitely."

"You want something to eat? Hudson's in the back, but I can put in an order for you if you're ready."

"Thanks, Piper. Hot wings with bleu cheese and a basket of cheese curds."

"Coming right up," Piper said. "Hey, Trinity."

Trinity took the seat next to me before I had a chance to turn and see her coming. "Give me whatever he just ordered."

"Hot wings and cheese curds?" Piper asked.

"Yep. And a beer. And put it all on his tab. He owes me," Trinity said.

"For what?" I asked, staring at her. Just being so close to her had me wanting to reach out and grab her. Hold her. Touch her. Kiss her. Whatever she'd let me do.

Trinity shrugged. "You always do something. I figured it was time I got a free meal out of it."

Piper chuckled as she set a beer in front of Trinity and left to put in our order.

"You just here to eat free food?" I asked her.

She sipped her beer and shook her head. "Nope. I got a call today. The guy said you caught the kid who stole my purse. And let him go."

She raised a perfectly arched brow at me and waited. Her brown skin glowed in the dim lighting above the bar. She looked ethereal, like a gift just for me. Except she wasn't mine and never would be. Trinity had never chosen to sit next to me. I had very little hope she would stay long. And I knew I'd be to blame for it.

"He's fourteen. And he was trying to get money to feed his ten year old brother."

She held my gaze for a long moment. "And you believe that's the truth?"

I nodded. "I do. I also know where he lives so if you want me to take him in, I will. But his mom works two jobs to pay the bills. His dad ran out on them years ago and saddled his mom with a bunch of debt. She's a good person, and she's just trying to make it all work. Joey, the kid, he didn't mean to hurt you or to scare you. He just wanted to make sure his brother had food."

Trinity nodded as I spoke then sighed. "Can I do anything to help them?"

Well, damn. I fell just a little bit in love with her at that moment.

"Help who?" Hudson asked, walking up on the other side of the bar.

"The kid who stole my purse," Trinity provided.

Hudson looked to me, and I nodded.

"It's a bad situation," Trinity continued, "and I'd rather help them than have him steal from someone else."

"I don't think they'll accept charity. I know the mom. She's a pretty proud woman," I said.

"Who?" Hudson asked.

"Anna Bradford. Now Anna Charlotte."

Hudson shook his head. "She's from here?"

I nodded. "She grew up in my neighborhood. She's younger than us. Married Nick Charlotte."

"Oh," Hudson said, catching on to all the things I wasn't saying. Nick Charlotte was known by pretty much everyone, even if only by reputation. What he did to Anna was public knowledge. She wasn't in too many circles over the last decade and a half since she was busy raising her boys, but everyone knew about Nick.

"Yeah," I agreed. "Her oldest is fourteen, the younger one is ten. They know Mom, but..."

"Fourteen means the kid can work. Has he tried for a job anywhere?" Hudson asked.

I shook my head. "He watches his brother while their mom works."

"Aren't there after school programs?" Trinity asked.

"The free ones are always booked up fast. And the rest all cost money. Usually a lot of money."

"Maybe I could cover the cost of that," she offered.

I shook my head. "I don't think she'd go for that."

"He can work here," Hudson said. "I could use a busboy. Obviously, that would mean finding a place for the brother to be. He can't hang out here while his brother works. I'd lose my license."

"Really?" I asked him. "You'd do that?"

Hudson nodded. "If you can find a spot for the younger

brother, send the older one to me. They might go for it since it's not charity."

I nodded. "Thanks, Hud. That means a lot."

He knocked on the bar top and walked away. I went there for advice and would walk away with a potential solution. It felt too easy, but it could work.

"I guess this is the guy everyone kept telling me about," Trinity said.

"What do you mean?" I asked her.

She huffed a smile and shook her head. "I mean, you really aren't an ass to everyone. Just me."

I leaned over and whispered in her ear, "I was very, very nice to you a few nights ago if you remember."

Her breath hitched and she leaned toward me. A dark stain rose on her brown cheeks and she licked her lips. "I haven't been able to forget."

Well, dammit. Just that quick, I was hard again.

8

TRINITY

Seeing James flustered was almost as big of a turn on as the angry sex we had the other night. I was telling the truth when I said I hadn't been able to stop thinking about it. About him. He'd become my favorite fantasy, and even though I hated him for it, I couldn't stop myself from remembering every second.

"Maybe we should do it again sometime," he said.

I snorted. Not because I didn't want to, but because we hated each other. I was not about to get involved with him. Not when all we did was argue. Or fuck. But that was a one time thing.

"Yeah, I don't think so. Anyway, I'm meeting someone here."

The fire in his eyes almost made me laugh. Pissing him off was fun, too.

"Are you staying here or did you want me to put your food at the table when it's ready?" Piper asked, stopping on her way past us.

"Table," I told her. "Thanks."

She nodded and smirked so James couldn't see her. I winked back and swallowed my own grin.

"You're up here flirting with me and you're on a date?" he spat. "Wow."

I shrugged, not giving him the satisfaction of an answer, and slid off the stool. "I just wanted free food. I didn't think you'd pay if you didn't know about it. Knowing you, you'd try to arrest me or something."

"Say the word and I'll be happy to get my handcuffs out," he said, his voice low and sexy. The glimmer in his eyes said he'd thought about it, too.

The man was potent. I didn't even have to spend ten minutes with him and I was ready to drag him to the bathroom and bend over the sink. But I couldn't do it. I couldn't fuck him again just because it was amazing sex. It was still with Officer James Rucker. The man who'd almost run me out of town. Who was nice to everyone but me. Who made it very clear he felt the same way I did.

"Trust me, I know you'd take any opportunity to drag me out of here," I said, letting the flirty words linger between us. "But not tonight."

He scowled as I turned away. I wound my way through the crowd, his eyes on my back. I knew when he saw where I sat down he would realize I'd been messing with him. I couldn't help but enjoy that he would know I wasn't on a date like he assumed, and that I was still available.

Except for the guy I was talking to online. But I didn't count that yet. We hadn't met or traded much personal info. He could become more than a connection, but I wasn't sure yet.

I reclaimed my seat between Laura and Finley. I took a sip of the beer I carried with me and glanced back at James. He shook his head and lifted his beer in salute, knowing he'd been had. I just smiled.

"What was that?" Piper asked, setting down my plate then Finley and Laura's.

"What?" I asked.

"You and James? I thought I was going to need to get the water hose," she said, fanning herself with her bar towel.

I laughed. "I like to mess with him."

"I thought you hated him," Finley said.

"Oh, I do. But I've realized it's fun to screw with him, too," I said, smiling at my own private double entendre.

"It feels like there's more to that story," Laura said, tilting her head and leaning forward.

I shook mine, letting my spiral curls bounce. "Nope. He was decent to me for the first time ever the night I was robbed. I got a call today that they found the guy, and it was just a kid. James let him go. I just wanted to ask him about it and see if it was true."

"Do you know who it was?" Piper asked.

"He said the name, but I don't know it. The kid's mom is from here and a little younger than him and Hudson, but I didn't recognize her name. Anna something, maybe."

Piper shrugged. "I don't think I know an Anna. Are you going to press charges?"

"No. He was trying to get money to buy food for his brother. I can't think of a better reason. He still shouldn't have done it, but I do understand," I told her.

Piper put her hand on my shoulder. "You're a better person than I would be. I'd love to say I'd be that forgiving, but I don't know if I would be."

"No one should go hungry. If he'd have asked, I would have bought him food. Maybe he'll learn that and do better next time. But forcing him to do community service or sending him to jail isn't going to solve anything for him. He needs to know there are other options."

"You sound like James," Piper said with a grin. "You two really would be perfect for each other."

I scoffed. "Except for the fact that we hate each other."

She shrugged. "Who said you have to like each other for some really good sex? We already had this conversation. You don't even have to talk."

I tried to smirk, but the memory of our spectacular sex against the door to my apartment flooded my memory. Piper was right. We didn't have to talk. At all. And for once, I didn't hate him. He felt so good I could barely breathe afterward. And if the opportunity arose, I would have a hard time turning him down again.

"I don't know," Laura said. "I still don't think I could have sex with someone I didn't like. Unless it was someone I didn't know well. But if I knew him and didn't like him, I don't think I could do it."

"You'd be surprised," Finley said. "I had a study partner in college that was an arrogant ass. I hated him. One night we were up late studying and ended up having sex. Hands down, the best sex of my life. The rest of the semester, we would study then have sex. I never saw him again after that, and I still think he's an ass, but the sex was amazing."

Laura snorted and shook her head. "I wish I was more like you. No judgement. I just wish I could do it."

"Who would you sleep with?" Finley asked. "If you had to pick someone you don't like, who would it be?"

Laura sipped her drink and leaned back. "I don't know. I haven't given too many men a second thought in so long."

"We really need to get you laid," I told her with a grin. "You'll feel better."

She laughed. "Think the guy would mind if I was imagining someone else?"

Finley put her hand on Laura's. "Oh, Laura. You never tell him that, and he'll never know!"

We laughed and nodded. Just like I would never admit I'd slept with James. Ever.

JAMES WAS ALREADY GONE when I left O'Kelley's that night. I half expected to find him waiting at my door when I got home. I tried not to be disappointed when he wasn't.

I spent the next few days recording videos and creating new designs. I liked the idea of sharing what I did with new people, people who were like me. Not everyone had the ability to buy jewelry, but that didn't mean they shouldn't look hot when they went out.

I had an appointment with Olive at Island Designs to show her some of my new pieces. I was hoping she would let me offer different options, but I was also holding back some of the items I liked the best for my own website. I felt a little guilty, but Olive assured me she understood completely. She liked the idea of only having certain things in her store, and she loved promoting local business. I was lucky to have met someone like her. Through Blake, of course.

I slung my bag over my shoulder then hesitated. Even though I knew the kid who grabbed my purse was a unique situation, it made me more aware of how careless I'd gotten since moving to MacKellar Cove. I knew what it was like to have to watch out for anything. Living in a small town, I'd forgotten. And it showed.

With my bag across my body, I set out to visit Olive. It was a beautiful day outside with the sun shining bright and the temperature still warm. I knew fall was coming, but for a few more weeks, it would feel like summer. I walked along the Riverwalk, facing the fear that had been inside since the night the kid stole my purse, and some of my trust. I wanted to forgive him and understand, but it didn't mean the fear would go away immediately.

People were kayaking in the cove, their bright boats bobbing along as they moved across the calm water. The MacKellar Cove Inn stood tall at one side of the entrance to the cove with the old MacKellar family home on the other side. Two massive structures that felt out of place in a town that was otherwise simple and quaint.

I turned up Joseph Street, cutting between Cove Antiques and Pop My Corn on my way toward Island Designs. I smiled at a few people I recognized. It still surprised me that after only a year people knew who I was.

Olive was behind the counter when I walked in. She nodded toward the back. I smiled and headed toward her unofficial office by the screen printing machine.

I opened my bag and removed the items I'd chosen to show Olive. I had some stock to replenish for her, but the new pieces were the ones I was hoping she'd take.

"I hear your videos are getting a lot of traffic," Olive said when she was close enough for me to hear her. "You're going to put me out of business."

"Not even a little bit," I said, glancing around her packed store. "You have so many things that people can't get elsewhere."

"That's the beauty of it. But I know it's a tourist trap. People come in here when they visit. The winter is always slow."

"Have you thought about closing in the winter? Saving a little money?"

Olive scoffed. "And do what? I'd be bored out of my mind without this place to come to. Even if I only get one or two people in here a day, it's more than I see at home."

I grinned. Olive was married to her work. She always said

if she could have gotten away with telling people it was her lover, she would have. She loved it, and she loved talking to people and telling them the stories she made up about the town.

"You have some new stuff for me? Any of it from your videos?" Olive asked.

I nodded and showed her two pieces that I'd made live on my YouTube channel. "I wasn't sure how these would turn out, but they're pretty great."

"Beautiful," Olive said reverently, lifting the one bracelet and examining all the beads.

It was a linked chain with beads dangling from different loops so it looked like it was twisted even though it wasn't. It had an elegance to it that was almost surprising because of the simplicity of the materials, but it worked.

"This will definitely sell. It's not an easy design, though. You think people could do this on their own?"

I shrugged. "If they have patience. I have some projects that are easy and some that take a bit more care, but I think I have something for everyone."

"Except kids," Olive said quietly.

"What?"

"Kids," Olive repeated. "Young people. I've gotten a few parents in here. When they see your signs, they say they wish you would do some videos of things that were easy for kids. I told them I don't think that's your target customer."

"No, I..." I paused. "It never occurred to me. Honestly, I'm not sure why. I started making jewelry when I was in high school, but there's no reason it can't be done by younger kids."

"You need to know how to teach them. Can you talk to kids?"

I laughed. "Of course. It's not that hard."

Olive shrugged. "Maybe. What about the youth center? Maybe go there and work with them before you get all cocky."

I smirked. "Maybe I will."

Olive nodded then tucked the pieces I'd shown her into a box. "What else do you have for me?"

I showed her the rest and handed over everything I'd brought with me. We talked price and I left with a check that would cover me for the next week.

After I stopped at the bank, I walked over to Catherine Park and sat in one of the chairs overlooking the Cove. When I first visited MacKellar Cove, I sat in the same chair and imagined what life would be like if I moved there. I'd grown tired of the hustle and bustle of the city and wanted a slower pace. A part of me imagined I'd find a man on day one and be settled down and married a year into living there, but that wasn't in the cards for me.

I looked up at Blake's mural of Ms. Georgia. I'd only met her once and didn't know her well, but I still thought of her often. She was an amazing woman who'd raised another amazing woman. I had no way of knowing how my life would have changed if Ms. Georgia were still there, but I couldn't imagine it would have been any better.

I smiled at her and stood, knowing she was watching me. Ms. Georgia was the guardian angel for all of us. I said a silent prayer that she would be with Karissa as she decided if she wanted a mastectomy or not.

On my way home, I spotted Piper on the Riverwalk sitting on a bench. Instead of walking past her like I would have done in the city, I stopped and sat down next to her.

"Hey, Trinity," she said brightly when she looked up. "How are you?"

"Good. Enjoying the sunshine?"

She nodded. "I am. I try to take my breaks outside as much as I can. It's hard to stay inside all day."

I chuckled. "I agree. I used to keep my slider open when I worked to get some fresh air."

"Used to?"

"Paranoid fear got to me."

Piper nodded in understanding. "Sorry. It sucks not feeling safe."

"Working in a bar I bet you have that feeling a lot."

It was Piper's turn to laugh. "Nope. If anyone ever laid a hand on me or anyone else, Hudson and James would kill them. Hudson doesn't play around with that kind of thing, and James is never far."

I snorted and shook my head.

"What's the real deal with you two?" Piper asked.

I shook my head again. "We don't get along. Never have, never will."

"See, I just find that hard to believe. Not with the way he stares at you."

"Like I said before, probably waiting to see something he can arrest me for."

Piper arched an eyebrow. "I think he's looking for something very different."

My entire body flushed with heat. I wanted to blame the sun, but it just ducked behind a cloud. I tried to push out words to deny what Piper said, but the dangerous glimmer in James' eyes when he pushed me said she might be right.

"Well, maybe I'm wrong," Piper said as she stood.

I nodded. "You are. He does not like me."

Piper stared at the water for a second then turned to me. "You're confident about that."

I nodded again.

She smirked. "Then he probably wouldn't have gotten so

upset when he thought you were on a date the other night. But what do I know."

She walked away without another word. All I could do was stare after her and try to convince myself she saw something that wasn't there. But I wasn't sure even I believed that lie.

Or wanted to.

9

I did everything I could to avoid James and O'Kelley's for the next week. The last thing I needed was Piper, or anyone else, thinking anything was happening between James and me. Piper didn't come to girls' night that weekend either, so it was even better.

But it left me feeling off. I couldn't get her words out of my head, and I couldn't stop dreaming about James. All night I imagined him climbing into bed with me and burning up the sheets together. During the day, I pushed thoughts of him ruthlessly out of my mind, but the number of times I had to do so was alarming. Like five alarm fire alarming.

The other thing I couldn't stop thinking about was creating training options for kids. I felt like there was more I could do. Too many kids ended up going to college and leaving with more debt than their earning potential, or never going to college because they couldn't afford it. Bringing in a steady income was a dream for many people. I had a skill that was taught to me by my grandmother. I'd kept learning and trying new things, but if I hadn't had her to encourage me to do it in the first place, I never would have.

I just wasn't sure I was good enough to teach kids. Like Olive said, it required a certain demeanor to get them to listen. Teenagers were more worried about social media and videos that entertained them than they were about learning a skill. Which meant I needed to learn more about how to talk to kids.

Dammit.

I was looking up information about the youth center when a notification popped up from Book Boyfriends Wanted.

JAYPO

I think I might have to dispose of my coworker's body. He's making me crazy today.

I laughed and shook my head.

DIAMONDGIRL

Probably not a good idea. I know a cop. I'd feel obligated to report you.

JAYPO

You know a cop?

DIAMONDGIRL

LOL, of course. Small town life means everyone knows everyone. I thought you lived near A-Bay?

JAYPO

I do. Sorry, fear got the better of me. I probably shouldn't be confessing something to someone I don't know.

DIAMONDGIRL

Probably true. I'd have to tell the cops that a guy whose name I don't know, whom I've never met, and who I can't describe told me he buried a body somewhere. I'm a wealth of info.

JAYPO

Good point. You're the perfect person to confess to.

DIAMONDGIRL

Hey! I'd be an accessory or something. I don't look good in orange.

JAYPO

I'd bet you look good in anything.

DIAMONDGIRL

Or nothing? Isn't that how that line is supposed to go? Of course it's better in person.

JAYPO

Then maybe we should meet sometime.

My smile faded as I processed his words. He was perfect inside the phone. He always said the right thing and he was kind and sweet and in my head, he was sexy with amazing hands and an even better tongue.

If we met, all that could change. What if he was rude to a server at dinner? Or if he was one of those people whose laugh was really obnoxious? Or if the spark only existed when we weren't live and in person?

JAYPO

Eventually. No pressure to meet now. How are things going?

A part of me breathed a sigh of relief but another part felt ridiculously disappointed that he gave up so easily. It wasn't fair since I had gone back and forth about even talking to him.

DIAMONDGIRL

Going okay. I'm considering expanding my business to try to reach kids. It's tough to think about, though. Kids have such a limited focus.

JAYPO

True. I was talking to a teenager the other day and he was not interested at all in what I was telling him. And he's one of the good ones.

DIAMONDGIRL

That's what worries me. I don't want to do something that ends up being useless. It's not that I need to earn money on everything I do, but I've seen the YouTube videos that are popular right now. That's not me.

JAYPO

You mean you're not an early 20's teen wannabe with bleached hair and a high pitched voice that makes you sound like you fell down the hill into the Valley?

I snorted a laugh.

DIAMONDGIRL

Not one word in that sentence described me.

JAYPO

Thank goodness for that.

DIAMONDGIRL

Am I safe to assume that's not you either?

JAYPO

Hell, no. That described me to a T. You should hear my giggle in my high pitched voice. I've been asked if I've gone through puberty yet.

DIAMONDGIRL

You're bad.

JAYPO

Yeah, well, talking to you makes me not want to commit murder. I wish I could hear your laugh.

DIAMONDGIRL

One day. Sorry. I'm cautious bordering on paranoid.

JAYPO

Don't apologize for being careful. Trust me, it's not a bad thing in my book.

DIAMONDGIRL

Thanks. I do like talking to you.

JAYPO

Me, too.

We chatted a few more minutes then he said he had to get back to work. I closed the app and went back to my search into the youth center Olive mentioned.

The address wasn't too far away so I decided to check it out. I grabbed some beads then paused and put them back. If I was there with a bunch of kids, they would want to make something themselves, not just watch me. I would just go see the place and take it from there.

I parked in the small lot next to the community center and looked at the building. It had definitely seen better days. The old brick was still in good shape but a pressure washer would do wonders for it. The windows and doors looked like they could have been repurposed from a prison. The cracked parking lot and sidewalks were an accident waiting to happen.

I shouldn't have been surprised by the falling down nature of the place, but after seeing how much care was given to most of MacKellar Cove, it was startling to see such a state of disrepair.

I sidestepped over the worst of the cracks and made my way up the four steps to the door. It was locked, and when I yanked on it, an intercom I hadn't noticed before crackled.

"Can I help you?"

I pushed the button and replied, "Um, yes. I wanted to check out the youth center and learn about opportunities to work with the kids."

The door buzzed and I rushed to grab it before the buzzing stopped. I walked into a vestibule with red carpet, zero windows, and a flickering fluorescent light. The door in front of me had no handle on it, and the window to my right was boarded up.

The telltale click of the lever on the opposite side being pushed warned me to step back before the door swung and caught my toes. An older woman with gray hair and a sharp look in her eyes scanned me.

"Follow me," she said without a greeting.

I nodded and moved behind her. She didn't go far, just to the office that was on the other side of the boarded up window, and gestured to the plastic chair near the door.

She moved to sit behind the desk, narrowly missing a stack of papers perched on the edge. I wasn't sure how they stayed put and wondered if the papers were simply too afraid of the woman to move.

"Name," the woman said, grabbing a pen and positioning it over a form.

"Trinity Mayer," I said automatically.

"Address."

I tilted my head and recited my address and phone number to her. I stopped when she asked for my social security number.

"Why do you need that?"

The woman looked up at me. "I thought you said you wanted to work with the kids."

I nodded. "I do, but why do you need all this information."

Her eyebrows shot up. She smiled, to herself, and nodded once. She set her pen down and folded her hands over the paperwork she'd been filling out.

"Ms. Mayer, do you know what this place is?"

"Um, isn't this the community center?"

She nodded. "It is. And this part is where the kids come. Some as young as kindergarten as we're primarily an after school program."

"Um, okay," I said, still not clear on why she needed so much information.

"Ms. Mayer, I'm sure you're a wonderful person, but not everyone who walks through that door is. There are people who come here to volunteer because they abuse children, they fantasize about children, they would kidnap or rape children if given the opportunity. When I start asking them questions like this, they bow out and say they don't have time after all. Because they know if I run a background check on them, it will come up with something they don't want me to find. So, forgive me, but you came to us. If you don't have time after all, please leave."

"I'm sorry," I rushed to say. "I didn't think. I apologize. No, I didn't mean…I'd like to continue, if that's okay."

The woman raised an eyebrow and nodded.

I answered every question she asked. When she said she needed three references, I gave her Finley, Karissa, and Laura's names and phone numbers. Only then did she ask anything that wouldn't be used to verify my identity or check up on me.

"Why do you want to work here?" she asked.

"I'm a jewelry designer, and I post tutorials online. I've realized there's a gap in the market where it comes to kids. I learned to design when I was a teenager, but younger kids could be interested. I wanted to get some insight, but also to give back a little."

The woman nodded. "I think it's a great idea. We have a good number of kids who would enjoy something like that. We do not have photography waivers from parents, though, so you wouldn't be able to record here. They could be your guinea pigs, but we would not be able to authorize filming or photos on site. I'm assuming you would provide kits for them to do the work."

I was surprised by the request but nodded. It was a great idea.

"Good. Unfortunately, we don't have a big budget, so we wouldn't be able to pay for too many. We are always looking for activities for the kids to do and don't have anything like this, so I think it will be a good fit. We will offer this as a class the kids could sign up for, but we would have to cap it depending on how expensive each kit is. I'm assuming your time is donated, right?"

She made notes and I nodded. "Of course. And I could provide the kits. Free of charge."

She narrowed her eyes at me. "Are you here for the right reasons, Ms. Mayer?"

I nodded. "I am. And please, call me Trinity."

"Okay, Trinity. I'm Amelia. Unfortunately, I need to throw you out because I will have kids coming in here soon. I'll get in touch with you once I've run your credit and background check and spoken to your references. Shouldn't be too long."

I stood when she did and let her usher me out of the office and back outside. I realized when I was driving away I never got to look at the place to see if there was a space we could use.

At the end of the day, it didn't matter. After seeing the place, there was no way I wasn't going to do something to help them out. Even if I had to buy tables for the kids to use when they were making their jewelry or do tutorials on a basketball court, I'd make it work.

I INVITED FINLEY, Karissa, and Laura over to dinner that night to warn them about Amelia and her potential phone calls. And because I missed my friends.

I still hadn't gotten used to having people around that I could call and they would be there without notice. In the city, it was a process to do things with other people. First, we had to decide on what to do, then figure out where to go, then what time worked for everyone with their schedules. It was too stressful and annoying. I never felt like I really fit with the people I spent time with. And the fact that we hadn't kept in touch since I moved away proved that we weren't that close anyway.

A knock on the door just before six had me smiling before I even got there. When I saw Laura through the peephole, I grinned even wider. "Hey," I said as I opened the door.

"Hey," she replied with a smile of her own. She looked business casual in her black leggings and lavender tunic with a large hobo bag thrown over her shoulder. Only the look in her eyes said she was not having a great day.

"What's wrong?"

She shook her head and rolled her eyes. "I'm being stupid."

"Nico?" I asked.

She nodded.

I wrapped my arm around her shoulders and led her inside. She sat on the stool I pointed to and I poured her a big glass of wine. She grinned in thanks.

"Want to tell me what happened?"

A knock interrupted us before Laura could answer. I went to let Finley and Karissa in. They were loud and boisterous and their usual selves, complete with a tray of something that smelled amazing.

"I invited you guys for dinner. You didn't have to bring anything," I told them as Finley unwrapped the dish. It looked even better than it smelled.

"Bacon wrapped mac and cheese cups," Karissa said. "I saw the recipe online and was procrastinating today. I wanted to try something new."

"I need one of those," Laura said, grabbing one off the tray. She bobbled it then dropped it onto the tray again. "Hot."

"They just came out of the oven," Karissa said. "Sorry. I should have warned you."

I set plates out so we could enjoy our appetizer before dinner. I poured wine for Finley and Karissa then refilled Laura's and poured my own.

"You're already on glass two?" Finley asked. "We need to catch up."

I gave Laura a look but didn't say anything. If she wanted to tell us what was going on, that was her call. I wasn't going to push her when she was obviously hurting.

"Nico is seeing someone," Laura said in a wobbly voice.

"He's not worth your time," Karissa said. "Look, I love the man, almost as much as you do. He gave me more time with my mom, and I will always be grateful for that. But you've spent too long wishing he would notice you. He's blind if he can't see you."

"I'm just his nurse. I'm not anyone special."

"How do you know he's seeing someone?" Finley asked.

"He told me."

"What?" we all gasped.

Laura drew in a breath. "He told me he needs to leave early tomorrow because he has a date in the city."

"Move on," Karissa said.

"I have to agree with her," Finley said. "It's not easy, but he's not the one for you."

She nodded. "I know. I should just stop thinking anything will change. He's never going to want me." She pulled out her phone. "I need to accept some of these requests and start putting myself out there. It's not worth it to be miserable and lonely and wonder if someone is out there."

"Good for you," Finley said, raising her glass. "You deserve better."

Laura nodded sharply and clicked her phone. We all stared at her for a minute, until she looked up. Her cheeks flushed, and she set her phone down. "Sorry."

"There's no reason to be sorry," I said.

"Unless you're using an app other than mine," Karissa said.

Laura shook her head. "Not a chance. I know if anything ever happened to me, you would provide all the information about who I'd been matched with to the police so they could find my body."

"Damn straight," Karissa said with a grin.

"I never thought about that," I admitted. "Of course, I try not to think about someone having to recover my body."

"It's the hardest thing for me about online dating," Laura said. "I have trouble trusting people. Knowing my friends and family would never know what happened to me if I disappeared is hard. Not that dying would be awesome, but I think we always want answers. We want to know what happened. We want to know why. I definitely would rather not think about dying, but if something did happen, I'd like to believe whoever was responsible would be brought to justice."

"That's dark," I said.

Laura shrugged. "It's just the way I think. But I'm done fearing the unknown person. I'm not happy right now, so I need to do something. Maybe I'll meet the guy I'm really meant to be with."

"I hope so," Karissa said. "Is that why you invited us over?" she asked me. "Did you meet someone?"

I scoffed. "No. Well, yes, but not like that. I went to the youth center today and volunteered. The woman there asked for references and I gave her your names."

"She already called me," Finley said. "I told her you kick strollers when you walk by and smack food out of the hands of the homeless."

"What?" I gasped.

Finley snorted. "Do you really think I'd say that?"

I chuckled with her.

"She asked how long we'd known each other and what I thought of your character. She's just doing her job. I wouldn't take it personally."

I shook my head. "I'm not. At least, not now. At first I wondered why I needed to give her so much information, but I get it. They have to protect the kids."

"Exactly. I think it's standard. I've done a little stuff there with their computers. The ones they have are pretty ancient. I'm trying to get a deal to buy a bunch of new ones. I've helped out with a few things, but I haven't worked with the kids. I think it's a great idea," Karissa said.

"Thanks. I'm looking forward to it. I think it'll be good

for me. And she gave me a great idea to create kits. I'm thinking I might even talk to Melody about adding a party basket to her options complete with a jewelry making kit and a private code to view a video just for the party. What do you guys think?" I asked.

"I think you're going to need me to expand that app I made for you," Karissa said.

"Ooh, you have an app," Laura said. "Let me see."

I handed over my phone and let Laura play with the app. They talked about it while I took the barbecue I picked up earlier out of the oven. My mouth watered as I added the sauce and mixed it all up.

We carried food to the couches and turned on a movie while we ate. We bounced ideas around about work and life and men. There was no doubt I'd found where I belonged. With these amazing woman as friends.

And maybe with my match as something more. Now that I knew Karissa could turn his info over to the cops if something happened.

Okay, so maybe I was still a little paranoid. But if Laura could be brave and try to move on from Nico, I could be brave and say yes to meeting JayPo sometime.

I opened the app and sent him a message asking if he still wanted to meet up sometime.

JAYPO

Hell yes. Whenever you're ready.

I took a breath and smiled as I put my phone down. I was ready for roots.

10

JAMES

The entire office was buzzing when I walked into work. There was a low murmur, like when something big happened or we caught a break in a big case. For a small town, it didn't happen frequently, so it put me on edge.

Colin Jones was standing in Captain Reynolds' office, nodding. His arms were crossed over his chest as he listened. He wasn't in cuffs, so I assumed he wasn't in trouble. Truth be told, I couldn't imagine Colin ever doing anything wrong, let alone something illegal.

"What's going on?" I asked the first guy who walked by me. He was young, one of the rookies who was only with us for a short time. Since all our precincts were small, we shuffled rookies around and all worked to train them.

"Donation. Must be a big one. I don't know how much, but someone said—"

"Okay, thanks," I said curtly and walked away. I didn't have time for rumors.

I sat at my desk and went through the reports that came in overnight. Not much happened. A medical call sent officers to check on a couple where the husband was having a heart attack. A domestic call brought officers to my old neighborhood. The last call was a public intoxication report from O'Kelley's for someone who was getting other people to order his drinks. That guy was sleeping it off.

The domestic call was the one I went back to. Oak Hill was usually fairly quiet and people kept to themselves. A call to the police meant someone was scared. It was also a good opportunity to check on Anna and her boys.

Captain Reynolds had Colin in our morning meeting. He looked wholly uncomfortable standing in front of all of us and accepting the praise he got for the donation he made. It was well deserved, the praise, but Colin was a behind the scenes kind of guy. He probably figured he'd get to drop off a check and leave. If he ever donated again, I was sure he'd send it through the mail.

"We can do a lot of good with this money," Captain Reynolds said. "We can't tell you what this means."

"Well, it's in memory of someone I've learned was pretty amazing," Colin said with a smile.

"Many of you remember Luke Carter. Mr. Jones is friends with his widow, and he wanted to honor them both with a donation. If any of you haven't been out to Jones Family Maple Farm, you should head out there this weekend and return the support to Mr. Jones here."

"That's not necessary," Colin said quickly. "I didn't do this to drum up business. It was a thank you to Mrs. Carter, one she asked me to give to the town. She loves MacKellar Cove, and she loves this force. I wanted to give back."

"Go to the farm, everyone," the captain said, ignoring Colin's words.

The rest of us chuckled.

"Thank you, Captain. I'll let you guys get to it," Colin said.

He nodded at me when he walked by. I held up a finger asking him to wait.

The captain ran through what was going on and where we were at with our open cases. Since Masterson and I didn't have anything open, we were on patrol for the day. Just what I was hoping for…a day stuck in a car with him.

Colin was sitting at my desk when I walked out of the meeting. I shook his hand and sat down in my guest chair.

"That was pretty awesome," I told him.

"You should have one of her pies. Those are awesome. Plus, she helped Elise and gave her a nudge toward me. I owe her."

"How are things going with you two?"

Colin nodded slowly, his lips curling up into a happy grin. "Great. She's the best thing that ever happened to me."

Trinity's face flashed in my mind with his words. I quickly banished it. Trinity and I weren't anything, let alone the best thing ever.

"That's great. You talk her into moving in yet?"

Colin chuckled and shook his head. "Not yet. But she does stay with me more often than not. We're down to about one night a week we spend apart."

"Must be nice," I said.

He nodded. "It is. You going to be at O'Kelley's tonight? You've missed the last few weeks."

I nodded. I was avoiding all the happy. After the way things went with Trinity, I didn't want to face my closest friends and end up telling them I'd screwed up with her. I still never admitted to any of them that I'd tried to arrest her the day we met. It was better they all thought we were just indifferent to each other.

"Good. See you then. I gotta head back. I didn't think this was going to take so long," Colin said as he stood.

"Next time," I said softly, "send it in the mail."

"Already planning on it," Colin agreed.

I moved back to my seat and had barely sat down when Masterson was in front of me asking if I was ready to go.

"I take it you are."

"I've been ready. Just waiting on you."

"Let's go then."

I gritted my teeth and forced myself to let it go. He was only going to be with me for a few more weeks, then he'd be on his own. I was looking forward to that day.

MASTERSON DIDN'T SAY anything when I drove out to Anna's before we went anywhere else. He raised an eyebrow at me, but he kept his mouth shut. I figured it was the best I was going to get.

My mom told me Anna is usually off on Thursdays, and since it was a school day, I hoped she'd be more willing to talk to me without the boys around.

Masterson said he was going to talk to some of the neighbors about the domestic case from the night before. I nodded and appreciated the privacy he was giving me to talk to Anna. I knocked on her door and waited, shaking my head once again that the front door wasn't secure like it was supposed to be. But since no one really claimed much of ownership for the property, it didn't surprise me. People who lived there learned to take care of things themselves, things they decided were important.

Anna opened the door with a dish towel in her hands. Her smile fell as soon as she saw me. Her gaze flickered behind me like she expected someone else to be there. She stepped back and closed the door after I walked in.

"What can I do for you, officer?" she asked softly, the defiance in her voice a tremor.

"I left you messages. Why aren't you returning my calls?"

"Listen, I know how most people think of me. I know I'm not a high class woman. I know I'm trash. But I'm not a whore. I'm not going to fuck you to keep my son out of trouble."

"Whoa, Anna, who said anything about that? I never asked for that. I want to help you."

"What about all the other people who live here? Do you want to help them, too? Are you knocking down their doors? Or are you just after the single mom?"

I rocked back and tried to picture things from her perspective. "Anna, I'm sorry. I never meant to make you feel uncomfortable. I really do want to help you. And it starts with one. If I can help you, maybe I can help someone else after you. Maybe you getting out of here will inspire someone else to do the same."

She scoffed. "You know how it is here, James. It's debilitating. It makes you feel like you'll never have normalcy. I was out. I was free. I had it all. And then it all disappeared. I'm meant to be here. I'm meant to live this life. I never should have thought I was better than this place."

She turned and walked back to the kitchen. A sink full of soapy water was waiting for her. She shoved her hands into it and started scrubbing something furiously.

I looked around her apartment and tried not to let the rush overflow my body. What she said hit me deep. Ever since I moved out, I had the same thoughts. I didn't deserve more than to live there. My house was precarious. I knew it could be taken from me in a heartbeat if I wasn't careful. Anna did everything right when she left. She got married, had a family, and tried to help her parents. And all the people she counted on fucked her over. People she loved, people who said they loved her. Why should she accept help from me?

I struggled to push aside my own fears of ending up back there and followed Anna to the kitchen. I stood in the middle, watching her do the one thing she could do to make the place better for her sons. My mom did the same. I asked her why she bothered cleaning when our apartment was such a dump. She always said it wasn't the fanciest place or the biggest place, but she was going to make sure it was clean and we were safe and healthy.

"A friend of mine owns O'Kelley's. He said Joey can bus tables for him after school."

"I don't want charity," Anna said without looking at me.

"How is offering him a job charity?"

She spun on me, her eyes blazing with fire. "Did he post the job? Is it something he was looking to hire for? Has he interviewed other people? Has he even met Joey?"

My cheeks burned with the answers to her questions.

"James, go away. Leave us alone. We will get by. We always have. There's no reason for you to worry about us now. You never have before."

The finality in her voice struck me. She was right. I didn't go back. I sat in my home and feared returning there. I was so wrapped up in my own shit that I lost sight of the fact that people are still there. Living in an unsafe environment, counting on the fact that none of them have anything worth stealing to keep people from breaking in. Trusting that none of them are any better than others.

"I'm sorry, Anna," I said quietly before I let myself out.

My mind was racing with thoughts and broken promises. My mom stayed there. She never wanted to leave. She was proud of the home she created for my brother and me. I was embarrassed by it forever, and I still was. I didn't tell people I grew up there. I didn't talk about it. I thought of myself as better, and I kept my nose up and acted like I was too good.

I couldn't do it anymore. I owed them more than that.

When Trinity's purse was stolen, I replaced her lock without thinking about it. It didn't cost me more than time, but it was still something that I didn't hesitate to do. I'd walked into Anna's twice in the last few weeks and both times walked right by the broken front lock without doing anything about it.

It was time I made a change for the people I used to be.

I was still considering what I could do when my shift ended and I headed to O'Kelley's. My phone dinged in my pocket as I sat down, and I pulled it out just before Piper set a beer in front of me.

"You haven't been around much lately. Everything okay?"

I nodded. "Just busy."

"Is that all it is?" she asked, a knowing look in her eyes.

I narrowed my eyes at her, trying to decide if she knew something or if she was trying to trip me up. I hadn't told anyone about sleeping with Trinity, but that didn't mean she kept it quiet. I didn't want to risk running into her at O'Kelley's, or anywhere else, since then. And I didn't want to listen to Ramsey and Colin and Ian talk about how great their relationships were.

"What else would it be?" I asked Piper.

She shrugged and grinned. "Just wondering."

She walked away, leaving me to think she knew something. My phone dinged again, and I abandoned thoughts of Piper when I saw a message from Book Boyfriends Wanted.

I signed up for the app one night when Karissa was bugging everyone to get it. I had no interest in online dating, and her app wasn't really any better for me, but I joined. I ignored the first few matches I had, but I traded messages with a couple eventually. It was low pressure and easy. I met up with one of the women I matched with. She was gorgeous and we had fun, but she felt more like a sister than someone I would fall for.

The one I'd been talking to lately made me laugh, something I hadn't done nearly enough lately.

> **DIAMONDGIRL**
> Still want to meet up sometime?

> **JAYPO**
> You name the place and time, and I'll be there.

When I brought it up the first time, she shut me down hard, but last week, she asked if we could meet. I didn't know what changed her mind, but I was up for it.

> **DIAMONDGIRL**
> What's your favorite drink?

> **JAYPO**
> Does beer count?

> **DIAMONDGIRL**
> Of course.

> **JAYPO**
> Good.

> **DIAMONDGIRL**
> What's the best thing about your job?

> **JAYPO**
> Helping people.

I answered automatically because that was always why I decided to be a cop, but the answer made my stomach turn. I wasn't helping enough people, and not in a way that mattered.

DIAMONDGIRL

Very noble of you. What do you like to do when you're not working?

JAYPO

Spend time with friends.

DIAMONDGIRL

Any other women you're involved with right now?

I hesitated. A part of me wanted to say yes, but Trinity and I weren't involved. Not really. It didn't matter that she was the one I thought about when I was alone, even before our one time together. If we were a thing, I wouldn't be talking to someone on a dating app.

JAYPO

No.

DIAMONDGIRL

Good. Life is too short to be unhappy. I'm trying to embrace that right now.

JAYPO

You and me both.

DIAMONDGIRL

I'm looking forward to meeting you.

JAYPO

Me too.

I waited for her to message me back, but she didn't. When I saw she'd signed out of the app, I closed mine and picked up my beer.

Ian claimed the seat next to mine as I took a drink. He

nodded and held up a finger for a beer. Hudson, behind the bar again, brought it over.

"I haven't seen the kid yet. Did you tell him about the job? I've been waiting for him to show up," Hudson said.

I nodded and groaned. "I've been calling his mom since we talked about it weeks ago. I went over there today, and she said she didn't want charity."

"How is offering him a job charity?" Hudson asked.

"I said the same thing, but she asked if it had been posted and if you'd interviewed anyone else or were even looking for someone for the job before. She also asked if you've met her son."

"Dammit," Hudson breathed.

I nodded. "Yep, my thoughts exactly. I get it, though. Living in Oak Hill, you give up on catching a break. You decide the world is against you and you're never going to have anything work out."

"But I'm trying to help," Hudson argued.

"I know. But Anna is the kind of person who wants help she's earned. If she gets paid an extra dollar an hour because she's working hard, she won't think twice. But if her son takes a job because you created one for him, she's offended that we think she can't take care of her family."

"I can understand that," Ian said. "Blake's the same way a lot of the time. When we first got together, her mom got sick all over her couch. Ramsey and I got rid of it for her, and she was upset about it because she wasn't used to people helping her without asking for something in return."

"Anna thought I was trying to get her to sleep with me," I admitted.

"Were you?" Hudson asked.

"No! I just want to help them. I've been her son. I've lived there and watched my mom struggle to keep things together. I know what their lives are like. I just wanted to help."

"So, help. Buy a bag of groceries, do a cookout in the parking lot, fix something in the apartment. Help them out," Ian said.

I drew in a breath. "I've been thinking about doing exactly that. Any interest in joining me?"

Ian and Hudson exchanged a glance and both nodded. "Absolutely."

11

By the time Colin and Ramsey arrived, Ian, Hudson, and I had almost a dozen ideas to help Anna and the others in her neighborhood. We filled them in on what we were planning and they wanted to do something also.

"I could offer free legal advice," Ramsey suggested. "Maybe even help some of them get loans or make connections with other people in the community."

"I think anything to give back works. I hate to admit I haven't spent much time there since I moved out," I told them. "I don't like going back."

"Going back is never easy," Hudson said, his gaze distant.

"Think you'll ever date again?" Colin asked him.

If any of the rest of us had asked, Hudson would have walked away, but Colin made everyone feel like he just wanted to know you better. Colin didn't know how to judge people.

Hudson hesitated then shrugged. "I don't know. I can't imagine being with anyone but Hillary. She was it for me. Not that things were perfect, but I loved her. The idea of feeling that way, and losing someone else, scares the shit out of me."

"I don't think that feeling ever goes away," Ramsey said. "I get to go home to Melody every night and I still have those fears. But I have the gift of hindsight and know how much it sucks to lose the woman you love and how great it is to be able to love her again. I know what you mean about not being sure how you could love again. When Melody and I were apart, the idea of her not being the last woman I kissed about killed me."

Hudson stared at Ramsey for a long moment and nodded. "That's why I wanted to slap you when you and Melody couldn't get your shit together. I'd give anything to have Hillary back. You don't let go of the woman you love. Not for anything."

"Never again," Ramsey said solemnly.

"Agreed," Ian and Colin said together.

"Since Hudson's not ready to date, how about you?" Colin asked me.

I chuckled and shook my head. "The last thing I need is a woman trying to tell me what to do."

"That can be hot," Ian said with a smirk. "I like it when Blake gets bossy."

Hudson shook his head and walked away mumbling something about not wanting to hear the rest.

"Elise is always bossy, but when she gets bossy in the bedroom...I don't mind those moments," Colin said. He grinned and sipped his beer, lost in his own thoughts.

"Wait until you have kids. I have two women telling me what to do. I still don't mind, though," Ramsey said. "When you have kids, you'll be wrapped around their little fingers."

I snorted and shook my head. "I don't have a woman and now you're giving me kids. Slow down some. And besides, I'm not sure I want kids. All the things I see every day?"

"Oh, please. This is MacKellar Cove, not New York City," Ramsey said with a snicker.

"So, this is where you hang out," someone said, sitting on my other side.

I turned and groaned when Masterson took the stool next to me.

"You going to introduce me to your buddies?" He nodded to them. "I'm Rowan. His new partner. I'm sure you've all heard what an asshole I am, wanting him to do things like arrest and ticket people."

Hudson walked over and asked Masterson what he wanted to drink.

"Whiskey. Over ice."

Hudson nodded and poured the drink then slid it in front of Masterson. "You opening a tab?"

He glanced at me to make sure it was someone Hudson could trust to pay a tab. I nodded. "Hudson, this is my temporary partner, Rowan Masterson."

"No, shit?" Hudson said with a grin. "In that case, first drink is on me. He deserves someone who's going to ruffle his feathers and piss him off a little."

"I already have one of those in my life. I don't need two," I said under my breath.

"Yeah, well, he ruffles just as many of my feathers. I still can't believe he let the guy who stole the purse go," Masterson said.

Hudson shrugged. "It's small town life for you. We watch out for each other. We're all talking about helping out the families in Oak Hill. We were tossing a few ideas around. If you want to pitch in, let us know."

Masterson nodded. "Sounds good. Maybe show the community that we're not all bad. Just you."

Ramsey and Ian snorted. I rolled my eyes. Hudson just grinned.

"You should come back. These fools come here almost every Thursday night. I live here," Hudson said.

"I might do that. Thanks. Assuming he doesn't shoot me tomorrow," Masterson said, getting up and sliding a bill across the bar.

"I said first drink is on me," Hudson said, waving him off.

"Then put it toward whatever you're going to need for this community project. It won't be free," Masterson said.

Hudson nodded, and Masterson said it was nice to meet all of them and walked away. It wasn't long before the questions started.

"He seems pretty great. Why don't you like him?" Hudson asked.

"Yeah, I expected an asshole, not a guy who harasses you and donates to a good cause," Ramsey said.

"I didn't know what to expect, but he can come back," Ian said.

"All of you suck," I told them.

"I just want to know who else in your life ruffles your feathers," Colin said.

"No one," I mumbled, wishing I'd kept my mouth shut.

"Oh, no, that's definitely not no one," Ramsey said. "Who is she?"

"Anyone we know?" asked Ian.

"Nope. I gotta go," I said, finishing my beer and tossing a few bills on the counter.

"Is it Trinity?" Hudson asked with a smirk in his tone.

I paused just long enough for the rest of them to pick up on it.

"Trinity? No shit. I didn't know you two were together," Ramsey said.

"We're not," I argued.

"But you want to be," Ian said, not asked. "You like her. Why didn't you tell us?"

"There's nothing to tell."

"She thinks he's an ass. Mostly because he is when she's around," Hudson said.

I glared at him, but he just rocked back on his heels and grinned.

"I like Trinity," Colin said. "She flirted with me the first time we met."

"Me, too," Hudson and Ian said.

"What about you, James? Did she flirt with you?" Ramsey asked.

"No, did she flirt with you?" I spat.

Ramsey snickered. "I'm wearing a wedding ring, so no. Why didn't she flirt with you? She's a friendly, flirty kind of woman. What about you did she not like on sight?"

I twisted my lips and tried to figure out a way to tell them without sounding like a complete ass. Hudson saved me the trouble.

"He tried to arrest her as a welcome to town gesture."

"You did what?" Colin asked.

The other assholes just burst out laughing.

"Okay, I have to ask why," Ramsey said. "Does she need a lawyer?"

"She was breaking into her car," I grumbled.

"Her own car? And you were going to arrest her?" Ian asked.

"I didn't know it was her car," I protested.

"No wonder she doesn't like you," Colin said. "I'd think you were an ass, too."

"How was I supposed to know?"

"Did you ask?" Ian asked.

"Do you know how many criminals lie?" I asked them.

"Probably all of them, but Trinity isn't a criminal," Ramsey said.

"I didn't know that!"

They all looked at me for a second then burst out laughing. Again.

I flipped them all off and walked out. I heard them calling my name, but I wasn't in the mood to listen to them. Mostly because if I ran into Trinity on the street now, I would have tried to help her instead of arrest her.

Like I did with Joey.

I drew in a breath and ignored the buzzing in my pocket. Hudson and the others would be fine. I needed to apologize to Trinity. Something that was long overdue.

I opened the door to her building and hesitated before I headed toward the stairs. I drew in a breath and shook my head. I couldn't show up at her home. We weren't friends, let alone friends who dropped in unannounced.

I turned to leave and stopped. Trinity was staring at me, an amused look on her face.

"What are you doing?" she asked.

I opened my mouth to say something and all my thoughts zeroed in on the tiny shorts she was wearing and the way her one tendril caressed the side of her neck.

"Are you okay?" she asked, her eyes narrowing as she moved closer to me.

"Yeah, I'm fine," I said harshly.

She took a step back and shook her head. "Have a good night." She moved around me toward the stairs, no longer concerned.

"I'm sorry," I blurted out.

"Don't worry about it," she said, not stopping.

"For trying to arrest you," I shouted after her.

That got her to stop. She turned back to me, her eyes blazing. She was halfway up the first part of the stairs and flew back toward me and got up in my face.

"Don't you dare come into my building and embarrass me like this. You're sorry? Fine. You're sorry. Whatever. You're forgiven. But don't try to make me look like I'm a criminal in my own home where people can hear you," she hissed.

She spun to walk away again and I grabbed her arm. She stopped and looked down at my hand.

"Let go of me. Now."

I released her and sighed. She stalked off, but I needed to say what I went there to say. "I'm sorry for the way I've treated you since we've met. For never giving you the benefit of the doubt. For always assuming the worst in you. I was quick to let Joey go, but I didn't extend the same courtesy to you. I talk to everyone about their situation, except you. I never should have treated you the way I did. And I wanted to apologize for making your life more difficult."

I held my breath while she stood on those steps, not going up or down. It was very possible she was going to walk away and not talk to me, but I hoped she wasn't.

Finally, she huffed a sigh. "If you're insisting on having this conversation, please let me put away my groceries and get out of the hallway so my neighbors don't report me for making too much noise."

I glanced around the empty lobby to the darkened world outside and nodded. "Okay."

I followed her up the stairs, doing my best not to stare at her ass the entire time and failing. The way her legs moved, parting with each step up the stairs, then caressing each other as they passed, her ass tightening on each step...that wasn't the only thing tightening.

We finally made it to her door and she set her bags down while she unlocked it and let us in. She carried her bags to the kitchen and started putting everything away.

"Can I help?" I offered.

"Do you know where my groceries go?"

"Um, no."

She gave me a *duh* look and kept moving around the small

space, fitting things into places that looked specifically carved out for them. I watched her while she moved, wondering if she even cared that I was there.

When she finished putting everything away, she opened her fridge and took out three containers of Chinese food. She set them on the counter between us and finally met my gaze.

"I figure I'll be better able to stomach whatever it is you want to say after I've eaten. Are you hungry?"

I nodded and kept my mouth shut. She was being nice to me. Relatively speaking. I would take it.

She put the food on two plates and heated them up before handing one to me and grabbing two beers from her fridge. She handed one of those over and carried her food to the couch. She put on a movie, acting like I wasn't there. It was almost comical, and definitely domestic. Like we fit together.

She ate her dinner and laughed at the movie, ignoring me while I did the same. When she was finished, she set her plate down on the coffee table and curled her feet up under her. She leaned against the arm of the couch and turned to me.

"Are you ready to talk now?"

I set my plate down and mimicked her pose, turning toward her and leaning against the arm on the other end of the couch.

She drew in a deep breath, preparing for me. In that moment, I saw how much my actions had affected her and I regretted them even more.

"The day we met," I began, "I judged you. I saw a stranger in a town that I have lived in basically my whole life, and I jumped to conclusions. I made a decision about you before I asked any questions, and that wasn't fair and it wasn't right. When I decided to become a cop, it was because too many people I knew growing up weren't given a chance. I wanted to make a difference, to help people. But I didn't do that with you and I'm sorry."

She let out a shaky breath and nodded. "Thank you." Her voice was small, like she was holding back her emotions.

"I know I've been an ass since then, and I'm sorry for that also."

She breathed a laugh and shook her head like she didn't believe me.

"You think I'm lying?"

She looked at me. "Do you really think I'm going to believe you've been an ass to me for a year and you're just going to say sorry and it's okay? What? Are we supposed to be friends now? You're still going to be an ass."

"And you really think saying that is going to fix this?"

She laughed and uncurled her body to stand. She carried her plate to the kitchen and put it in the sink then glared at me. "You came into my home. You showed up at my home. You said you wanted to talk to me and apologize. You're the one who started this. Am I not allowed to have my own feelings about it?"

"I'm trying to apologize and you're acting like I'm doing something wrong."

She shook her head. "No, you're acting like you've never done anything wrong. Do you know what it's like to live in a town where you aren't sure if you're going to get arrested at any given time because you've been targeted? Or to worry any little thing you do is going to piss someone off who has the authority to toss you in jail? You had some epiphany or something today and you show up at my home and demand that I listen to you, and now you tell me I'm not being kind and forgiving enough. Just get out."

"No," I said. I stood and walked toward her.

"Why the hell not?"

"Because you don't really want me to leave, Trinity."

She scoffed. "I don't know what you're talking about."

"I think you do," I said softly, moving closer to her. "I think you're just as hot right now as I am. I think you want me to throw you on that couch you just stalked away from and fuck you until your neighbors scream. I think you're dying to have me inside you again, just like I'm dying to be inside you."

I paused, emboldened by the way her eyelids dropped to half mast and her tongue darted out to wet her lips.

"I don't know what the hell is going on between us, Trinity, but I'm not walking out that door right now unless you tell me you don't want me as much as I want you."

"I don't want you," she breathed, her voice hitching with the lie.

"Yes, you do," I said softly. "But if you can't admit it to me, when there is no one else around, I'm not going to push."

I went back to the couch and picked up my plate and beer. I finished the beer and carried both to where she stood in the kitchen.

The air between us pulsed with desire. I brushed against her as I set my plate in the sink with hers and leaned in close when I put my beer on the counter behind her.

"We were good together last time, Trin. Maybe one day we can find out if that was a fluke or if we burn up the sheets every. Single. Time."

I kissed her cheek, lingering as I drew in a breath of her to take with me. I started to pull away and she grabbed my arms.

"I hate you."

"I never asked you to like me."

"I hate that I want you."

"Trust me, the feeling is mutual."

She groaned as she lunged for me, wrapping her body around me like she worried I'd leave.

If she only knew.

12

TRINITY

My brain tried to tell my body to pull back, but there was no chance my body was going to listen. I wanted him. It was more than that. I needed him. Not just sex, but him. I needed a man who wouldn't try to sweet talk me or be gentle and loving. I just needed sex.

His hands scorched up and down my back while his tongue danced inside my mouth. I groaned and sucked on his tongue, loving when his fingers dug into my hips. He leaned over, the difference in our heights forcing me to bend with him, and steered me toward the living room.

We stumbled and kissed and rushed to the couch, clothes already flying by the time we reached the soft landing. He pulled me down on top of him, his cock settling between my thighs and hitting me just right.

The last time we had sex, I came, but I rushed off right afterward because I wasn't done when he was. The last thing I wanted was to ask him to help me out. Nope. I just needed a few more minutes alone and the desire that was already pulsing through me to finish.

This time, I wasn't sure I was going to be able to wait until he left to use the memory of him to scream my way to another orgasm.

"Come here," he whispered, drawing me down to him.

My bare stomach hit his and we both sucked in a breath. His skin was warm and soft against mine, a sharp contrast to the rough feel of his calloused hands on my skin. I leaned forward as he leaned up, both of us claiming the kiss that hung in the air between us.

He thrust against me, his cock sliding deeper between my thighs, and cupped my ass, holding me against him as my body squirmed for a release. My panties were soaked, and my nipples were hard, the soft padding of my bra doing nothing to block the feel of him on the other side of the cotton.

His hands trailed up and quickly unhooked my bra, drawing it down my arms until his hands worked between us and cupped my bare breasts.

I pulled back from his kiss with a moan, and he pushed me up, his hands the only support for my oversized breasts. He kneaded and teased my flesh before rolling my nipples in his fingers and groaning.

"You're so fucking gorgeous," he murmured.

I looked down at him, but he wasn't looking at me. It was the first time I wasn't disappointed to find a man talking to my chest instead of my face and I almost laughed.

James leaned up and licked one of my nipples. My head fell back, the feel of his soft, wet tongue on my body turning my insides molten. I rocked softly on his lap, enjoying his body as he enjoyed mine.

He moaned his approval and traded sides, licking my other nipple into his mouth and sucking hard on it. A yelp escaped my lips, but he didn't stop. He smiled against my flesh and nipped me before pressing his tongue flat to my breast.

I held his head in place and rode him shamelessly. I enjoyed sex and had enough lovers to know what got me off, but I wasn't always free with a man and rarely took what I needed. With James, I didn't care what he thought of me. He already judged me. Sex wasn't going to change that, so I was going to enjoy myself.

"Fucking hell," he groaned, rocking up into me as I bucked against him.

The orgasm I wanted was just out of reach. I tried to get there, but there were too many layers between us. My cotton shorts and panties didn't conceal much, but the shorts he wore were too thick to let me feel him the way I needed to.

I groaned and pulled back, teetering between ready to give up and ready to do it myself. James pressed my shoulders until the center of my back hit the arm of the couch. I still straddled him, his legs pinned between mine. He skimmed his hands up my thighs and slid a finger beneath the edge of my shorts.

My entire body jerked at the intimate touch. He pulled my shorts and panties aside with his other hand and traced my seam with one delicate finger.

"Don't hold back on me, Trinity," he said, meeting my gaze for the first time since I threw myself at him.

The connection in that moment scared the hell out of me. He saw me. Not just physically, but me. All of me. He peered into my soul and a piece of me knew he was the only one who would ever see as much of me as he did in that moment.

Then his gaze fell to my parted thighs and he teased my clit. My body tensed. I was already sensitive and on the edge, and just one touch had me ready to lose my mind. James knew it and quickly moved away from my clit, spreading my flesh apart as he explored lazily.

His finger barely entered me before he pulled out again. He dragged the wetness around me, his fingers providing zero relief.

"Please," I groaned, jerking my hips toward him.

"Are you sure you're ready?" he asked, a teasing hint in his eyes.

"This is supposed to be sex, James. Nothing more. We don't like each other."

The mocking smile smile slid from his face. For half a second, I worried I hurt his feelings. Then I worried he was going to leave.

Then he pushed two fingers into me and pressed his thumb against my clit and I nearly came instantly.

"Oh, yes," I groaned. My body stretched to fit his fingers as it clenched around them. The pressure on my clit was just right. Close. So close.

Slickness coated his fingers as he pumped them in and out. My eyes fell closed as the orgasm raced toward me, climbing up my throat and freezing in my lungs. James pumped harder, his fingers slamming deeper into me, his thumb slipping over my skin.

The air conditioning kicked on, the cold air blasting on my exposed body and reminding me how open and vulnerable I was for a man I told myself I didn't like.

Then he whispered, "Come for me, Trinity. Come."

My name on his lips sent me over the edge. I groaned and screamed and dug my nails into him. My mind went blank and all I could do was let my body release everything James built up inside me.

As I came back down from my high, every nerve ending inside me said to go right back up there. His fingers lazily stroked in and out of me, setting a pace that lit me up in a different way. The first one was fucking, but the slowness was something else. Something deeper. Darker. Something that threatened more than just my body would want him.

I couldn't do it.

"Inside me," I said firmly. "Now."

His gaze snapped to mine and he withdrew his fingers. I stood while we stripped off the rest of our clothes. He dug out a condom and sat on the couch to roll it on. Then he looked up at me and reached for me.

I never liked being on top. My thighs were too big for me to fit over most men, and I hated the way my body jiggled and bounced with my every move. It made me feel like the fat girl who didn't really belong.

But the heat in his eyes when they flickered down my body said he didn't see any of those things. James saw the woman I tried to be. The woman with the curvy figure who was proud of her body. The woman who liked to eat and enjoy all life had to offer.

Including him.

I crawled on top of him and moaned when he fitted us together. His cock swelled inside me, filling me up. I sat there for a few seconds, getting used to the feel of him.

I put my hands on his shoulders and his went to my hips. Together, we set a rhythm, our bodies meeting then sliding apart, then crashing back together. We moved faster with each stroke, like we couldn't get enough.

All thoughts flew from my mind. It was no longer Officer James Rucker between my thighs, but James. It was a man who drove me crazy for more than one reason. He was gorgeous and kind, and he cared about the people in his life. He was a good man, and one I knew I could fall for if I let myself.

But I couldn't let myself. I couldn't fall for him.

His hands slid up my thighs, across my stomach, and

cupped my bouncing breasts. He brought one to his mouth while I kept going. The added sensation of his lips and tongue and teeth on my nipples sent me racing faster toward another orgasm.

I threw my head back and abandoned all give-a-shit and let go. I rode him hard, grinding down onto him and taking exactly what I needed. He sucked harder on my flesh and thrust up against me, letting me set our new pace and drive us both insane.

My energy waned with each punishing stroke. My body wasn't used to that level of exertion for so long. As my strokes failed and my orgasm shrunk back inside, James took over.

He pushed me off and scrambled off the couch, guiding me to lay down quickly. He settled between my thighs once more, rushing silently to get right back to where we were. His first thrust was hard and deep and told my body to get ready because the O-train was coming in fast.

"Oh, God," I moaned, spreading my legs wider to allow him deeper.

He pumped into me, his face floating above me in a mask of determination. Sweat beaded on his forehead as he clenched his jaw and drove into me again and again. He closed his eyes at one point, then opened them to stare between us and watch where he entered me.

He held himself up on one hand and reach the other between us. His fingers found my clit and teased it. The gentle stroke of his fingers and the punishing stroke of his cock confused my body. One move pushed me higher and the other drew me back, over and over, until my body raced full steam ahead and fractured.

I shouted again, screaming his name and clutching him to me. I needed to feel his weight on me, to have his body pressed to mine. The enormity of sensations overwhelmed me and made me feel painfully alone without his touch.

He sank onto me, pressing me into the soft cushions. He kissed my neck and shoulders and up to the soft spot behind my ear. He didn't say anything, just reassured me that he was there with his kisses.

The whole time, his body stroked in and out of mine. Long, gentle strokes. Lovemaking strokes.

It was sex. All we had was sex. There weren't feelings involved. We didn't like each other when we weren't naked. But it didn't feel that way when he held me and kissed me and made love to me.

I drew in a shaky breath and tried to push aside the emotions threatening to rise up and wrap around everything else I felt about James. I didn't want to like him. I wanted to use him and throw him out.

He pulled back enough to meet my gaze. The same war I was having with myself was reflected in his eyes. He brushed the hair back from my face and kissed the tip of my nose. He watched me, his gaze flickering from my lips to my breasts to my eyes, scanning all of me while he slid in and out of my body.

The only warning I had that he was about to come was when his eyes fluttered closed for a second. He whispered my name then stilled deep inside me, his cock swelling then releasing into me.

He lowered himself onto me, once again kissing my bare skin. I wrapped my arms around him and just let myself stop fighting all the feelings inside.

How much I actually liked him scared me. I didn't want to like him, but I did. A lot. We got off to a rocky start when we met, but if the situation had been different, we might not dislike each other so much.

Hell, the way we just lit my couch on fire, most people would say we didn't dislike each other at all.

My skin finally started to cool, and James pulled back. He didn't look at me as he withdrew from my body and stood. He walked into the kitchen, giving me a fantastic view of his bare butt, and grabbed a paper towel.

When he came back, he grabbed his clothes and started to get dressed. There was a part of me that was disappointed he wasn't trying to stick around, but another part of me knew him leaving as quickly as possible was for the best.

I grabbed my clothes and dressed quickly, ignoring my bra and panties since I had no plans to leave home.

"I didn't…" he started. He wasn't looking at me. He took a breath and tried again. "I didn't come here for this. Any of it. I just wanted to tell you I'm sorry for the way I've treated you."

I nodded. "Thanks."

He hesitated, like he was debating saying something else. His gaze drifted to my lips then snapped back to whatever he found so fascinating behind me.

"Uh, so, I should go."

I nodded and followed him to the door. He turned back to me, and I almost ran into him.

"This…I don't know what this is."

"Does it need to be anything?" I asked.

He opened his mouth then snapped it shut. He opened the door and nodded once. "Lock it behind me."

I nodded again.

He looked at me once more then gave me a tentative smile and pulled the door closed between us.

I locked it, watching him through the peephole as he walked down the hallway until I couldn't see him anymore.

I breathed a sigh and leaned against the door. Everything that had to do with him was all mixed up for me. I didn't know if I liked him or not. If I wanted to be with him or not. If we worked together or not.

Or if he wanted any of that. He showed up, twice now, and we fell into each other. I always thought people who said they didn't know how it happened were stupid, but now I got it. There was a pull, an invisible force, that made me feel like I had no choice but to sleep with him. And not because he was there and he was convenient or because he forced me, but because he was James. He was a man I hadn't been able to resist since we met. Whether it was sparring verbally or in bed, I couldn't resist him.

I pushed away from the door and went into my kitchen. When everything else felt topsy-turvy, cleaning helped me to focus. It was a task I could accomplish, something I felt in control of. I needed that.

I'd just turned on the water when there was a knock on my door. I sighed and turned the water off, only remembering my bra and panties were in the middle of the living room when I got to the door. It was likely Finley or Karissa, but I still checked the peephole.

I pulled back when I saw James standing on the other side of my door. I unlocked it and asked, "Did you forget something?"

He nodded and stepped into me. He slid an arm around my back and yanked my body flush with his. His lips came down and sealed over mine, his tongue darting into my surprised open mouth.

He leaned us back, forcing me to grab ahold of him before falling over. The kiss was urgent and insistent, demanding I pay attention to it, and to him. When he pulled back, almost as quickly as he lunged at me, he stared at me until I could focus on him.

"This is definitely something for me, Trinity."

"Oh."

He kissed my cheek, then let go of me and walked away.

I stared after him, a smile curling my lips up.

"Lock your door," he called down the hall just before he turned the corner.

"I will," I called back. "Good night."

"Night," he said, already out of sight.

I went back inside and locked my door, then sank against it again and grinned.

13

"I met someone," Laura announced at girls' night on Sunday.

"Congratulations," we all said, like she was someone who had a hard time meeting men.

Laura was beautiful. She was sweet and funny and an amazing person. But she moved to MacKellar Cove because of Dr. Allison. She found his practice online and decided to make a change to her life. She was impressed by him before she ever met him, and her impression became infatuation once she started working for him.

I didn't blame her. He was a good looking man. I hadn't met him, but I looked him up. Yum. What bothered me about him was the way he didn't seem to notice her. Ever.

"Where did you meet him?" Elise asked.

"Book Boyfriends Wanted. We've been talking for a week but I wasn't sure about it. He lives in A-Bay so we decided to meet up last night," Laura explained.

"And I take it things went well?" Blake asked.

Laura nodded, a smile ghosting her lips. "It did. We didn't fall into bed or anything like that, but we had fun. He's a really good kisser. And I'm looking forward to seeing him again."

"Good for you," Finley said. "It's about time you move on from Dr. Clueless."

The rest of us nodded in agreement. Laura smiled sadly. "I know. I wanted things to work out with him, but it wasn't meant to be. So, I'm going to see who else is out there and try to find my own happiness. I still love my job, but I don't have to love my boss. Or be in love with my boss."

"Good for you," I told her. "It's not easy to let go, but I think it's the right thing for you."

She nodded. "I agree. Okay, enough Laura is pathetic. What's going on with everyone else."

"Well, I'm teaching my first class this week at the youth center. I got the call Friday that I was approved to volunteer there," I told them.

More congratulations circled the room. I was excited about the opportunity. To be able to reach the people I wanted to work with, but to reach them before they became adults, was awesome. I hoped I would find a few kids who were really into it and who wanted to learn. I was sure there would be some who were somewhat indifferent, but Amelia said there were a lot of opportunities for the kids so they wouldn't join me unless they had some interest.

"What are you going to teach them?" Karissa asked.

I held up my wrist and showed everyone the bracelet I made that afternoon. It was a fairly simple looped design that was less exact. If they did something wrong, it wouldn't show in the final product.

"That's cool looking," Piper said. "And probably easy for those kids to pick up. You should do gifts for Christmas or holiday themed stuff. That could be fun."

I nodded. "I've been thinking about some options like that. Amelia said the kids are young, so I need projects that are easy. They don't have kids older than eighth grade there, and even that age group is very limited. Mostly it's elementary kids."

"Which means you need it to be quick before they lose patience. Amber would love to practice with you sometime if you need a guinea pig. She's young so it would be on that end of the scale. Have you thought about having two projects that are really similar so both the older kids and the younger kids can work on them?" Melody asked.

I shook my head. "What do you mean?"

"Amber can only focus on something that challenges her for about ten minutes. She gets distracted when things are tough. Older kids, kids that are in fifth or sixth grades, can focus for longer. If they have a similar design that's a little more complicated, I think it would work for everyone," Melody explained.

"That makes sense, but I never thought about that. I'll have to try to figure out how hard I think this design is. This whole thing is all a lot more complicated than I expected," I said.

"But it'll be fun. And once you get some kits ready to go, I'll add that option to my website so I can start shipping them as a party activity. I think kids will like it, and if you have a suggested age group, parents will love it," Melody said.

"I hope so. I'm excited about that option," I said with a smile. I was looking forward to seeing pictures and videos of kids creating their own jewelry.

"And we can add a link to Melody's site on your app to connect the two," Karissa said.

"You have an app?" Piper asked. "How do I miss everything? I need to come here more often."

I shook my head. "Karissa built me one, but I haven't asked her to activate it yet. It's beautiful, though. See?" I handed over my phone.

Piper swiped and tapped her way through the app, showing things to Blake as they looked at every detail. I sat back and ate my slice of Finley's vanilla bean cake.

"This is great. You should definitely activate it. Karissa did an amazing job," Piper said, handing my phone back to me.

"I really did," Karissa said with a grin. "I keep telling her it will help her business to have an app and be able to reach her customers more easily. She can send out alerts when she has new stock and offer sales to app users only. It's perfect."

"So modest," Finley teased her. "But seriously, she's right. It's nice to be able to send out something to my customers. I have people who don't want to sign up for email but who collect apps and are happy to download the app. I have a sign at the register with the QR code for them to download it right then. And for new app users, I give them a discount, so people want to get it. There's really not a downside."

"I don't feel like I'm big enough for an app. I think that's it. Like I am still just playing with my grandma's beads and not someone who should be making money doing something I enjoy so much," I confessed.

"Trust me," Finley said, "I get that. I started reading my mom's romance novels when I was in elementary school. Poor Blake was scandalized when I read her a section of one really juicy book. We had no idea what all the words meant, but we knew they were dirty. And now I get to do that every day, except I know what all the words mean."

"But I'm still scandalized when you read them to me," Blake teased.

"You're such a prude," Finley joked back.

"Compared to you, absolutely," Blake said with a smile. "But that's what I love about you. You keep me guessing, and laughing."

Finley blew Blake a kiss.

What Finley said really hit me. She was right. We were lucky to be able to do things we loved, to have jobs that fit with who we were and who'd we'd been. I was feeling like I wasn't enough because I didn't have a bunch of fancy degrees or tons of training, but I loved my job. I loved sharing it with people. And I was holding back for no other reason than I was afraid.

"You know what, Karissa?" I said. They all looked at me. "Turn it on."

"That's what she said," Elise said with a snicker.

Everyone else cheered and laughed.

"Good for you," Laura said. "You should share your talent with the world. You're going to be so happy you did that."

I nodded. "I hope so."

I had a lot of things to think about, but my work was not something I needed to debate. I loved my job, and Laura was right. It was time to share it.

I PACKED up my bag on Tuesday afternoon and nervously zipped it closed. I was as ready as I was going to be, but I was still anxious. I had never taught a group of people before, let alone a group of kids.

I had no idea how many would show up, so I packed up twenty kits. I followed Melody's advice and made some of them a little smaller for the younger kids, and more bigger for older kids. I figured a bracelet was easy enough, and since it wasn't that big, it could be finished in under twenty minutes for most of the kids.

I parked in the lot and made my way to the door. I waited for someone to buzz me in, smiling at Amelia when she opened the door.

"The kids should be here soon. You need to get set up before they invade you. I have you up on the stage. When you're done, you need to sweep the area very well because a dance class uses that stage later tonight. We can't have a bead roll under someone's foot and they get hurt," Amelia told me as she walked.

I hurried to follow her across the wide open space of the gym. Basketball hoops were at both ends with extras on each side. Faded lines on the well worn floor made it look like other games could be played on the same surface, but the rack of basketballs made it obvious the kids didn't choose another option.

Amelia climbed the five steps to the stage and stopped in front of the first table with her hand on her lower back.

"Are you okay?" I asked her.

She huffed a laugh. "No, but I'll live. Is there anything else you need? You can move the tables around if you'd like. I wasn't sure how you wanted them."

"I might. I'll think about it for a minute."

Amelia looked at her watch and grimaced. "You don't have much more than a minute. The elementary school lets out right now. Kids will be here soon. I asked them to sign up, but not many did. More will likely filter in if you have space for them. We'll see how it goes for today."

I nodded, feeling more than a little deflated. If not many kids signed up, was I wrong about them wanting to do this? I could be home working on new pieces instead of teaching kids.

I shook my head and chastised myself. Even if I only had one kid show up who was interested in learning, it was one I wouldn't reach another way. I was going to try, and maybe more kids would come next week.

I decided to leave the tables how they were and focus on getting the kits out so the kids could sit down and start to explore. I wanted to find small work stations for them so the beads wouldn't roll off the table, but I wasn't able to get anything like that locally. I had twenty on order, but it was going to be another week or two before they arrived, so we needed to be careful.

The slam of the door startled me and I dropped one kit. It hit the table with a clang that was quickly drowned out by the shouting of the kids rushing into the building.

Boys raced for the basketballs before taking off their backpacks, grabbing the one they wanted to claim as their own. Some of the girls joined them, trying to wrestle away equipment to use themselves. It wasn't long before Amelia walked out and blew a whistle to get their attention.

"You all know to put your things away in a cubby and then you can start to play. If you have a backpack on, go put it up now or the basketball in your hand is mine. And don't forget, Ms. Trinity is here with us for the first time today. If anyone wants to learn how to make a bracelet, she has kits for you and will walk you through how to do it," Amelia said over the chatter.

A few kids glanced my way and I smiled, doing my best to look friendly and welcoming. I saw two little girls watching me and pointing, debating between joining me on the stage and staying with the other kids on the court. I waved, and the one waved back. Her friend didn't look too excited, but they both walked toward me.

"Hi, ladies," I said too cheerfully. "I'm Trinity. It's nice to meet you both."

The one girl smiled and introduced herself as Heather. The other girl said her name was Meghan. I asked if they wanted to sit and work on a bracelet for a few minutes.

"How long will this take?" Meghan asked.

I shrugged. "That depends on you. For a lot of people, it takes about twenty minutes."

Meghan sighed dramatically. "That won't give me much time to play."

"Well, why don't you try it. If you're fast, it might not take you so long," I offered, smiling again and hoping she would stay. Heather was already looking at the beads on the tables and scanning for a set she wanted to do, but if Meghan bailed, I knew Heather would also.

"Fine," Meghan said. She flopped down on the chair closest to her and picked up the bag in front of her. "What do we do with this?"

I smiled and grabbed the bag Heather was eyeing and handed it to her. She smiled up at me gratefully and I took the bag in front of her to use as a demonstration.

"First, we're going to get out the ribbons. At the end, your bracelet will look like mine. We're just going to weave the ribbon through the beads. You can do it any way you want. I would suggest keeping the beads in your bag so they don't roll away."

Heather took her three ribbons and slid one bead onto all three together like I showed them. She added one bead on two of the ribbons and slid it close to the first bead. Then she switched which two ribbons she added a bead to and kept going, making her bracelet look like a seamless, flowing unit.

Meghan went a different route. "This looks dumb," she said, tossing her bracelet on the table. She added all her beads to one ribbon and used them all before she could add beads to the other ribbons.

I grabbed another bag from the next table and handed it to her. "Why don't you use these beads on another ribbon?"

She glared up at me, all the attitude in her little body focused on me like a laser beam. If she wasn't so tiny, I would have been intimidated, but she couldn't have been older than third grade. She was a feisty one, though.

"Those don't match. It'll look even more dumb if I do that."

I forced a grin and went to the table a few over and brought her those two bags. They coordinated well enough for her to use them. She rolled her eyes at me, but she went back to work.

"How does this look?" Heather asked.

"That's beautiful," I complimented her. Her bracelet was something that could be sold in a store. She definitely had a natural talent for design, even down to the beads she used on each ribbon.

"Thank you. How do I wear it?" she asked.

"I can help you to finish it," I told her. I took the bracelet from her and added the opposite end to the ribbons after checking that it would fit on her small wrist. She smiled and put it on, showing it off to her friend.

"What do you think, Meghan?"

Meghan shrugged and scowled at her own piece. "It's fine. Better than mine."

Heather smiled and said, "I like yours. It looks cool. I like all the beads you used."

Meghan shrugged but her lips curled up just slightly on the edges. "Thanks."

"Heads up!" someone shouted, right before a basketball slammed into the edge of the table the girls were sitting at.

Meghan dropped her bracelet and half the beads bounced off. The open bags on the table shook with the vibration of the basketball and beads spilled out. The basketball bounced against another table and rolled around the stage, like a pinball machine.

"Can we have that back?" one of the boys shouted up to us.

I turned and stared at him, but he didn't understand why it would be better if he came up and got the ball. I huffed and picked it up, throwing it back to him. "Try to keep it down there," I said.

"We'll try," he shouted back, already taking off and ignoring me.

"Are you okay?" I asked the girls.

"Well, this was a waste of my time," Meghan said with a roll of her eyes. "I knew I should have said no. My bracelet is dumb and now it's ruined. This is stupid. I just want to go play."

Meghan tossed her bracelet onto the table and stomped off. I gawked at her back, wondering what I was supposed to do.

"Can I take this home?" Heather asked quietly.

I stared down at her as she scooped the beads that came off Meghan's bracelet into a bag and added the bracelet she was making.

When I didn't answer right away, she looked up at me and said, "It's okay. I know it costs money and I can't get things for free."

I shook my head. "No, Heather, it's fine. Are you going to finish it for her?"

Heather nodded. "I want to. I think she did a good job, but Meghan doesn't like to be girly. She wants to be a boy, but when it's just us, she says she likes girl stuff. She only has a dad, though, and he wants her to do boy things."

My heart went out to the sassy little girl who didn't know how to be who she was. At the same time, my mind spun with options that could work for boys or girls. Maybe I could find beads that looked like basketballs or baseballs or other things like that. Something that would allow Meghan to do something girly but in a way that she wouldn't resent.

"I think it's very sweet of you to want to help your friend. I think she'll like that. And she did a great job. You both did.

Thank you for coming up here today. Hopefully you two will join me again next week."

Heather nodded eagerly and grinned widely. She stuffed the bag into her pocket and raced off the stage in search of her friend.

I looked around the open space and not one kid met my gaze. They were more interested in what they were doing. But my day was a success because I reached one girl, maybe two.

I stayed up there for another thirty minutes, just in case someone got bored with basketball or video games, then I started to pack up my supplies. I didn't think we dropped any beads on the floor, but just in case, I was going to sweep like Amelia said to.

I set my bag to the side and folded up all the tables so I could move them out of the way. There was another stack in the corner, so I added to it and found a broom nearby. I'd just carried the last table to the stack when I heard footsteps on the stage.

Thinking a kid changed their mind, I pasted on a grin and turned to welcome someone. Only to come face to face with a not so happy looking James.

14

JAMES

The last person I expected to see at the community center was Trinity. A glance at my mother told me she knew Trinity and I knew each other, but she didn't want to tell me. I was going to have to talk to her later. First, I needed to know what Trinity was doing there.

"Why are you here?" I demanded.

Her gaze slid over my crossed arms and down to my wide-set stance before returning to my face. She didn't look any happier than I felt. "I'm working."

"You work here?" I blurted out. If she was having money problems, the community center was the last place she should take a job. My mom started working there when my brother and I were in elementary school so we could attend for free. She also worked as a waitress at night and at a gas station when we were in school. None of them were full time, and none of them paid well.

"Volunteering, really. I…I wanted to teach some kids how to make jewelry. I learned when I was in high school and moved in with my grandma, but there's no reason younger kids can't learn. It's a skill that could help them when they get older," she explained. Her half shrug said she didn't like having to defend herself.

"Mr. James!" one of the kids called from the basketball court. "Are you going to play with us today?"

I turned and had no trouble smiling at the kids who were hovering at the edge of the stage. I nodded. "I'll be there in just a few minutes. I wanted to talk to Ms. Trinity. Did you guys meet her today?"

Another boy rolled his eyes and said, "My sister was up there, but that stuff is for girls. We played basketball."

I rolled up my sleeve and showed them the bracelet I wore. It wasn't glittery or fancy, but it was still a bracelet and it was one Trinity made. "Boys can wear jewelry, too. Boys can wear anything they want. And so can girls. If it's not for you, that's okay, but it shouldn't be not for you because you think it's only for girls."

The boys nodded and slowly wandered back to the basketball court. I hadn't gotten through to them yet, but I wasn't giving up on teaching the boys who hung around that girls and boys didn't have lines drawn about what they can or can't do.

One boy took a little longer to make it back to the basketball court, and I thought he might ask Trinity something, but one of his friends called him away and he rushed off without a word.

I turned back to Trinity. She was looking closely at me, her dark brows drawn together. "What?" I asked.

She shook her head and walked past me with the broom and dust pan. "I'm still trying to figure you out."

"What you see is what you get with me," I lied. It couldn't be further from the truth, but she didn't need to know who I really was. Although it was likely she'd figure it out soon enough.

"I don't think that's true," she said.

When my mom asked me to set up the tables and chairs on the stage, she didn't tell me why. As Trinity started sweeping the empty stage, I realized why I took an hour the night before getting things ready. It was for Trinity.

And she cleaned it all up on her own and was sweeping the floor.

"I can do that," I offered, reaching for the broom in her hand.

She spun away. "I got it. I told Ms. Amelia I would clean up. There's a dance class later tonight and she wanted to make sure no one gets hurt."

I nodded. I knew that already since that was why I was there. Mom asked me to stop by to put away all those tables and chairs I set up the night before.

I didn't mind helping out. Some of the best memories I had growing up were at the community center. The youth side was set up like a clubhouse for the kids so they could do homework, play games, and spend time with friends. A bus brought the kids there from the elementary and middle schools so the kids weren't walking, and parents picked them up after work. It was a safe place for kids to be when they didn't have a parent home at the end of the day.

It was the one job my mother never quit. She left the restaurant and gas station when a better paying job came along at a doctor's office, but she refused to give up her job at the community center. Now, she worked as the director and oversaw all the youth programs.

"Why are you watching me?" Trinity asked over her shoulder.

"I offered to help."

"And I said no. Go away."

"I'm here to help."

She scoffed. "You didn't even know I would be here, and

now you're telling me you're here to help me. What does that even mean?"

"Thank you for cleaning up, Trinity," Mom said, joining us on the stage. "Is my son giving you a hard time?"

"Son?" Trinity stammered, her gaze dancing between us. She took a breath and forced a smile. "I didn't realize he was your son."

"Is that a problem?" Mom asked, narrowing her eyes at me. "I thought today went very well, and I was hoping you'd be willing to come back again. Maybe on a different day. We have some kids who only come on Tuesday and Thursday, and some who only come on Monday, Wednesday, and Friday, so if you could alternate which days you come, you'll hit different groups of kids. But if this is an issue…"

Mom trailed off, letting her threatening words hang in the air. It was clear she would choose me over Trinity, and I didn't want Trinity to give up something she wanted to do.

"It's fine, Mom. We're just surprised since neither of us expected the other to be here," I said firmly.

"I'm not sure why it matters."

I shook my head. "It's doesn't. It was just a surprise." I glanced at Trinity, who was nodding silently.

"Okay, good. So, Trinity, are you going to be able to come back next week?"

She smiled and nodded. "Yes, I'd be happy to."

"Good. Well, since Trinity moved all the tables and chairs, you're off the hook, Jimmy. You can go. I know you don't like being here. Too many memories of when you were a kid."

I smiled. "I was going to stick around and play with the kids, if that's okay."

Mom brightened, her brown eyes lighting up. "Of course. The kids would love that. They're always asking when you're going to come visit."

Mom patted me on the cheek then thanked Trinity for being there and left the stage.

"Did you tell her to let me do this?" Trinity breathed.

My eyebrows shot up. "I had no idea you were going to be here. I set the tables up last night and was here to take them down before dance."

"She had to do a background check. How did you not know she was letting me work here?"

I took a breath and blew it out slowly. "That's one of the many questions I intend to ask her later."

"Do you want me to stop working here?" she asked quietly.

"No. I would never stop you from doing something you enjoy. It sounds like you had a good turnout, too."

Trinity snorted and walked the broom back to its spot against the wall. I followed her, wanting a minute without so many prying eyes.

She stood facing the wall for a long moment and shook her head.

"What's wrong?"

"I had two girls," she hissed, spinning to get in my face. "Two. I thought I'd have twenty kids, but I had two. I want to be happy that I even reached one, but it makes me feel like I failed. That's not a good turnout. It's pathetic."

I grinned, which only served to make her more angry.

"You think that's funny?"

I shook my head. "I'm not laughing at you for having two kids. I'm laughing at you for thinking that's a bad thing. These kids...these kids come here because life at home isn't great. A lot of them only have one parent at home. The programs are cheap because many of these kids are also the kids who get free or reduced price lunches. They come from families who don't have much. And with all that going on, they are already different from their classmates. They are already picked on and trying something new isn't easy. These kids want to blend in, not stand out. So two kids who were willing to join you…that's a great turnout in my book."

A ghost of a smile turned up her lips.

I jerked my head toward to basketball court. "Why don't you come let me show you how to shoot a basketball?"

Her brows lifted and she grinned. "I think I can do that."

THE WOMAN WHOOPED my ass at basketball. I was all big and bad for about five minutes, showing her how to hold the ball and flick her wrist, then I told her to line up on the free-throw line to take a shot. She sunk it. Nothing but net.

I knew I was in trouble. Not only could she shoot hoops, effortlessly, but she looked good doing it and had all the boys falling for her.

They weren't the only ones.

"I think you owe me a victory dinner," she said with a wide grin.

I shook my head. "I think you owe me dinner since you hustled me."

"I did no such thing. You made an assumption that since I make jewelry, I can't play ball. You're all talk, telling those boys they can do everything, then you think I'm a helpless woman who can't even hold a basketball let alone kick your ass."

"Ms. Trinity, you can't say that word," one of the little girls told her.

Trinity's cheeks darkened and she crouched in front of the girl. "You're right, Heather. I should not have said that word. Thank you for correcting me."

Heather beamed then ran off, the praise making her happy.

"Where did you learn to play?" I asked her.

She stared at the hoop and said, "My dad. He loved to play. We had a basket above our garage growing up. When we moved, I only played during gym class. I wanted to try out for the school team, but we moved before the season and they'd already chosen the team at my new school. By the next year, I was making jewelry with my grandma."

"It looks like it was like riding a bike for you."

She smiled. "It kind of was. Plus, it was fun to beat you."

I barked a laugh and shook my head. "I still think I was hustled."

She shook her head. "You're a sore loser. Where did you learn to play? I knew you played baseball, but I didn't know you played basketball, too."

"Checking up on me?"

She snorted. "Hardly."

I grinned and looked around the beat up gym with the faded paint and the wood floor that was older than me. "I learned here. On this floor."

She narrowed her eyes and tilted her head in question.

"My brother and I were these kids growing up. Single mom, living in a rundown apartment, not enough food most of the time, and counting on a stranger to teach us something because our mom worked three jobs just to try to make ends meet."

She held my gaze for a minute. I wasn't sure if she was judging me or trying to decide if I was lying, but it was out there.

I never told anyone about the way I grew up. I hated it. I was constantly picked on for the free lunches I got from school and the hand-me-down clothes I wore. The richest kid in school donated something and my mom brought it home for me. I didn't realize it had been his until I showed up at school wearing his discarded clothes and he called me out. I'd never been more ashamed in my life.

Being at the community center was different. It was the only place I felt like I wasn't being judged. Everyone else was the same as me. We were all a little ragged around the edges and a little behind on everything.

That was why I credited the community center for making the baseball and basketball teams in high school. Baseball was my sport, but we didn't have the money for me to play Little League. It wasn't until I could play for school, and have equipment provided for free, that I played. But the confidence I gained in myself and use of the free weight room at the community center made all that happen.

Waiting for Trinity to laugh at me and say I wasn't good enough for her felt like someone slowly pulling my insides out. MacKellar Cove wasn't a wealthy town, but I knew I didn't even measure up by MacKellar Cove standards.

The last thing I expected was for her to step closer to me and say, "If you think I'm going to let you out of paying for my dinner, you haven't been paying attention to who I am."

She smiled one of those come get me grins and turned, adding a little bounce to her step as she taunted me with her curvy ass.

Dear God, she was perfect.

"She's a nice woman," my mom said from next to me.

I was so lost in watching Trinity that I didn't even notice my mother approach. "She is. Although I would have told you that if you called me about her."

Mom shrugged.

"Why didn't you call me?"

She crossed her arms and turned to me. "You're not the only person I know at the station. Besides, asking you to help always feels like I'm circumventing the system."

"Why? You know I don't mind."

Mom shrugged. "I figured you wouldn't want to do this one."

"Why?"

"The references she gave me were people you've mentioned. I figured you knew her, and I didn't want to put you in an awkward position or to violate any confidences. So I asked someone else to do it."

"Who?"

Mom shrugged and looked away.

"Mom, who?"

"Your partner."

"Masterson," I growled.

"He's very nice."

"No, he's not. He's an ass."

"Jimmy Rucker. Do not use that language in this place."

I clenched my jaw until it cracked. I shook my head because there was no reason to argue with her. My mother always ruled with an iron fist, but she had plenty of moments where she was soft as a feather with my brother and me. Talking poorly about someone and swearing were two of her hard lines. She never let either of them go. Ever.

"I don't like him, Mom. I think he's an arrogant jerk with no compassion for the people in this town. He wants to arrest everyone."

"Isn't that your job?"

I rolled my eyes at her. "Aren't you the one always telling me to look beyond the first impression of people? That if you only see the surface, you'll miss the best parts?"

"Yes, which is why you need to look for more from Rowan. He's a good man, and you aren't giving him a good chance."

"But—"

"Jimmy, you're not going to change my mind on him. Let it go. Are you going to come over for dinner soon?"

"Why don't you come to my house?"

She shook her head. "Your house is too fancy for me. Why don't you come to the old apartment?"

I sighed. "I'll see, Mom."

She nodded and kissed my cheek. "Get out of here, honey. I'm going to finish up and head home. I love you."

"I love you, too, Mom."

I walked out, skipping over the cracks in the sidewalk, nearly tripping over a few new ones. I spun my keys around my finger and whistled as I walked to my truck.

And dropped my keys when I walked around the end and found Trinity leaning up against my door.

"Hey," I said, bending to grab my keys and feeling like an idiot.

"Hey. I was starting to think I should just go."

"Sorry. I didn't know you were waiting for me. I was talking to my mom."

"Is everything okay?"

I nodded. "Yep, all good. Just catching up."

"Do you see her often?"

I raised an eyebrow and leaned against my truck next to her. "Did you really wait out here to ask me about my mom?"

She grinned and ducked her chin. Then she shook her head. "No, I didn't."

"Then why are you still here, Trinity?" I asked, my voice dipping low.

"Because you owe me dinner," she said.

I chuckled. "Okay. Where do you want to go?"

"Ooh, and I get to pick? I think I'm going to enjoy this."

I laughed and nodded. She wasn't the only one.

15

I half expected Trinity to pick someplace ridiculously expensive for dinner, but she surprised me with the suggestion of takeout and a picnic at Catherine Park.

"Are you sure this is okay?" I asked her as we sat. I didn't have a blanket for us to sit on so we grabbed a couple chairs and balanced our food on our laps.

She nodded and sipped her milkshake. "It's perfect. Tonight is beautiful. This is my kind of weather. Cool but not uncomfortable to be outside. I'm trying to soak in as much of it as possible with the fall coming soon."

"You don't like fall?" I asked, unwrapping my sub and taking a bite.

She shook her head. "No, I love fall. I'm just not a big fan of what comes after it."

I laughed. "Winter?"

She shuddered. "Don't even say it."

I laughed again. "Didn't you grow up in Syracuse? It's not like it's warm there."

She shook her head. "I didn't say I wanted to go back

there or that it was warmer. Just that I don't like the cold. I've seriously considered moving somewhere like San Diego where it's always seventy, but I think I'd miss having four seasons."

"So, you don't like winter, but you aren't willing to give it up?"

"I never said I made any sense or was easy to figure out."

I grinned. "That's definitely true."

We shared a smile and ate our subs in silence for a minute. A young couple with a dog threw a frisbee on the grass in front of us. An older couple held hands and walked along the water. The soft sounds of the town drifted around us. The water lapped at the edge of the shore. Gulls flew around our heads. It was good to spend time with her.

"Do you help your mom out a lot?" she asked, balling up the wrapper and throwing it into the bag.

I nodded and put my trash with hers. "I try. I have kind of a love / hate relationship with the place. We spent a lot of time there growing up, and as soon as I could, I got away from everything that reminded me of my old life."

"But you still live here?"

I chuckled. "I've considered moving a ton of times. My brother left for college and never came back. He's married and has a kid and a dog and a white picket fence. He's happy, and he does not want to come back. But my mom's still here. I don't feel like I can leave her."

"She seems to be pretty independent."

I snorted. "You have no idea. I think she only asks me to help her so I have to go see her."

"You don't go see your mom?" Trinity asked.

"I do. I try to get her to come to my house, though."

Trinity nodded. "I get that. I don't think I could go back and visit my mom in the house I grew up in. Losing my dad and our lives changing so much...it would be hard to be there. My grandma's house is different. It doesn't bother me as much to be there."

"I've tried to get my mom to move. I even offered to let her live with me—"

"Seriously?"

I shrugged. "I don't want her in that place. Oak Hill is run down and it's not safe. Especially as a woman living by herself."

"Do you really think she can't take care of herself?"

I took a breath and debated saying yes, but deep down it wasn't the truth. I looked at Trinity. "I hated growing up there. I hated growing up the way I did. I was always responsible for my brother, and we were home alone most of the time. My mom worked three jobs. Going back there, I feel like a failure. Like I never should have gotten out of there. And Anna…Joey's mom?"

Trinity nodded in understanding.

"I grew up with her. She lived there. Seeing her and her boys…"

"It makes you feel guilty," Trinity provided.

I held her gaze and nodded. "I do. Why did I get out and she didn't? And even worse, I was jealous of her when she got married. I wanted that. I wanted a family. I resented her for having it."

"It's not your fault that things didn't work out for them," Trinity said gently.

I smiled. "I know, but I still feel like an ass. You've told me I am plenty of times."

She grinned. "Well, you usually are to me."

I smiled and held her gaze for a long moment. Long enough that her eyes went dark and lusty. For a minute, I forgot where we were and leaned closer to her. Then the dog barked, and we snapped out of our trance.

"Um, so, uh, should I walk you home?"

She stood and grinned. "I think I can handle going a few blocks on my own."

"How about you let me walk you home anyway?"

She tilted her head, her dark curls sliding over her shoulder. The look in her eyes said she wasn't sure what I was thinking, but my intentions were definitely honorable. This time. I wanted to spend a few more minutes with her. I liked her. A lot.

She nodded and waited while I took our trash to the closest garbage and stuffed the bag inside. When I made it back to her, she bumped me with her shoulder then wrapped her hand around my arm.

I looked down at her and grinned. "You're willing to be seen with me in public and let people know we like each other now?"

She shrugged. "Would you rather I let go?"

"Fuck, no."

She grinned and slid her hand down to thread her fingers into mine. "I still don't like you."

I chuckled. "Understood."

We walked past O'Kelley's, letting the roar of the crowd be our conversation for a moment. When we were beyond the noise, without getting interrupted, I asked Trinity, "Did you know my mom worked at the community center before you went there?"

She shook her head. "Not until she said it today. Why?"

I shrugged. "I just didn't realize you were thinking of working there. And she kind of went out of her way to not tell me. She asked my partner to run a background check on you."

"Is it a problem?"

I shook my head. "No. I'm just...I don't let a lot of people into that part of my world."

"Are you saying you don't want me to volunteer there?" she asked, pulling away.

"No. Trinity, no. I...I like you. I know things between us have been..."

"Weird?"

I huffed a laugh. "We can go with that. When people see where I came from, there's a shift. It's not a good shift."

"You think I'm going to hate you now because you grew up without a lot of money?" she asked.

I didn't answer, which was enough of an answer.

"Well, I didn't like you before, so that really isn't going to change anything."

I barked a laugh and shook my head. "I really want to kiss you right now."

I looked up at me and smiled. "Thank you for trusting me with your past."

"Thank you for not running away from me."

We kept walking in silence. I held the door for her to walk into her building and followed her up the stairs. When we got to her door, she fumbled with her keys.

"Do you want to come in?"

I nodded and leaned closer. She looked up at me, desire in her gaze. "I'd love to, but I'm not going to."

She blinked away the haze and narrowed her eyes. "What? Why?"

I tucked her curls behind her ear and kissed her forehead. "Because I don't want to just fuck you, Trinity." I kissed her cheek. "I want to touch you." I kissed her ear. "I want to hold you." I kissed her jaw. "I want to drive you crazy until you can't stop yourself from falling in love with me."

She let out a shocked laugh.

I kissed her nose. "I told you before this isn't just sex for me. I had fun tonight. I want to see you again. And I hope you'll agree to that."

She hesitated a moment then nodded.

I leaned in slowly, holding her gaze until her eyes drifted shut and our lips sealed together. She parted her lips under mine, letting me in and taking control all at once. Her tongue glided along mine. She wrapped her arms around my neck and pulled my body flush to hers. She moaned softly into my mouth and hummed her approval when I wrapped my arms around her waist and held her closer.

We pulled back with matching pants, staring at each other with nothing but a breath between us.

"I should go," I breathed.

She nodded. "I know."

I kissed her again, slowly and deeply, until I wasn't sure I could stop.

She pulled back once more. "Good night, Officer."

I shook my head and took a step back. "Good night."

She let herself in and closed and locked the door between us. I couldn't stop myself from smiling the entire way home.

FOR THE NEXT FEW DAYS, I debated what I should do about Trinity. I really liked her, and we were definitely getting closer. I hadn't seen her since the night we had dinner, but I wanted to see her over the weekend.

Which meant I needed to call it off with the woman I'd been matched with on Book Boyfriends Wanted.

I knew it was a dick move, but I'd been talking to both of them for a while. Things with Trinity…I never expected that to happen. The woman on the app…she was great. Easy to talk to, funny, kind. I could really like her. But she still wasn't real to me. Trinity was.

I needed to end things with the woman on the app, but I wasn't sure the best way to do that without being an ass. The only reason I was ending it was because it wasn't fair to Trinity or her that I was talking to both of them. It wasn't because I didn't like her. If I could mash them together into one person, that would be perfect.

I was staring at my phone, the app open, with a new message ready to send to DiamondGirl when Hudson stopped in front of me with a beer.

"You okay?"

I nodded. "Trying to figure out how to end things with someone I've never met."

"At least you know she won't throw a drink in your face or do something crazy," Hudson said.

I looked up at him and followed his gaze to where a couple was arguing. The guy was dripping wet, wiping what used to be his drink off his face. The woman was standing above him shouting at him.

After a few seconds, she stalked off and he looked around like he thought everyone in the bar might not have noticed.

I grimaced for him. "Yeah, there's that."

"Who are you ending things with?" Hudson asked. "And why?"

"I've been talking to this woman on that app Karissa made. She's great, but I need to end things with her."

"Because of Trinity?"

I pulled back. "Yeah. And how the hell did you know that?"

Hudson snorted. "Please. You're always doing stupid shit around her. You're a lucky son of a bitch that she even bothered to give you a second glance."

I nodded. "I know. And I don't want to screw it up by continuing to talk to this other woman. When Trinity and I...the first time just happened. She wasn't happy about it, and—"

"What do you mean she wasn't happy about it?" Hudson growled, leaning close and getting in my face.

I calmly met his gaze and shook my head. "Not like that. It was completely consensual. I would never force myself on a woman."

He stared me down for another minute before he nodded and backed up.

"Anyway, she's hated me for so long that she wasn't happy we slept together, even though I didn't force her. The second time was different, but I still wasn't sure how she felt. Then she volunteered at the community center."

Hudson's brows went up and he leaned back, arms crossed. "Really?"

I nodded. "I went there Tuesday night to help Mom, and Trinity was there teaching some kids to make jewelry. We got talking and had dinner, and it was good."

"And now you're ready to call it quits with this other woman."

I nodded again. "I need to. I like her, but I don't know her real name or anything. I'm not going to throw away whatever I could have with Trinity for a maybe with a stranger. But I don't want to be a total ass when I end things."

"Hillary always told me to tell the truth. Even when it felt worse, be honest."

I sipped my beer and drew in a deep breath. "Hillary was a smart woman. Except for the marrying you part."

Hudson flipped me off and shook his head as he walked away. But I saw his grin and knew he wasn't pissed.

Hudson and Hillary were the kind of couple everyone wanted to be a part of. I didn't know her well, but it was obvious to anyone who met them that they were made for each other. Hudson had never been happier in his life, and Hillary was perfect for him. When she died, he barely held it together. She was his reason for living. They had moved back to MacKellar Cove, but he withdrew from everyone in town after Hillary died. He sold the house they had and bought a bungalow on the edge of town. He barely left home for months, but one day he pulled himself out of it and said Hillary wouldn't want him to throw his life away because of her.

It still took him a year or two to get himself together, but when he did, he threw himself into making O'Kelley's a place everyone felt at home. I was sure Hillary would have been proud of him.

Losing Hillary was hard on all of us. She was a bright spot in MacKellar Cove while she lived there. Hudson told me once she was the reason he moved back. She wasn't close to her family, and even though his family had left the area, she knew he loved it. She wanted them to live in a place that felt like home, no matter where they went in town.

When I got back after the academy, I was happy to have my friend back in my life. And I was happy he brought the wisdom of a smart woman with him.

I typed a quick message to DiamondGirl and hit send before I could stop myself.

"Hey, you," Trinity said from right next to me.

"Hey," I said, tucking my phone away before she could see the screen.

Her phone dinged with an alert. She pulled it out and narrowed her eyes at the screen.

"Everything okay?"

She nodded and put it back into her pocket. "Yep. No big deal. I didn't know you were going to be here tonight."

"It's Thursday. Ian, Ramsey, Colin, and I usually get together."

"Oh. I've seen them a bunch of times, but not you. I'll let you enjoy your night."

I turned to her. "I'd much rather spend it with you."

She smiled and shook her head. "You need your friends. I'm not one of those women who will demand all of your time."

"I didn't think you were, but I haven't had much of your time at all. I want to see you again."

"Yeah, okay. I'm sure we can figure something out."

She nodded and slid off her stool. She waved and smiled and disappeared into the crowd. I looked for her, but I couldn't see where she ended up.

"Everything okay?" Hudson asked.

I turned back to him and shook my head. "I don't know."

"I take it telling her about the other woman didn't go well."

"I didn't tell her about the other woman. I told the other woman I met someone in person and didn't feel right leading her on. I didn't tell Trinity anything."

Hudson sucked in a breath. "That's gonna bite you in the ass. She should know."

I shrugged. "There's nothing for her to know. I never met this woman. Nothing happened."

"It's called an emotional affair," Hudson said. "For women, that's just as bad."

"It's not...I don't think it's a big deal."

My phone buzzed in my pocket before Hudson could reply. He went to serve drinks to someone else while I pulled it out. DiamondGirl replied.

DIAMONDGIRL

Totally understand. I've been trying to figure out a way to tell you the same. Good luck.

I typed back *thanks, you too,* and closed the app. That was done. Nothing to worry about.

16

TRINITY

I watched as James put his phone back in his pocket. The app gave me the alert that he replied. It was a coincidence that he was sending someone a message the same time I was getting one. I was pretty sure it was too big of a coincidence for it to not be him sending me messages.

I shook my head. James was JayPo. The guy I really liked and wasn't sure if I could keep talking to because of James… was James.

And he just broke up with me for me.

I was trying to decide what I should do when Piper brought over a beer and set it in front of me. "From the guy at the bar," she said, nodding to the end James wasn't sitting at.

I glanced over and saw a cute guy with his glass in the air. He had dark brown hair and lighter brown skin. His smile was friendly, not creepy. Normally, I wouldn't think twice about accepting a drink from a stranger, but I felt awkward when I was involved with someone else.

"What am I supposed to do?" I asked Piper.

She raised her eyebrows and grinned. "Well, usually you tip the glass up and drink from it. I can get you a straw if you'd rather."

I rolled my eyes. "You know what I mean."

"Your options are accept the drink and know he's likely going to come over here and talk to you, or decline it and miss out on a free beer."

"I'm not available," I confessed.

She grinned. "Yeah, I know."

"You…We'll talk about that in a minute. What should I do about the drink?"

"Whatever you do, do it fast because he's coming over now."

Piper hurried away, leaving the beer on the table in front of me. And right behind it was the man who sent it over.

"Hi," he said, flashing me that welcoming smile again.

"Um, hi."

"Do you mind if I sit?"

I stared up at him, trying to figure out how to answer his question. From his perspective, I took the drink. He had no idea what I was talking to Piper about.

I glanced at James, but his back was to me. I looked back up at the stranger and nodded. "Sure."

He took the seat and held out his hand. "I'm Adam."

"Nice to meet you. Trinity."

"Beautiful name for a beautiful woman. Do you live around here, Trinity?"

I nodded. "I do. How about you?"

He shook his head. "No, but it's beautiful. I'm finding it hard to imagine going back to my boring life in New York."

"You're from New York?"

He nodded and sipped the beer he brought to the table with him. "I am. Born and raised. Every once in a while, I try to get out and explore the rest of the world. Slow down some. I think we all need a slower pace."

I nodded. "I agree. That's why I moved here. I loved the scenery but I also loved the people. It's a great place to live."

"Is your place close?"

I nodded again, second guessing it as soon as I did. I was just robbed, and I was telling a complete stranger I lived close. Not to mention I was seeing someone and hadn't mentioned that tidbit yet.

"Maybe you can show me," he said, leaning close and gliding a finger down my arm.

"Time to go, buddy," James said, lifting the guy from his chair and shoving him toward the door.

"Whoa, man, what the hell?" Adam said, trying to shake James off.

"She's not available," James said.

"She never told me that. How was I supposed to know?" Adam argued.

James stopped in his tracks. His gaze flickered to mine then to the beers on the table in front of me and back to mine. He released Adam and took a step back. He nodded once and said, "Sorry about that. I must have misunderstood the situation."

Adam shrugged it off and nodded back. James stepped around him and stormed out the door.

I was out of my chair and racing after James before Adam could take two steps toward me. He tried to catch me, but I brushed past him and hurried outside.

James was stalking away in the opposite direction of my apartment, moving fast. I called out to him, but he ignored me and kept going.

Cursing myself for wearing sandals when it was mid-September, I walked / ran down the sidewalk after him. I could see his silhouette walking up the hill in Catherine

Park, and tried to move faster before he left the park and disappeared. I realized in that moment I didn't even know where he lived and couldn't track him down if he went home.

I raced up the hill and looked around but it was quiet. No one was walking. A car drove by, but it wasn't James' truck. I had no idea where he was.

"Dammit," I said out loud.

"Problem?" he asked, sitting in a chair a few feet from me.

I jumped at the sound of his voice. He was hidden in the seat, invisible from behind. But he made his presence known.

I took the seat next to him and said, "I didn't invite him to sit with me."

"And you didn't tell him you were seeing someone. Maybe…"

"Maybe what?"

"Maybe I'm more invested in this than you are."

"You mean like ending things with your match on Book Boyfriends Wanted?" I asked.

He turned to look at me, his brows drawn together in question.

I raised an eyebrow. "Are you JayPo?"

"How the hell do you know that?"

"Because I'm DiamondGirl. You ended things with me earlier."

He tilted his head, clearly not sure what to think.

I unlocked my phone and pulled up the app. I went to our conversations and handed him my phone so he could read the words we'd written to each other.

He laughed. "I guess I didn't have to end things with you earlier. Since I was ending them because of things with you. How long have you known?"

"Since I was getting messages at the same time you were contacting someone."

He shook his head. "I guess I should have figured that finding one woman was hard enough. Finding two had to be impossible."

I laughed with him. We sat quietly together for a minute.

"I ended things with virtual you because I didn't want to be unfair to real life you. I need to know if we're in the same place. If not, that's okay. But if you're still looking for options, I'm not sure I can handle this."

I shook my head and reached for his hand. He let me wind our fingers together but he didn't look at me. "That guy sent me over a drink. I asked Piper what I should do since I'm not single, but before we could figure it out, the guy joined me. I didn't tell him I was seeing you because I didn't have a chance. He asked my name and if I lived here, said he was from New York, invited himself back to my place, and then you removed him from his seat. I would have said no and told him why, but I didn't have a chance."

James squeezed my fingers and released my hand. He leaned forward and put his elbows on his knees. "My dad left us when I was a kid. He used to go out of town a lot, and one day he didn't come home. He had a girlfriend somewhere else and she got pregnant. He was starting a new family with her instead of finishing raising the one he started with my mom.

"It was hard on all of us, but it was the worst on my brother. He didn't understand how Dad could have a second family. He was young. I'm six years older, so I understood it enough. But I vowed to myself I would never be in a relationship with someone if we weren't both in it all the way. I know things happen, but I'm not okay with cheating or lying. I never will be."

"I wasn't—"

"I know. You didn't do anything wrong. But I jump to conclusions. My mom never saw it coming. She was blissful and stupidly in love with my dad. For years, she convinced herself he would come back to her. She just knew there was some other reason, something else going on. My dad wouldn't cheat on her. She insisted. But he never came back. And watching her hope for so long…that was the hardest part for me. Having her believe that he still loved her when he'd completely moved on and forgotten about us made me wonder if we ever really know a person. If the person you put all your trust and faith in cheats and lies and leaves you, do you ever really know another person?"

"Everything in life is fragile. My mom taught me that lesson," I told him. "My dad died in a car accident. It just happened. There was no warning, no preparing, just there one day, gone the next. For a while, I convinced myself that I had to squeeze as much of life in as possible before my time was up. Then I decided to be happy and not let fear rule me. But now I realize that it doesn't matter what we do, life is fragile and we can either treat it with kid gloves and worry about everything or we can trust that even if it breaks, it's still there."

"I'm not sure I understand," he said, turning his head to give me a wry smile.

"I don't want to be afraid of everything. Life is meant to be lived. We only have one. If we decide to go through it with caution at every turn, we might miss out on something. If we decide to throw caution to the wind, we might miss out on something. There is no one rule. Life is meant to be enjoyed, and if we aren't willing to try to do that, whatever that means for each of us, then what's the point?"

"So, you're saying trust doesn't matter?"

I shook my head. "I'm saying your mom trusted your dad, got her heart broken, but she also got two sons. My dad didn't betray my mom, but he's still gone. You would never say he broke her trust, but she's still heart broken from losing him. I'm saying it doesn't matter which path we choose, life is going to shit on us and lift us up in all of them."

"Hopefully it lets us wash off the shit before it lifts us up for everyone to see," James said with a grin.

I chuckled. "I hope so."

He leaned back in his seat and stared out at the town. "I think I like what you're saying. Whatever we do, we're going to have some regrets and we're going to have some joy and life isn't about eliminating one or the other, it's about choosing more things that we think will bring us joy."

I nodded. "Yep."

"You're pretty smart. You know that?"

I shrugged. "Well, I did pick you twice."

He barked a laugh. "I don't know how I got that lucky."

"You chose joy," I told him.

He turned to me and raised an eyebrow. "I know a way I could choose a lot more joy." He pulled me out of my chair and onto his lap. He kissed my throat and said, "A lot more."

"Yes, please," I breathed.

"Your place is closer."

He pushed me off his lap and grabbed my hand as we rushed through town toward my condo. We made it up the stairs and inside without being stopped by anyone. A small miracle in a town like MacKellar Cove.

As soon as the door closed behind us, we were stripping each other's clothes off and reaching for each other. He followed me to my room and collapsed onto my bed with me, him on top, pressing me into my mattress.

He kissed his way down my throat and licked a circle around my belly button. I squirmed and moaned at the feel of him, his shoulders pushing my thighs wide. His teeth pinched at my hips and he kissed his way down my legs. When he got to my feet, he licked his way back up, pausing to kiss and suck on my inner thighs and between my breasts.

By the time he pressed his lips to mine, I was panting for more of him. He stretched out on top of me and kissed me lazily. He intertwined our fingers and brought them above my head, kissing and sucking on my throat.

I drew my foot up his leg, enjoying the feel of him notched between my thighs. He kissed me like nothing else mattered outside of the two of us.

When he pulled back and looked at me, I waited for him to say something, but he just stared at me. He brushed my wild mess of curls back from my face and kissed his way around my face, lingering long enough to whisper, "I can't wait to be inside you again."

I moaned softly at his dirty words. "Please."

"Soon." He dragged his tongue between my breasts and traced the edges of my bra. "Take this off so I can lick you."

I lifted myself up to reach my bra while he drew my panties off. I laid back on my bed completely bare and open to him, trusting him.

He stood at the foot of the bed and looked at me. His gaze slid from my face down my body and back up to meet my gaze. Panic threatened to overwhelm me, to make me cover up. Was he going to walk away and leave me there, wanting him? Was he going to laugh and say he didn't really want me? Was he going to join me on the bed again and choose joy with me?

I held my breath while I waited for him. When he stripped off his briefs and rolled on a condom, he said, "Thank you for trusting me."

He crawled onto the bed and kissed me. The kiss lingered as he once again slid down my body. This time he stopped between my thighs and pressed his lips to me.

A long, low moan forced its way out of my mouth. I was already close. He wasn't wasting time with foreplay that didn't lead anywhere. James was the kind of man who knew exactly how to play my body and he was going to get me off as quickly as possible.

My orgasm built and quickly stole my breath and all my sense. I tried to hold back the intensity of it, but James didn't let me, pressing his tongue to my clit and thrusting two fingers into me. I came hard, my entire body going hot then cold as I erupted at his expert touch.

"I love the way you come," he whispered against my hip. He slowly withdrew his fingers, toying with my body as he kissed his way to my lips.

He held back from kissing me, but I pulled him to me. He growled and dove in, fitting himself between my thighs and thrusting into me while we kissed. He pumped in and out, supporting his weight above me while he drove me crazy with his kisses. I wrapped my legs around his hips and moaned when he sank in deeper.

"You feel so damn good," he groaned against my neck. "So fucking good, Trinity."

"You, too," I said.

I let myself get lost in James, choosing not to get too deep into what was happening between us. If it were any other man, I would be thinking about a future with him. But James was different. If I let myself fall for him, I wouldn't be able to crawl back out. I would lose myself in him.

Just like I did every time we were together.

Another orgasm raced toward me, overwhelming me as he thrust into me. He held himself up and watched me. I couldn't look at him. I needed to keep a little bit of distance between us. But I couldn't look away.

My orgasm demanded to let go, and I let my eyes fall closed for it to happen. I screamed his name and held onto him while I fell harder.

"I got you, Trinity," he whispered in my ear as I shouted. "I got you."

My body trembled with aftershocks as he thrust deep inside and found his own release. I held him when he collapsed onto me, not wanting to let go any time soon.

Our bodies cooled as our heartbeats slowed. The stickiness of sweat and the euphoria of sex combined to make me feel amazing. I wanted to never let go of the feelings he brought out in me.

He made a move to get up and I reluctantly let him go. He glanced around then went into my bathroom. When he came back, he looked like he wasn't sure what to do.

"Do you want to stay for a drink?" I asked, propping myself up on my elbows.

He looked at me and grinned. "Yeah, I do."

I smiled back and climbed ungracefully off my bed. "I'll meet you out there in a sec. Feel free to see what I have. If you want to stick around for a little while."

He nodded. "I'm not going anywhere."

I smiled. Maybe joy was not strong enough of a word because I was feeling a whole lot more than just that at the moment. But I wasn't ready to use that other word yet.

17

James had to work through the weekend, so we didn't see each other much for a few days. I decided to share that we were seeing each other with everyone at girls' night on Sunday. After insisting we didn't like each other, I wasn't sure how it was going to go and kept putting off saying something.

"Have you heard from your match lately?" Finley asked me once we all finished our raspberry cheesecake from Melody.

I nodded and leaned back in my seat. "He actually ended things. He met someone in real life and thought it was for the best that he doesn't talk to both of us at once."

"That sucks but it's honorable of him," Blake said. She scrunched up her face. "Especially since you were thinking about meeting him."

"That must be going around," Laura said with an eye roll. "Things ended with me and the guy I was seeing." She sounded indifferent but her eyes said she was bothered by it.

"Really? You just met him last weekend," Elise said.

Laura nodded and huffed a laugh. "Yep, but he said there wasn't a spark. I seem to have that effect on men."

"You'll find someone," Elise assured her.

Laura smiled and shrugged. "I don't know. I'm thinking I might just let things happen for a while. Not worry about finding someone, just try to enjoy life. I used to be that way. I used to date whoever I found interesting. I want to enjoy life again."

"Choose joy," I said.

Laura pointed her fork at me and nodded. "Exactly. I've spent too long wishing Nico would look at me, and he's not. I need to move on from him, which I am, but I also need to move on from wanting what the rest of you have. Not forever, but for right now. If I try to hold onto that dream too tightly, it's going to slip through my fingers."

"If that makes you happy, then do it. Have some fun. Sleep with some hot guys. Go visit Peyton for a few days," Elise suggested.

I'd heard of Peyton, but I didn't know her. Laura told me she was her old boss and good friend from where she lived near Buffalo. I also knew she was one of the people who made it possible for Ms. Georgia to marry Eddie before she died. I hadn't met her, but I liked her just for that reason alone.

"Maybe I will. I haven't been there in far too long. She's due with baby two in a month. I should go before things get too crazy for her," Laura said.

"Can I go with you?" Karissa asked, leaning toward Laura. "I'd love to see all of them again, and I need a break for a few days, too. Long weekend?"

Laura nodded sharply. "Yes, let's do it. I'll talk to Ally and see when I can get off in the next few weeks. Peyton won't mind. This will be fun."

"I'm sleeping with James," I blurted out while everyone

was focused on Laura. I hoped maybe they wouldn't notice, but of course, they all did.

"You're what?"

"I knew it."

"James Rucker?"

"Since when?"

I leaned back in my chair and tried not to burn up with embarrassment. I was happy I wore an oversized sweatshirt and could pull my hands into the sleeves and hide a little. My hair was tied back in a loose ponytail. I was prepared for the onslaught of questions, but having them thrown at me still made me anxious.

"How long have you been together?" Blake repeated.

"A few weeks."

"After your purse was stolen?" Finley asked.

I nodded.

"How did you get together?" Karissa asked.

I sighed and told them about finding him at my door the one night after girls night and it just happening.

"Wait, but you insisted after that that nothing was going on," Karissa said. Her gaze was sharp.

I nodded and drew in a breath. "Yeah, because I thought it was a one time thing. We didn't talk. It was that angry sex where we just went at it. I thought there was nothing to tell. And then it happened again. And last week he was at the community center when I was there. Did you guys know his mom is the director?"

They all nodded.

"You didn't know that?" Laura asked.

I shook my head. "No. I had no idea until she said something. He thinks she was trying to keep him from finding out I was volunteering there."

"Why would she do that?" Piper asked.

I shrugged. "I don't know. James doesn't seem too happy

his mom still works there. Or that she lives in the apartment where he grew up. I think he wants to erase his past or something."

"He definitely does," Finley said. "A girl in our grade grew up in the same neighborhood as James." She nodded at Blake. "She told us how hard things were for her family. She was grateful for a place to live, but she said a lot of the families in Oak Hill were barely holding on. But I think Amelia is trying to make it a better place. She started a community garden a few years ago and has all the neighbors help when they can. She's tried to make sure everyone knows each other so they feel more comfortable asking each other for help. It's not easy feeling so alone, though."

"Hudson was talking about a project to help out there," Piper said. "He said something about the woman whose kid stole your purse."

I nodded. I hadn't met them yet, but I knew she was close to Hudson and James' age.

"They want to do something to help the people who live there. Maybe a community cookout or something," Piper continued.

"They should reach out to Amelia," Elise said. "If she's already trying to help the neighborhood, she would know what would be of the most help."

"I'll tell him," Piper said. "I think he'll be open to that. He's looking for as many volunteers as he can get. I already said I was in for whatever they decided on."

"Count me in, too," Finley said. "Maybe we can donate some books to the parents in the neighborhood. I'll put out a box near the register for people to leave their gently used copies that they don't want to hang on to."

"That's a great idea," Elise said. "You could create one of those mini libraries in the neighborhood so people can trade the books."

"Great idea," Finley said.

We kept talking about other things we could do to help the neighborhood. I kept thinking that I wanted to give back more. I was teaching at the community center, but I knew there was more I could do. There had to be. I just had to figure out what it was.

I TRIED to focus on work over the next few days but found myself continually distracted. Karissa activated my app, and it sent me a notification for everything. There was one when a new app was downloaded. Another when someone ordered something. One more when someone left a comment on one of my videos. It was making me crazy.

I decided to get outside a little while on Wednesday and enjoy the fresh air. Fall was moving into town and bringing the crisp air and colorful leaves I loved, but the nights were getting colder too fast for me. I couldn't open my slider in the evenings anymore without my heat kicking on.

The pavilion at Catherine Park was quiet when I got there. With kids in school and most of the town at work, very few people were out and in the middle of the afternoon. It gave me a chance to sit and think but also to watch the sun glittering off the water and the large boats glide seamlessly by.

The peacefulness of MacKellar Cove reminded me why I moved there. I could never find that kind of relaxation in the city. There were parks, but I was always tense. I felt like I was waiting for the next thing to happen. In MacKellar Cove, I wasn't waiting for anything. I was enjoying life.

My phone buzzed in my pocket and I ignored it until it buzzed again, telling me it was a phone call and not an alert. I dug it out and smiled before I answered.

"Hi, Grandma."

"Hello, sweetheart. How are you?"

"I'm good. How are you?"

"Oh, good. I just felt like I should call you for some reason. Is everything okay?"

I chuckled. "Yes, grandma. Everything is good. How are you and Mom?"

My grandma liked to think of herself as somewhat psychic. She did have a sixth sense at times and would call when I really needed someone to talk to, but she also called when she hadn't heard from me in a while and decided she was going to check in.

"We're good. Your mom is working today. I'm making some more of these bracelets you showed me. I'm going to run out of friends to give them to before long."

"You should sell them, grandma. You make beautiful pieces."

"Psh. You know I don't do this for the money," she argued.

A lightbulb went on in my head. "Would you be willing to do it to help people?"

"Of course, but I'm not sure how making jewelry could help people."

"I'm working on a project with some friends. There's a neighborhood that is pretty bad off. From what they've told me, the people who live there have no other choice."

"We know what that's like," grandma said.

I nodded. "We do. But Mom and I had you to help us out. These people don't have anyone. To some people, a piece of jewelry is not a big deal, but to someone who doesn't have much, it could mean a lot. Would you be willing to make some pieces and donate them?"

"Of course," grandma said without hesitation. "What else can we do?"

"I don't know yet, but I think I need to do more. There

are too many people who don't have enough. The right accessory could make them feel confident enough to get a new job or get through the day or maybe go on a date."

"I always told you people underestimate the power of feeling good about yourself."

I smiled. "You have. And I think I've forgotten that lesson, too. I keep thinking I want to give back in some way and help more people, but doing so doesn't have to mean helping everyone at once. It means doing what I can now and then doing more later."

"There will always be more to be done," grandma said.

"Always. Thanks, grandma. I'm happy you called."

"When are you going to come for a visit?" she asked.

I smiled. "Soon. But I might bring a friend if that's okay."

She chuckled. "Of course. I look forward to it."

I hung up with her and nodded. I felt better already, but I wanted to talk to Hudson about the ideas I had. I didn't know everything he was planning, but if we all chipped in with something, we could make the event a huge success.

O'Kelley's was quiet when I walked in. Hudson was behind the bar, so I took a seat on a stool and dove right in.

"What are you planning to do to help Oak Hill?"

His eyebrows shot up. He grabbed the bill of his cap and adjusted his hat then shrugged. "I don't really know yet. We talked about a cookout or something. I'm trying to gather some ideas. Colin offered to fix things since they don't seem to have a maintenance person. I'm not in charge of anything, though."

"Who is?"

"James. All this was his idea. He wants to give back. We all do, but he was the one who said if we're going to help, we can't just help one person. Anna…I offered her son a job and she wouldn't let him take it because I didn't consider other people. She was right. I was going to hand him a job to help them out. There are a lot of people who need help. James knows we can't help everyone, but he wants to try to help more than just one family."

"I thought Piper said you were in charge?" I asked.

"What did I say?" Piper asked, appearing next to me and tying on an apron.

"I thought Hudson was in charge of the event to help Oak Hill?"

Piper shook her head. "No, he's helping and O'Kelley's is likely to be the home base since everyone is here all the time, but James is taking the lead."

I nodded. "I didn't realize. Thanks."

"Of course. What are you thinking about doing?"

"I was talking to my grandma about making jewelry we could donate. Is that stupid?"

Piper shook her head. "Not at all. I put on something every day when I come here. Sometimes it's a pair of earrings, sometimes it's a necklace. I don't wear a lot, but it makes me feel like I'm putting in a little extra effort. You're always wearing something great."

"I keep wondering if it really matters. I've been teaching at the community center for a few weeks and I enjoy it, but it's something to keep the kids busy. And I feel kind of selfish because I went there to help my career. Am I really helping people to give them jewelry?"

Piper shrugged. "Some people, probably not. That's just the truth. There will be some people who don't see the value in a new item. But I'm the kind of person who wears lace bras and panties because I want to feel good. I want to know that underneath my black tee and jeans, I'm wearing something amazing and I feel sexy in it."

"It's like lace panties on the outside," I said.

Piper laughed. "Exactly. You could totally use that in your marketing. Lace panties on the outside."

I laughed with her. "I'm not sure anyone else would get it."

Piper nodded. "True. But honestly, I think it could help people. What if someone has a job interview or a date? If that one piece gives them a little boost of confidence, it's worth it."

I nodded. "That's what I was thinking, too."

"I'm happy you're on board with this. I think it's going to be good for the community. And for those of us giving back. I know I don't do enough of that."

"Neither do I, but I want to change that."

"How are things going at the community center with your classes?" Piper asked.

"Really good. I was discouraged the first week because only two girls wanted to participate. James said that was a good turnout. This week they brought another friend."

"Really?"

I nodded. "It's not much, but they both came back so I'm happy."

"Wow. That's awesome."

I grinned. "Yeah. It's going well. A part of me wishes I could do two days a week, but I think it would be too much. Maybe when I have more kids than I can handle in one session I'll do two."

"That would be a good problem to have."

"Very true."

"Are you going to be here for a while? I need to check in with these people?"

I nodded, and Piper walked off. Hudson set a drink in front of me and said, "Thanks for helping. I know it'll mean a lot to James to have you participate."

"Do you know why he didn't ask me?"

Hudson shrugged. "Probably because all this started because of you. Joey stole your purse. You agreed not to press charges. It's made James face some tough things, but he feels like he already asked a lot of you by not pressing charges. He can't ask more."

"I didn't let it go because of James. I let it go because no kid should have to go hungry."

"It would be nice to make that a reality."

I nodded. I definitely agreed with that thought.

18

JAMES

"Got a case for you two to look into," Captain Reynolds said, dropping a file onto my desk. "MacKellar Cove Inn had a break in last night. Mrs. Holbrook was pretty shaken up. She said she heard the noise and went to see what was going on and must have scared them off. She has video cameras but she doesn't know how to send us the footage. Need you to go talk to her and get everything."

I nodded. Mrs. Holbrook owned the Inn forever. I couldn't remember anyone else being there. It sat opposite the MacKellar home at the entrance to the Cove. The two properties were the biggest structures in town, and both had been there longer than anything else. The rest of the town was built to support the families that built the homes.

The MacKellar family owned more land and decided to name the cove and the town they were building for themselves. The Robinson family, the family who built what became the Inn, had a feud with them. Supposedly, both sons were in love with Catherine Winters when they were children, and she chose Travis MacKellar. Harry Robinson hated being around them and left town. His parents, without any other reason for being there without their son around, also left.

The family home sat vacant for years. No one wanted to spend the money they were asking for the property, and no one could afford to. They finally dropped the price, and the Holbrooks bought it and turned it into a local inn. Travel to the area was just starting, and it was a good investment. They added a private residence in the back for the family after a few years, and upgraded the house overtime to one of the nicest places to stay in the area.

Mrs. Holbrook was getting close to eighty, so I was surprised she hadn't retired and sold the place. If nothing had convinced her before, it was possible a break in might.

"Introduce the new guy to Gina. Make sure he's nice to her," Captain Reynolds said quietly.

I nodded. "Will do, Captain." I carried the folder to Masterson's desk and handed it to him. "We need to go. How good are you with computers?"

"Very good. Why?"

"We might need your skills. Let's go. You can read on the way."

Masterson flipped through while I drove us out to the Inn. When we arrived, he asked, "How old is this place?"

"One of the original homes here. The one across the way is the other." I pointed to the MacKellar home. "Two families that settled here. Supposedly good friends at one point, but the MacKellars had more money than the Robinsons and the sons fought over the same woman, and both created problems. The Robinsons left and the house sat vacant for years before Mrs. Holbrook and her husband bought it and turned it into what it is now. He died years ago, and Mrs. Holbrook has been running the place alone for years. The guy who maintains the lighthouse helps, but for the most part, she's on her own."

"No family?"

I shook my head. "No. Never had kids. She has a niece and nephew who used to come up here for the summer, but they haven't been back in a long time."

"That sucks."

I nodded, wondering if Masterson actually did have a little bit of compassion for others.

We walked to the door and let ourselves in the front. A bell chimed, telling Mrs. Holbrook we were there.

"Be right there," she called out.

Masterson and I looked around the lobby. It used to be the sitting room for the house and showcased pictures of some of the renovations the Holbrooks took on over the years. The entire outside was redone with new siding and the roof replaced. They had the home almost down to the studs to do both since there was so much neglect after years on the market with no one to look after the house.

"Any chance the people across the way had anything to do with this?" Masterson asked quietly.

I followed his gaze out the windows to the MacKellar home gleaming in the bright morning sunshine. I shook my head. "The only one who lives there is a caretaker. The family hasn't been in town in years. The guy who maintains the property keeps to himself mostly. He's a good guy, and friendly with Mrs. Holbrook. I can't see Andrew having anything to do with this."

Masterson nodded and went back to looking at pictures of the home. The shuffle of feet and the tap of a cane signaled Mrs. Holbrook's arrival.

"Well, good morning, gentlemen. How are you?"

I turned and grinned at her, and she smiled and reached for me.

"Jimmy Rucker. I didn't know I would be seeing you today. How's your mama? And your brother?"

"Both good. Mom is still at the community center. Johnny is married with a little girl. They're in Albany and loving it."

"Oh, that's so nice. Please tell them I said hello."

"I will, Mrs. Holbrook."

"Good. So, what brings you here, and in your uniform?" she asked, looking between us.

I nodded to Masterson and explained, "Officer Masterson and I were asked to come check on you after the break-in last night. Captain Reynolds said you have some video cameras and thought Masterson might be able to help you get the footage."

"Oh, these things. Sebastian insisted I hook them up, but he knows I don't know how to do anything. He should be here soon if you can wait. Why don't I make us some tea? And you boys can have breakfast."

"We really need to see that footage, ma'am," Masterson said.

Mrs. Holbrook waved her hand. "Why such a hurry? You have your whole life, officer. Come have breakfast and we can talk."

I shrugged and followed Mrs. Holbrook. There was no way to go to visit her and not leave at least five pounds heavier and smiling. She was the kind of person who insisted on taking care of everyone around her, and she didn't care what you said about it.

Masterson glared at me as I took a seat at the worn wood table in the dining room. Mrs. Holbrook was already pouring me coffee and setting a plate of danish in front of me.

"I can make you boys some eggs if you'd like. Or French toast. What about some bacon?"

"You don't need to fuss, Mrs. Holbrook," I told her.

She looked at Masterson. "I'm sorry there isn't anything here you're interested in. What can I make for you? Pancakes? Waffles? I think I have sausage, too. I baked a fresh loaf of sourdough last night."

I raised my eyebrows at him, hoping to convey that he better choose something and eat or we'd never get out of there.

He finally sighed and said, "Sourdough and bacon sounds wonderful. Thank you, ma'am."

She grinned and patted his cheek with her free hand. "Such a handsome man. And such sweet manners. I'll make you some eggs, too. How do you like them?"

"No, I don't need eggs," Masterson said.

"Are you allergic?"

"No, but—"

"Okay, then I'll fix some eggs. I have to be careful with allergies. So many people are allergic to different foods. I ask everyone. But I know Jimmy isn't allergic to anything. I'll be right back. You boys make yourselves comfortable."

I nodded and lifted my coffee cup in salute. Masterson glared at me again until Mrs. Holbrook disappeared behind the swinging door into the kitchen.

"Listen, she's gonna feed us. If you go with it, we can get to business faster."

"This town is ridiculous," Masterson groaned.

"No one is forcing you to stay," I told him with a smile.

I earned another glare for that.

Masterson poured himself a cup of coffee and took a seat across from me. I offered him the plate of danish, but he shook his head. We didn't speak as we waited for Mrs. Holbrook to come back with his breakfast and whatever else she fixed while she was in the kitchen.

It wasn't long before the bell above the door rang. I

turned to see who was letting themself in and grinned when I saw Sebastian Parks with a bag of groceries.

"Well, hell, I wasn't sure I'd ever see you again," I told him.

I stood and went over to him, shaking his hand and clapping him on the shoulder. He looked a little more ragged than the last time I saw him, which was years ago. Sebastian oversaw the lighthouse and kept to himself, no small feat in a small town. He was two years older than me but could have been a decade older by the look of him. Weathered skin, full beard, and more than a little gray sprinkled through his hair.

"Good to see you, James. You here about the break-in?"

I nodded. "We are. And getting the full treatment."

Sebastian grinned and ducked his head. "Well, I just wanted to check in with Gina and drop off some groceries. She's been having more and more trouble getting around lately. Keeping up this place isn't something she'll be able to do much longer."

"Have you talked to her niece and nephew?" Masterson asked. "Rucker said they're her only family. Would either of them be able to help?"

Sebastian stiffened at the mention and shook his head firmly. I wasn't entirely sure what that was about, but it was clear he didn't want to talk about it.

"Did she have a falling out with them?" I asked him.

"No, but they aren't interested in ever coming back here. That's been made very clear," Sebastian said firmly. "I need to check on Gina."

He left the dining room without another word, leaving both Masterson and I to wonder what that was all about.

"Do you think he had anything to do with it?" Masterson asked quietly.

I shrugged and took my seat again. "I don't know what the hell that was, but I think we need to find out."

We ate in silence until Mrs. Holbrook brought out a plate

piled high with eggs, bacon, sausage, and toast. Mrs. Holbrook insisted Sebastian sit and eat with us, and he agreed reluctantly.

Mrs. Holbrook chatted like nothing out of the ordinary was going on, telling us all about her garden and the way she wanted to decorate the inn for the holidays and then what her niece and nephew were doing.

Sebastian grew quieter with each topic of conversation but he excused himself when Mrs. Holbrook mentioned her niece, Zoey.

I followed him into the kitchen and found him white knuckling the edge of the countertop in front of the sink.

"Everything okay?"

He spun, not having heard me walk in. He glanced behind me and shook his head. "I haven't seen Zoey in ten years, since her last summer of college. I shouldn't be this bothered by it, but I still can't breathe when I hear her name."

"What are you talking about?" I asked him.

"Zoey and I were together. I thought you knew. It seemed everyone knew."

I shook my head. Zoey and her brother, Gavin, visited a few summers, but they never lived in MacKellar Cove. She was younger than us, a lot younger. Gavin was a couple years younger, but Zoey had to be almost ten years younger, so for Sebastian and Zoey to be together…

"What happened?"

"She wanted to move here after college. She planned to. We were going to be together and have a family."

"Why didn't she come back?"

Sebastian shrugged. "I don't know. I tried to get in touch with her, but she changed her number and disappeared. I asked Gina about her a few times, but it was clear she had no idea we were together. Zoey got married and had a couple of kids. I stopped asking after that, and I can't be in the same room when Gina starts talking about her."

"That's why you were acting crazy when Masterson asked if you'd talked to either of them?"

He nodded. "I love Gina. I watch out for her because she's like family to me. I'd do anything for her, but I can't listen to her talk about Zoey."

I nodded. "I understand. Do you have any idea who would have broken in here?"

He shook his head. "Wish I did, but no. I assumed it was likely someone who was looking for cash and thought she might keep some on hand, but she doesn't. I take her to the bank every day to deposit her cash. She keeps a few hundred dollars here, but she doesn't like having a lot of money around."

"I'm guessing the same, but we want to look at the footage if you can help us out with that."

"Of course," Sebastian said. "Want to get your partner?"

I grinned. "No, I think he needs some time to get to know Mrs. Holbrook."

Sebastian snorted. "You're cruel."

"Trust me, he deserves it."

ONCE SEBASTIAN GAVE me the footage, I grabbed Masterson and we headed back to the station. He grumbled about me leaving him with Mrs. Holbrook, and I tried not to laugh, but I failed.

"She's what MacKellar Cove is all about, Rowan. If you're going to stick around, you need to get to know people. You don't have connections here, so you need to make some."

He grimaced and snarled but didn't argue. Maybe the town was growing on him. I kind of hoped not.

We reviewed the video of the break-in and got a few decent shots of the two men. One of them was a person of interest in another case we had, so we brought him in for questioning. He rolled on his friend and by the end of the day, we had both of them in cells and could tell Mrs. Holbrook the good news.

"Things never get solved that fast where I'm from," Masterson said as we walked out at the end of our shift.

I shrugged. "That's the beauty of a small town. When you already know who the guilty party is and where he lives, it's easier to catch the bad guys. Obviously, everything isn't always that easy, but when we can solve a case within twenty-four hours, everyone is a little happier."

Masterson stopped next to my truck with me and tilted his head. "Is everyone like this? Wants to talk to everyone else and tell them their life story?"

"What do you mean?"

"That Mrs. Holbrook…she wanted to know everything about me. She told me the history of the inn and everything she knew about the owners before her. She even went on about her family and how her niece and nephew used to come up here for summers but haven't in years. She talked about some of her guests. It was kind of a lot."

I grinned. "It means she liked you. And yeah, pretty much everyone is like that. I get that being in a city is different. People keep to themselves. But being here…it makes people feel safe to know their neighbors. It doesn't mean bad things don't still happen, but you're not as likely to steal something from a friend as you are from a stranger."

Masterson snorted in a way that made me wonder a little more about him.

"What brought you up here?"

He shook his head. "Needed a change of scenery."

"Yeah, well, you don't seem like you're too thrilled with this particular one. Are you sticking around?"

He looked at me and for the first time I felt like I was actually seeing him. He was a little broken, a little fragile, and a little unsure of himself. Usually, he seemed like a cocky asshole who could do no wrong. Maybe there was more to him than what he seemed on the surface.

"For now," he finally said. "Are you going to O'Kelley's again tonight?"

I nodded absently, wondering what secrets he had deep inside.

"Mind if I tag along? I know that's your group, but they seemed like they might be good guys."

I met his gaze and nodded. "They are. And they sure liked you, so yeah. We're usually there around six or seven."

Masterson nodded. "Thanks."

I nodded once and watched him walk to his SUV. Maybe there was a human side to him after all.

$\mathcal{H}$udson raised his eyebrows at me when I walked into O'Kelley's with Masterson. I shrugged, not knowing what was going on either.

Hudson played it off as though Masterson was always there with us and asked what he wanted to drink. He set a beer in front of me and asked if we were eating dinner.

"Yeah, I'm starving," Masterson said. "Burger?"

Hudson nodded. "Sure. What do you want on it? Fries, onion rings, or mozzarella sticks on the side?"

"Cheddar, bacon, and ketchup with fries. Thanks."

"Same for me," I said. It sounded good.

Hudson went to put our orders in, leaving us to drink in awkward silence when we didn't have work to talk about.

"Hey, Rowan," Ian said, clapping us both on the back and taking the seat next to me. "Glad you could join us again. How's this guy treating you?"

"He stuck me with an old lady who told me the entire history of the MacKellar Cove Inn today," Masterson grumbled.

"Mrs. Holbrook?" Ian asked.

Masterson nodded.

Ian laughed. "Oh, she's a good one. You need to go to Island Designs sometime and hear the unofficial history of the town from Olive. Those two bring out the character in MacKellar Cove."

"That's one word for it. I'll tell you, though, she knew everything that's happened there. She showed me a mark on the wall from a grease fire in the kitchen. The repair guys didn't notice it until after they were done but she said they never painted over it to make sure they remembered to be safe," Masterson said.

Ian and I traded a grin. "She tells everyone that story," Ian said. "She loves that place. I wonder what's going to happen to it when she dies."

"Dude, a little respect," I said.

"What? She's not dead yet, and it's not like she's going to live forever. I'm just saying I'm curious," Ian said.

"Curious about what?" Colin asked. "Hey, Rowan. Thanks for coming out to the farm last weekend."

Masterson nodded. What the hell?

"You went to the farm?" I asked him. He nodded again like it was no big deal.

"I was curious what's going to happen to MacKellar Cove Inn when Mrs. Holbrook dies. She doesn't have kids," Ian said, answering Colin's question.

"Who doesn't have kids?" Ramsey asked.

"Gina Holbrook," Ian said.

"He's wondering who gets the Inn when she dies," Masterson provided.

"I assumed her niece and nephew," Ramsey said. "Or she would sell it, but if she dies before she sells it, I would think they would get it."

"Why?" Masterson asked.

"I forgot about them," Ian said. "They were younger than us. I think they were both younger than Blake and Finley."

I shook my head. "Gavin isn't too much younger. Maybe only a year younger than you. Zoey was a lot younger. Did you guys know she and Sebastian were together?"

"Sebastian and who were together?" Hudson asked, delivering our burgers.

"Zoey Holbrook," I said.

"Sebastian Parks? No. He's older than me," Hudson said.

I shrugged. "Colin and Elise are eleven years apart. I don't know if age matters that much."

"When she was a teenager it did," Hudson argued.

I shook my head. "I'm not going to disagree with that, but I think they were together when she was in college. He said she was supposed to come back here after she finished but never did. Got married and had a couple of kids."

"Ouch," Ian said. "No wonder he stays at the Inn and the lighthouse and doesn't get out much. I'd be drunk half the time if that happened to me."

"Without a doubt," I said.

Ian turned to me with a smirk. "Well, since you brought it up…Trinity? I can see you two being good for each other."

I shook my head and laughed. It was only a matter of time.

"You're telling people now?" Hudson asked.

"Oh, no, he didn't tell me. Trinity told Blake and everyone else on Sunday. This chicken shit just sat on it," Ian reported.

"Did you want me to call you so we could gossip?" I asked, mocking dialing a phone.

Ian shoved me and laughed. "I'm happy for you. I guess now you can use your cuffs for something other than trying to arrest her."

Masterson choked on his beer. "You tried to arrest your

girlfriend? I'm not touching the other comment." He shuddered.

"It's a long story," I said.

"Genius here thought she was breaking into her car. He didn't know it was her car," Hudson said.

Masterson's brows went up. "You were actually going to arrest someone? Damn. Although maybe that's why you won't do it anymore. You want to make sure your girlfriend isn't jealous?"

I rolled my eyes at him while the rest of them hooted like children. "I arrested someone today."

Masterson nodded. "I know. I was there. Had to make sure you still remember the words to the Miranda Rights."

I flipped him off and bit into my burger, choosing to ignore him for a minute.

"I really like him," Ramsey said with a grin and a salute of his beer.

I shook my head and ignored all of them.

"So, Rowan, how do you like our small town so far?" Ian asked.

"It's quiet."

"Is that a good thing?" Colin asked.

Masterson shrugged. "Haven't decided yet. I'm used to a lot more going on. Being a cop in a big city is both easier and harder. You have a lot more cases and bring in a lot more bad guys, but a lot more go free because there's not a lot of evidence sometimes."

"We have the same issues here," I said.

Masterson nodded. "True, but it's on a bigger scale. The good days are better, and the bad days are worse."

I nodded, understanding what he meant. I'd only been a part of one murder investigation in my career. There were more than that, but it was rare to have dangerous crimes in MacKellar Cove, or in the towns nearby.

Which made me think of Joey.

"I think we should do something for Oak Hill soon. Maybe an outdoor fair type of thing. Free food, but maybe some games for the kids, a few new contacts for the residents, and a big push to fix things up as much as we can," I said.

"Good idea. I've been collecting funds and have a good stash to put toward whatever we need. And a handful of people willing to give time to help out," Hudson said.

"Sounds like we have things started. Let's set a date and make this happen," Ramsey said, pulling out his phone. "How about two weeks from Saturday?"

We looked around and nodded.

"That works. We'll start putting the word out. Talk to your mom," Hudson said.

I nodded. "I will. She already knows, but I'll tell her the day so she can start talking to people. A lot of them are too proud to accept charity but no one can resist free food on a grill."

"Damn straight," Masterson said. The others agreed.

With the date and the beginning of a plan, we were making things happen for the people I'd turned my back on for years. It was more than a little ironic that Trinity was a big part of the reason I was doing something for my old neighborhood.

"Hey," a woman said, taking the empty stool next to Masterson.

He turned to her. "Hey."

"You want to buy me a drink?"

Masterson nodded slowly as his gaze slid down her body. "I'd be happy to. What are you having?"

"Slippery Nipple," she told Hudson.

Ian snorted. Ramsey covered his mouth with his hand.

Colin drank his beer and pretended it was a totally normal night. I just shook my head.

"Want to get out of here?" she asked as she lifted the shot to her lips.

"Sounds good." He climbed off his stool. "Thanks for dinner," he said to me with a nod.

I shook my head and watched him walk out the door with the woman.

"Miss that?" Hudson asked me.

I shook my head again. "No. I'm actually wondering if I ever fell for lines like that."

Ramsey laughed. "You were the ones using lines that like."

I chuckled. "Probably true. I don't want to go back to that."

"Are you telling us things are that serious with Trinity?" Ian asked.

I shook my head. "I'm not saying anything. Just that if things don't work out, I prefer trying to get it right to trying to get it right now."

"Aw, he's growing up," Hudson teased.

I glared at him and reached for my bottle. Someone else took Masterson's seat. Someone curvy and beautiful who smelled amazing.

"Hey," I said to Trinity. "I didn't know you were going to be here."

She smiled and waved to the other guys. "I was hungry. Thought I'd see if I could get you to buy me dinner."

I shook my head. "Seems to be the plan for everyone tonight."

"Hey, I gotta go," Ramsey said, getting off his stool.

Ian and Colin went with him. "Yep, us, too. Thanks for dinner."

"Hey! What the hell?" I shouted after them.

The assholes just waved.

Hudson walked over and said hi to Trinity then asked where the rest of them went.

"They just skipped out," I told him.

Hudson looked toward the door. "Really?"

"Yep, they left me with their bills. Assholes."

Hudson chuckled and shook his head. "What are you having, Trinity?"

"Cheeseburger and fries," Trinity said with a grin. "On his tab."

She grinned at me and I shook my head. Then I stole a kiss. She gasped in surprise but melted into me after a few seconds. Her hand cupped my jaw and she smiled against my lips.

I pulled back and smiled.

"What was that for?"

I shrugged. "Just wanted a kiss. How was your day?"

"Good. I filmed a few videos today and have a new project for the kids at the community center. Plus, I sold a few pieces from my app today." She grinned widely.

"Yeah? I take it that's good?"

She nodded. "I didn't really want the app, but Karissa made it and it's amazing. I didn't think it would be something my customers wanted. She knows better than I do. She's amazing."

"Well, it's a good thing you listened to her. Hey, we set a date for the community event at Oak Hill. Are you still interested in helping out?"

"Absolutely. My grandma and I are making jewelry to give away. What else do you need me to do?"

"We need to get the word out. Do you think you could help with that?"

She nodded. "Not a problem. I'll take care of it."

Hudson delivered her burger and fries. "Anything else?"

"All good. Thank you," she said.

Hudson tore off the bill and made a show of setting it in front of me.

I raised an eyebrow at him. "Really?"

He shrugged. "I wouldn't want to have to call the cops because you skip out on the bill."

I glared at him and handed over my card. "So you know I'm good for it."

He chuckled and took the card. He ran it and handed it back to me with the slip to sign. "Make sure you tip your server."

I shook my head and gave him a good tip, then signed it and wrote *the customer is always right* on the bottom.

Trinity looked over my shoulder and laughed. "You're funny. And thanks for dinner."

I winked at her. "Any time. For you. Those other guys owe me next time."

She chuckled and took a bite of her burger.

WE WALKED out of O'Kelley's and paused. "Are you heading home?"

Trinity nodded. "I was planning to. You can join me if you want. Or we can do something else."

"You can come to my place," I said. I'd never invited her over before. I could tell by her pause that she knew it was a big deal that I was opening up to her like that.

She wrapped her hand around my arm and nodded. "Sounds good."

I led the way to my truck and opened the door for her to get it. I took a deep breath and hurried around to the driver's seat.

We chatted about nothing on the ride to my house. I was

anxious. Did I clean the toothpaste out of my sink? Did I put the dishes away? When was the last time I dusted?

None of it mattered when we walked inside and she took it all in then acted like she'd been there a hundred times before, settling on the couch and turning on the TV.

"Movies?"

I sat next to her and we found a movie to watch. She settled against me and I wrapped my arm around her. I couldn't remember the last time I felt so comfortable with another person.

When the movie ended, she said, "Show me around. I want to see your house."

We stood and went to the kitchen. "Small kitchen, but it works for me."

"It's not as small as mine. I like it. These cabinets are gorgeous."

I grinned. "Thanks. I refinished them when I bought the house. The kitchen was kind of rough. A lot of it was. That's how I could afford the place."

"How long have you lived here?"

"Nine years."

"Wow. I've never lived anywhere for nine years. I'm a little jealous right now."

I laughed.

"What else did you do around here?"

I smiled and showed her through the rest of the house. She oohed and aahed over the refinished floors and the remodeled bathrooms and teased me about the sparse decorating that left it looking like a dorm room.

"You don't even have a picture of your mom in here," she said when we made it to the bedroom.

"Well, my mom is the last person I want to think about when I'm in my bedroom."

She rolled her eyes. "I meant in the entire house. Why

haven't you decorated? I could help you. Go shopping sometime."

I hesitated a little too long, and she backtracked.

"Sorry. I wasn't thinking like that. I didn't mean I should decorate your place. Or that…I'm sorry. I didn't intend to overstep."

I shook my head and wrapped my arms around her. "You didn't overstep. Can I tell you something?"

She nodded against my chest.

"I told you about how I grew up. How we didn't have anything. Every time we got something, we felt like we were on the top of the world. We were adopted by families every year for Christmas, but by mid-January, we were trying to figure out how to afford food again. Lots of people want to help around the holidays, but what about a Tuesday in February or our birthdays or going back to school. There were moments that were okay, but there were so many more that weren't. And the lows felt even lower after a high. Going to bed hungry was normal in the summer. Going to bed hungry on December twenty-seventh sucked."

"I'm sorry," she said softly.

I nodded. "I'm not telling you all this for sympathy. This is why I'm trying to help Joey and his family. But it's also why I…I've never decorated because I'm afraid all this is going to disappear. I want it easy for me to walk away from. I keep pretty much everything in my life like that. I chose a job I can do anywhere. I have a home I can leave in a heartbeat. Everything."

"You don't want to stay here? In MacKellar Cove?"

I shrugged, and she tensed. "I have no plans to leave, but it's where I'm from. It's where I grew up. I never went anywhere else and put down roots. I just stayed put."

"There's nothing in your life that you want to hold on to?"

I shook my head. "It's not that exactly. It's more that I

know how fragile everything is. I know how easily it can all disappear. And I don't want to get too attached."

"I'm the same in a way because of my dad. I moved every few years after college. I never stayed in one place. I never felt like anyplace was home. But being here…I love MacKellar Cove. I love having friends I can count on and people I care about. I could work from anywhere, but I'm getting attached."

"A lot of people feel that way."

"You're really not attached to anything? Your mom? Your friends?"

"I can't imagine starting over. Leaving my mom, even though I know she'd be fine. Finding new friends. I don't want to do it. But it's not easy for me to sit back and trust that everything is going to work out. That people will still be there on that random Tuesday when I have nothing to eat."

She stepped up closer to me and went up on her toes. She pressed her lips to mine and smiled. "I'll be there, James. I want to be. If you're okay with that."

I nodded and slid my arms around her back, holding her to me. "You're the last person I expected, but I'm pretty happy I tried to arrest you that day. I don't think we'd be where we are now if we'd just gotten to know each other through everyone else."

She smiled. "I don't know. I'm still pretty upset about that. Maybe you should make it up to me."

"Oh, yeah? And how do you propose I do that?"

"Well," she said, stepping back. She grabbed the hem of her shirt and lifted it over her head. "You could start with a kiss. And we'll see where things go from there."

I grinned and did as I was told. All night long.

20

TRINITY

My time at the community center was quickly becoming one of my favorite parts of my week. Knowing that I was giving the kids something different to focus on for a few minutes was exciting for me and helped me to see how easy it was to give back, especially to kids.

I'd just finished setting up everything for the day when Amelia walked up on stage. Typically, she let me in and went about her business, so for her to approach me, I wondered what was going on.

"I've heard good things about your projects," she said, looking across the tables. "It sounds like the kids are enjoying it."

"I think they are. They're a lot of fun to work with."

"Good. These kids don't let people in easily. I hope you plan to stick around for a while."

I nodded. "I do. I love working with them. I'm trying to make sure I come up with ideas that any of them can do, so we've done some different things. Today's project is for a key chain because a few of them told me they always lose the key for their home. I thought we could do something that will be useful instead of just fun."

Amelia nodded. "That's a good idea. You seem to really understand these kids and what they're going through."

Her question was pointed. I smiled at her and gave her the answer she was looking for. "I don't. Not from personal experience. But I know someone who does understand them and have gotten some advice."

She crossed her arms over her chest. "I see."

Before she could say anything else, the children burst into the room. The flurry of activity always drew her undivided attention. She walked purposefully across the stage and down the stairs to remind the few kids who went straight for the basketballs to put their stuff away before they started to play.

I smiled and waited for a few kids to join me. I was surprised when a boy left his friends on the basketball court and walked up the stairs.

"Can I make something today?" he asked me.

"Of course," I said. "My name is Trinity. What's your name?"

"Mark."

"Hi, Mark. I'll tell you how to do each step, but you can pick how you put this together. Today, we're making a keyring. Do you have keys for your home?"

He nodded. "Yeah, but they always get shoved in the bottom of my backpack."

"I have the same problem with my purse. That's why I thought we could make this today. What do you think?"

He smiled at me and walked slowly through the tables. "Can I pick any one I want?"

I nodded. "Absolutely. And if you like more than one, you can mix and match them or make two."

"I can make two?" he asked, his eyes wide.

I grinned. "Maybe even three."

His smile matched his eyes. He nodded and chose a seat. He opened the bag in front of him and started looking through the pieces inside.

Heather and Meghan raced up the stairs and said hi to Mark and me then chose their seats. Two other girls weren't far behind them.

Five kids. It was a good day.

"Is everyone ready?" I asked them.

They all nodded enthusiastically.

"Good. Today we're going to make keyrings. As always, I will help you if you have trouble, but I want you to use your imagination and create something you love. Are you ready?"

They cheered, even Mark.

"All right. First, take everything out of your bag and put it on the tray in front of you. If you want, you can arrange your beads in the order you want them to be." I held up the keyring I created to practice. "This is what it's going to look like when you're done."

"Wow, that's awesome," Heather said.

I grinned. "Then let's get started."

I waved at Mark's mom when he showed her what he made and pointed to me up on stage. She smiled back, looking more than a little grateful to me. He was so excited to have something to show her. And he told me when he made the second one that he was going to give it to her for her birthday. He was a good kid. They all were. And getting to know James only helped me to be open to seeing that.

When I first went there, I was looking to help myself and my career, but every time I went back, I hoped I was helping the kids as much as they were helping me.

I was cleaning up the supplies when I heard footsteps behind me. I stopped what I was doing and turned in case it was another kid who decided late to make something. It had happened before where they saw the craft I had for them and decided they wanted to do it. I tried to be ready for it.

But this time it was Amelia again.

"Hey," I said with a smile.

"Was my son the person you mentioned earlier? That has helped you see these kids?"

I nodded slowly. I didn't know how close James was to his mother. He told me he didn't like going to her house and that he only went to the community center to help, but I had no idea if they talked regularly or if they went out to lunch or dinner or anything.

"What is going on with the two of you?"

"I like him. A lot."

"And he feels the same about you?"

I shrugged. "I don't know, but I hope so. Does that upset you?"

She shook her head. "James is a very private person. He doesn't share who he is. When I mentioned, the first day you were here, that he's my son, it was so you knew not to say anything about him that you wouldn't want his mother to know."

"Um, okay."

She tilted her head. "He trusts you. And if he trusts you, it means he likes you. He doesn't let people in. Especially women. I hope you understand how important that makes you to my son."

Emotion welled up inside me. I would rather hear it from James, but I wasn't ready to tell him how I felt either, so I would take it. I nodded, unable to squeeze any words out.

"When I asked if you're going to be around, I wasn't just

talking about for the kids here. I meant for James also. He has had enough loss in his life."

"So have I, Amelia. I don't have any plans to leave, and I really like your son. I'm not going to 'hurt him."

She held my gaze for a long moment then nodded once and walked off the stage.

I continued cleaning up the leftover supplies and put all the tables and chairs away. James was working late that night so I knew he wouldn't be by to help out and I didn't want Amelia to have to do it herself.

When I was finished, I grabbed my bag and set it by the edge of the stage. I walked down the stairs and smiled when one of the boys passed me a basketball. I bounced it a few times and took a shot from where I stood.

It hit the backboard and swished into the net. The boys all cheered. Ever since the first day I played basketball with James and the kids, they'd been trying to challenge me.

"How do you hit every shot, Ms. Trinity?" one of them asked. I hadn't learned all the boys names yet, but I was going to eventually.

"You know what? I miss a lot. And I missed even more when I was growing up. But I love basketball, so I keep play-ing, even when I miss."

"I love it, too," another boy said. "The only time I get to play is when I'm here. I asked my mom if I could have a basket at home but she said we don't have enough money for that."

"They're expensive," I said. "But you guys get a lot of time here to play. Are there any nets at school or anywhere else that you can play on the weekends?"

A few of them shook their heads, but one boy nodded. "I went to a park with my dad and we played on an old court. By the soccer fields."

The other boys nodded and said, "Oh, yeah."

"Maybe you guys can go there sometime," I suggested. "That could be fun."

They nodded in agreement and dropped back. "Hey, Ms. Trinity, can you hit it from here?"

I smiled and walked over to them. I bounced the ball a few times and lined up my shot, and sunk another one.

By the time I left the community center, it was getting darker outside and most of the kids had gone home. I'd just set my stuff in my car and slid behind the wheel when my phone rang.

I didn't recognize the number, but it was local so I answered it.

"Hello?"

"Is this Trinity Mayer?"

"Um, yes."

"Hi, Ms. Mayer. My name is Elizabeth Joseph. I'm a reporter with the Thousand Islands Times. I was in Island Designs last week and the owner, Olive, mentioned you to me. I picked up one of your pieces and fell in love with it, and Olive suggested I take a look at your videos and your website. You seem like a bit of a powerhouse business woman. I was wondering if I could do a story about you?"

"Wow, well, I'm flattered, but I'm not sure I'm really that interesting."

"I have a weekly column that talks about local businesses, and the owners, and how they're doing different things. It's a chance to show people that there are other jobs around here than working in tourism, especially since that's a seasonal job for most people. I want to show our locals that they can create their own careers and provide for their families."

"That's why I've been working at the community center," I said, staring up at the large brick building. "I want to give back to the community and help kids from an early age know they can create something amazing."

"Wow, I didn't know you were working there also. I'd love to come by and get some shots of you at the community center."

I shook my head even though she couldn't see me. "I'm sorry, but that's not allowed. They don't have photo releases."

"Is there anywhere else that you will be so we can take some pictures and talk?"

I thought about the Oak Hill party James was planning and nodded. "Actually, I think I have the perfect place. What do you think about highlighting more than just me?"

"How so?"

"Well, there's going to be an event at Oak Hill next weekend. A few local business people are going to be out there helping to serve food and fix up the apartment. We're going to have giveaways and swag bags, and there will be a few locals who run businesses that you could connect with. Maybe book your schedule for a few weeks. And you get to report on something great that's happening in the community."

"I like it. That sounds like a great idea. Can you tell me a little more?"

"Of course," I said. I promised James I would get the word out. This was definitely going to help.

I WAS SO excited about all the people who were starting to talk about the Oak Hill party. By the weekend, it seemed like everyone in town was buzzing.

Colin said I could put some flyers out at the farm to make sure even more people saw them. Instead of just dropping them off, I made plans with Elise for the day.

She and Colin were kissing in the barn when I walked in,

the loud squeak of the door breaking them apart. "Sorry!" I said.

Colin just grinned. Elise scowled at me. "You couldn't have given us five more minutes?"

Colin squeezed her hand. "We have plenty of time later."

Elise grinned at him. "I intend to make good use of it. What I meant to say was hi, Trinity!"

I chuckled and shook my head. "Hi, Elise. How are you guys?"

"Good. Thanks for doing this, Trinity," Colin said. "I think this is going to be great for the community. James seems really excited about it."

I nodded. "He is. I think he feels bad that he isn't more involved in the neighborhood. He thinks he turned his back on all of them and he wants to help. Joey really got to him."

"Are you okay with all of this?" Elise asked.

I nodded again. "I understand why he took my purse. I wish it hadn't happened, but I get it. I also haven't seen him since, so I'm not sure I'll feel as generous when I'm face-to-face with him, but he's a kid. He was trying to help his family. I've never been in a situation like that. I've never had to choose between helping my family and getting in trouble."

"It's not an easy choice," Colin said. "Hopefully, Joey learned not to do it again."

I smiled. "I hope so."

A customer walked in, and Colin went to go greet her. Elise helped me set the flyers out in a few places around the barn so people would see them and grab one. We were good with the items we had for the residents, but we hoped to pick up a few more volunteers to cook and plan some activities, and maybe help fix up the place since that seemed to be the biggest part of the project. James was really excited and going all out for the event.

"You look happy," Elise said to me as I fingered a soft scarf.

"I am," I told her. "There's a lot to be happy about right now."

"James?"

I nodded. "He's definitely one of the things I'm happy about."

"Good," she said. "I've decided to move in with Colin."

"What?"

She shrugged. "I stay here almost every night anyway. He told me he wants me to live with him, but he's not going to push. I've been staying here most nights for months. It's time."

"Is it time because you feel like you should or because you want to?" I asked.

Elise held my gaze and smiled. "Because I love him and I don't want to spend another minute away from him if I can help it. I never let myself imagine I'd find someone like him, but he's unbelievable. He's kind and considerate and so patient with me. And I love him. So much."

"That's great news," I told her. "I'm so happy for you."

She smiled. "Thanks. I'm happy, too. I hope everyone else finds someone like Colin. Or James."

I chuckled. "They will."

"Did you want to stay here, or do you want to go for a walk?"

"Definitely a walk. I haven't seen much of the farm. It's gorgeous, but I don't do a whole lot of nature by myself."

Elise laughed at me and nodded toward the back door. "I'll keep you safe from all the nature. We wouldn't want it to get too close and touch you."

I shuddered and shook my head. "Nope. We can't let that happen."

Elise led me down a path through the trees. We walked

and talked about everything and nothing, from men to jobs to our friends.

"I'm glad Piper has been coming to girls' night," I said. "She's funny."

Elise nodded. "She is. I've invited her before, but she always worked Sunday nights. I don't know her well."

"Neither do I, but we're getting there. I think she's getting more comfortable with us."

"Yeah, especially after last weekend when we were talking about our favorite positions."

I laughed. "Yeah, I think we scared her a little."

"She joined in eventually. Remember when Blake and Ian got together and she was afraid to talk about him in front of Finley?"

"I can't say I blame her. If James had a sister, I wouldn't want to tell her about our sex life. It's bad enough his mom asked me about us."

"His mom asked about your sex life?"

I shook my head. "No, not that. She just asked if we were together and what's going on with us."

"What did you tell her?"

"That I really like her son."

Elise stopped and studied me. "Really like him? Like…?"

I shrugged and smiled. "Yeah, like that. I never saw him coming, but yeah. I'm pretty much done. He's it for me. I'm just not sure he feels the same."

Elise grinned. "I think he does. You don't have anything to worry about."

I snorted. "Except getting my heart broken."

Elise waved her hand. "You'll get over that. Just focus on the good stuff. And have faith."

I huffed a laugh. I hoped she was right.

21

My phone rang as I locked my door to go to girls' night. I fumbled with my keys and managed to get them put away without dropping them and answer my phone before it stopped.

"Hello? Hello!"

"Hey," James said, his voice deep and so welcome.

"Hey. How are you? Are you off work?"

"Yeah, I'm off today. I was hoping I could see you."

I hesitated for a minute, but I didn't want to miss girls' night. "Um, actually, I'm on my way out."

"Oh, sorry. I didn't realize."

"It's fine. A bunch of us get together at Finley's on Sunday nights."

"That's right. Book club girls' night. I've heard talk about it. Never paid much attention." He chuckled.

"You never had a reason to. I'm sorry, though. Unless you want me to miss it?" It wasn't a trap but I really hoped he said no.

"Absolutely not. You need time with your friends. We all do."

"And this is coming after I ambushed your night with your friends," I said, feeling sheepish.

He laughed. "I didn't mind that at all. You're a lot nicer to look at than they are."

"Well, thanks, I think."

He laughed again. "Maybe I'll see you later? Or tomorrow? I'm off for a couple days and then working most of the week."

"Are you off Saturday?" I asked, hoping he wouldn't miss the event he worked to bring to life.

"I am. Captain Reynolds wants to show support for the community and when he heard Masterson and I were going, he made sure we had the day off. But he doesn't expect us to be there as cops or in uniform, just as citizens."

"That's a good thing," I said.

"Yeah, it is. Hey, I'll let you go. I'll see you soon."

"Sounds good. Thanks for understanding."

"Of course. Bye."

"Bye."

I hung up and smiled at my phone. I missed him more than I thought I would after only a few days apart and a few weeks together.

I thought about my talk with Elise the day before and realized I wasn't the only one. She felt the same about Colin. I thought he was cute on sight, but he wasn't a man I couldn't resist. Once it was clear to me he was interested in Elise, I had no problem backing off. With James, I always noticed him and who he was with. Even when I didn't want to.

I arrived at Book Boyfriends Unlimited before I realized it. I knocked on the door and glanced around at the other people walking by. Finley unlocked the door and let me in, but I was still in a daze.

"Are you okay?"

I nodded. "Yeah. Just thinking."

"About what? Did something happen?"

I shook my head. "No, just lots of things going through my head."

Finley gave me a look and led me to the back where she announced, "Trinity has the face."

"What face?" I asked.

The rest of them just looked at me and laughed.

"She definitely has the face," Karissa said.

"Yep," Blake agreed.

"We talked about it yesterday," Elise added.

"We talked about what?" I asked her.

"That you're in love with James and aren't sure if you're in it alone," Elise said matter-of-factly.

I groaned and took a seat. "I don't like any of you right now."

"Actually, you love all of us," Finley said, "because we're going to help you."

"How?"

"By helping you see that you're not the only one who's lost their mind," Melody said. "Trust me, you need the help."

I grumbled in agreement but knew she was right. They were all right. I was free falling and was confident no one was going to be there to catch me.

"He went to you the first time you slept together, right?" Elise asked.

I nodded.

"And the second?" Finley confirmed.

I nodded again.

"And he's the one who asked you out?"

"We just sort of started seeing each other. We were paired on BBW and talking there, and sleeping together, even though we didn't really like each other, and it all just sort of happened," I said.

"Just like Pride and Prejudice," Finley said. "You hated each other but were falling in love the entire time."

"But I…"

"What is wrong with loving him?" Blake asked. "I was terrified of letting Ian in, but I couldn't stop myself from loving him. But I let William in and never really loved him. What are you feeling with James?"

I shrugged. "I've never really cared about anyone like this. It's…"

"Terrifying?" Elise said.

I nodded. "Yeah. My mom lost herself when my dad died. She didn't know how to do anything. She let him handle stuff, and when he died, she lost not just a part of herself but she didn't know how to do things like pay the bills. I never wanted to be like that. I hoped for love and believed in it, but I think I held myself back because I saw it as a weakness. Giving so much of yourself to someone else means they get to keep that piece of you. If things go wrong, they have a part of you that you will never get back. That's scary."

"It is," Elise said. "I know Andy will always hold a part of me. Not that I still love him, but I trusted him. I never imagined I would be in a relationship like I was with him. And being with Colin…he's so different. He's so patient and calm and amazing. Letting myself trust him was crazy hard. I had no interest. But he showed me who he is. He showed me that he's not the same person as Andy."

"I know who James is, but I also know his job is dangerous and he could get hurt any day just because he goes to work," I said.

They all nodded, but Piper leaned forward.

"I think when love is real, it doesn't matter how long you get to hold onto it, just that you were there for it. I know things didn't work out with my old boyfriend because we weren't meant to be together. There is a part of me that will always love him because he was my first in so many ways. But he won't be my last. He wasn't meant to be. And I can let that break me or I can accept that there might be someone else out there who is better for me. Someone who wants the same things I want.

"I'm not trying to tell you that if James isn't perfect you shouldn't be together. I'm just saying that love is something we take for granted when we have it and miss when we don't. Love makes the world a better place. And even unrequited love can still be beautiful. Because love is love. We can learn something from it each and every time we fall in love, and we will have multiple people we love in different ways that will help us find the one person who we are meant to love forever. We all deserve that."

"Well, damn. If that doesn't put me in my place and convince me to tell him how I feel, nothing will," I said. "Thank you."

Piper grinned. "Any time."

FINLEY LOCKED up while Karissa and I waited. The wind whipped down the street, making me retreat into my jacket.

"Man, it's getting cold fast," Karissa said.

"No kidding. I hope this weekend is good. I want this party to go off without any issues," I said.

"It will. I think it's great that so many people in town are coming. And that you got that reporter to agree to attend. It'll be really good to have people there who want to help and give back. Things weren't always easy, but my family never knew the kind of suffering so many do," Karissa said.

"Mine either," Finley added. "I was pretty oblivious to it growing up even. I knew kids who lived in Oak Hill, but I didn't realize there was anything to think twice about with them. They were just other people in my class."

"I think that's what anyone wants. To feel like they are like everyone else," I said. "I started playing basketball at the community center with the kids so they knew I was just another person."

"You do?" Finley asked. "That's pretty cool."

"I enjoy it, and it helps the kids relate to me. They talk when they play, and I can turn those conversations into ideas."

"Everything changes when you get people to let their guards down," Karissa said. "That's why I created an app where you can't upload photos of yourself. If you don't know what a person looks like, you're going to automatically judge them on their personality. We let attractive people get away with some crappy things that we judge less attractive people for. If you suck as a person, it doesn't matter how hot you are."

"So true," Finley agreed. "I met this one guy at O'Kelley's one night who thought it was okay to tell me I needed to lose some weight. He was gorgeous and he thought that flirting with me was enough of a payment for acting like an ass."

"I can't stand men like that," Karissa groaned. "They think they are God's gift to all womankind. I wish they'd realize we all talk about them behind their backs."

We laughed.

"They never will. If they found out, they would think we were ridiculous women for not being fooled by their good looks and zero charm," I said.

"So true. How could we not see that they're amazing?" Finley joked.

"Right? Ugh. I've had enough of men like that," Karissa said. "I guess I'm going to be single forever. Especially once I go through with my surgery."

"You decided to do it?" Finley asked.

Karissa nodded. "I am. I'm too anxious all the time. If I don't do it and end up with breast cancer like my mom, I'll regret it. If I do it and end up single because no man wants a woman without breasts, I'll regret it. But I'll regret breast cancer more than I'll regret being single."

"We're going to live together forever anyway, so it won't matter," Finley said with a grin. She threw her arm around Karissa's shoulders and hugged her to her.

"Yep, we are. We don't need men," Karissa said with a wicked laugh.

"You guys are too funny," I said.

"We'd invite you to live in our man free zone, but you've already gotten sucked in. You're lost forever," Finley said dramatically.

I snorted a laugh. "We'll see about that."

Karissa wrapped her arm through mine. "You and James are good together. I wouldn't worry at all."

I smiled. "I hope not."

We said bye at their floor and parted ways. I made it up to my floor and stopped when I saw James sitting in front of my door.

"Hey," I said with a smile.

"Hey," he said, getting up. He held out his arms for me to walk into.

"What are you doing here?"

"I wanted to see you so I figured I'd stop by. Is that okay?"

I nodded against his chest. "Absolutely. Let's go in and you can relax for a while and tell me about your week."

He let me lead him inside and to the couch. He was exhausted.

"Why didn't you go home? You're falling asleep right here," I said.

He shook his head. "I missed you. I wanted to spend some time with you."

"How about a movie? Or we can just go to bed."

He waggled his eyebrows at me. "I like option number two. All the time."

I chuckled and shook my head. "You're bad."

He smiled. "You love it."

"Yes, I do," I admitted.

He winked at me and led me to the bedroom. We stripped slowly, both pausing to watch the other. By the time he took off the last of his clothes, he was hard and I was wet.

"Even exhausted, I can't get enough of you," he said in a low, gravely voice as he rolled a condom down his length.

"You're not the only one with that problem," I said.

He smiled and reached for me. We moved to the bed together, our bodies meeting before we hit the mattress. James positioned himself between my legs, his weight pressed on top of me, and kissed his way from my jaw to my neck and back up to my lips.

The kiss was slow and sensual, like a seduction. He licked his way into my mouth then pulled back and kissed my lips with gentle pecks. He didn't touch me with his hands, but he used his body to drive me crazy. A gentle lift of his torso rubbed his chest against my aching nipples. And shift of his hips had his erection digging into my clit. A rub of his thighs had me spreading wider for him and trembling.

Every move made me want him more. Made me love him more. He knew exactly what he was doing to me. How crazy he was making me. The languid pace was only making it harder to resist him.

But I didn't want to resist him any longer.

I parted my thighs and shifted so we lined up. He pulled back just enough to see my face. We locked eyes as he pushed inside me. And in that moment, I knew he felt the same way I did. I'd never seen that emotion before, from anyone.

He held my gaze and stroked in and out. He acted like we had all the time in the world, and a part of me felt like we did. I was done worrying and searching and thinking about forever. I'd found it, I'd found him. I loved him. I never expected it, but I did, and I knew he loved me, too.

"Trinity," he breathed, his eyes slipping closed. His jaw clenched and he trembled just enough that I knew he couldn't hold out. He wanted to wait for me, but he wasn't going to last much longer.

I slid my hand between us and touched my clit. A brief touch was all it took to send me flying over the edge. My channel tightened around him, and he followed me over into bliss.

He collapsed on top of me, letting all his body weight hold me in place. I held him, my heart so full of love for him that I could barely contain it.

After a minute, he shifted and went to the bathroom. When he came back, he curled himself around me and held me tightly.

"How was your week?" I asked him.

"Exhausting. Night shift sucks. I don't have to do it often, but when I do, I hate it."

"Sorry."

He shrugged. "It's okay. How was your week? How did things go with the kids?"

"Good. I had a few new kids on Tuesday. Even one boy."

"Wow, Trin. That's awesome."

"Thanks. I'm also getting some publicity about the event on Saturday. A local reporter is going to come out and do a story about it. And we're getting the word out."

He snuggled closer to me and kissed my shoulder. "That's awesome. Thank you. I couldn't do this without you."

"Of course. I'm happy to help. Anything for those kids. And anything for you."

"Mmmhmm."

We were quiet for a minute, relaxed and sated together. James never stayed the night so I knew it wouldn't be long before he was up and on his way to the door. The one night I went to his house, I stayed over, and waking up the next morning in his arms was the best feeling ever. I wanted that again.

"You don't have to go if you don't want to," I said. "I don't mind if you stay."

"Mmmhmm," he murmured. He kissed my neck and burrowed in deeper.

I smiled to myself and slid my hand over his arm. He squeezed me gently.

I closed my eyes and took a deep breath. Then I whispered, "I love you, James."

I waited for him to say something or do something. For him to get up and run or to return the words. But there was nothing. It was like he wasn't even there.

I turned to face him and found his eyes closed and his mouth parted slightly. His arm was dead weight on top of me.

I huffed a laugh and kissed his chest, then settled in to sleep with the man I loved. Since that was all he could handle at the moment.

22

James rushed out the next morning and we didn't talk much through the week. He was putting in extra time at work to be off for Saturday, and I was doing the same. I wanted to have pieces to give to everyone who was there, if I could make it happen. Even with my grandma helping, it wasn't an easy task, but I wanted to do it.

Saturday morning, Karissa and Finley came up to my condo so we could all ride together to Oak Hill. I told them about Elizabeth Joseph and they were both excited at the opportunity to be interviewed by her also.

"Have you heard from James today?" Finley asked as we walked downstairs with all the supplies for the day. We were bringing our own stuff to giveaway to people and had contributed to the food and drinks that James and Ian were getting to the event.

I shook my head. "I haven't talked to him much this week. Not since I whispered *I love you* Sunday night when he was asleep."

"You did what now?" Karissa asked, stopping in the middle of the sidewalk.

"It was dumb, but it just felt right to me. I was pretty sure he was feeling the same way and I said it."

"While he was sleeping?" Finley confirmed.

I nodded. "I didn't know he was asleep, but yeah."

"Are you sure he was asleep and didn't just ignore you?" Karissa asked.

I shrugged. "I don't know. He seemed like he was out. Do you think he would do that?"

"If he didn't want to say it back, then maybe. You haven't talked to him all week?" Karissa asked again.

I shook my head and wondered if I'd read everything with him wrong. He didn't say or do anything that made it seem like he felt the same way. It was a feeling I had. Could it have been one I made up?

"I'm sure he was just asleep," Finley said. "We all said we think he's in love with you. Don't worry about it."

I nodded and gave her a weak smile. Inside, I was a mess. Did I screw up the best relationship I'd ever had?

I couldn't think about that. We had an event to run and people to help. This whole thing started because of Joey and me, and I was going to come face-to-face with him for the first time today. He wanted to apologize to me, and I agreed to it.

I climbed into Finley's car with Karissa and Finley up front and chewed on my nail on the drive over. Hudson brought a massive grill, and Ian and James were bringing all the food. Ramsey and Melody were in charge of games for the kids. Colin had tools to fix just about anything that needed to be fixed. It had become a block party type of thing with lots of fun things instead of just food and gifts that felt more like charity and less like helping.

I unloaded the car woodenly, unsure how the day was

going to go. A part of me thought the people in Oak Hill were going to be upset and not want us there, but James said his mom talked to everyone and got them all on board. They wanted to contribute and many of them were bringing a dish to share or were loaning themselves to help out in whatever way they could. It was a way for people to give back and not feel as though they were just there to take something for free.

Karissa, Finley, and I dove into helping set up tables and chairs and making space for everything. We had tables for free giveaways that people could go through and take what they needed. Some local business people were going to be mingling with the crowd and handing out cards, but others wanted to leave things on the table and just have conversations.

"Good morning," Amelia said, grabbing the other side of a table I was struggling to move into place.

"Good morning. How are you?"

She nodded. "Good. Thanks for helping out with this."

I smiled. "I'm happy to. I've been looking forward to it. And to meeting Joey."

"Do you want to meet him now?" Amelia asked. "He's here, helping set up."

I looked out at the crowd of volunteers we already had and didn't recognize him. I never got a good look at his face, but I still thought I would recognize the person who stole my purse.

Sweat beaded on my forehead and my hands felt clammy. The cool air suddenly felt like the middle of summer. I took a deep breath and nodded, knowing I needed to face him sometime and hoping it was better to just get it over with.

Amelia led the way through the groups of people and waited for me to catch up to her. She nodded toward a young family of three, two sons and a mom who looked like she hadn't gotten nearly enough sleep lately.

"Come on. I'll introduce you," Amelia said.

I nodded and appreciated her presence as we moved closer. Fear climbed up my throat even though my mind knew I was completely safe. Everything was upside down, especially when I got within earshot and heard Joey and his brother teasing each other.

"Is your girlfriend coming today?" his brother, Matty, teased.

"Shut up. She doesn't like me like that," Joey hissed.

"But you want her to," Matty said, his smile wide.

"Whatever. I don't really care."

Matty snorted. "Yeah, you do."

"Stop picking on your brother and get to work," Anna snapped at them.

"Yes, ma'am," the boys said together.

"Good morning," Amelia said, directing her greeting at Anna.

"Hey, Amelia," Anna said, sinking into a hug with her eyes closed. For just a second, she looked like she was at peace.

"I wanted to bring Trinity over to say hi," Amelia said.

Anna looked at me and froze, shame and fear on her face. She turned to her boys and reached out an arm for them to come to her.

"What do you have to say?" Anna asked Joey firmly.

Joey stepped forward and struggled to meet my gaze. When he did, he clamped down on his lip. "I'm sorry, Ms. Trinity. I'm sorry for taking your purse and getting you hurt and for scaring you. I'll never do anything like that again. To anyone."

I nodded and forced a smile. Standing in front of a teenager who was so ashamed of himself that he couldn't even look at me broke my heart. It was a time of his life when he should be kissing girls and playing sports and enjoying being a teenager. Instead, he was worrying about his brother and his mom, trying to take care of them and make sure they had food.

"Joey, what you did…I won't say it was okay, but I understand. You were willing to do anything to help the people you love, and I get that. I know asking for help isn't always easy, but sometimes it's the best answer. Now that we know each other, if you need something, ask me. I will do what I can to help you." I looked up and met Anna and Matty's gaze. "All of you."

"Thank you, Ms. Trinity," Joey said. "I don't deserve your forgiveness, but I hope one day I can earn it."

I shook my head. "You already have it, Joey. I know today is a drop in the bucket and that there are a lot of other days where you'll feel forgotten, but hopefully this starts something and helps out a little."

Anna looked like she wanted to say something but wasn't sure if it was okay. I met her gaze and smiled, hoping to encourage her.

"They're good kids. I am doing my best with them, but it's not always easy. I know I should do better, and I'm sorry you were hurt because of it," Anna finally said.

I shook my head and moved toward her. "I'm not a parent. I don't know what it's like to live in your shoes. I'm not here to judge you because that wouldn't be fair of me. We all do things we regret, and the biggest thing is learning from those actions so we don't repeat them. I think you're raising two amazing boys, and I'm happy to have met all of you."

Anna stepped forward and asked, "Can I hug you?"

I chuckled. "Of course."

She embraced me, her body shaking with her tears. "I've been so afraid you would change your mind and have him thrown in jail. I don't know how I can ever thank you enough for letting him go free."

I squeezed her tight. "No one should have to live with the

fear that they might go hungry. I know you are doing your best, and I'm not judging you. I'm saying I understand Joey, and I hate that your family, any of these families, have experienced that. I wish there was more we could do. Something beyond just today to help."

"Honestly, we are proud people. We don't accept charity easily," Anna said.

"No one does," I agreed. "But all this isn't charity. It's giving back to people who need a little help. If a friend asked you for help moving, or needed a babysitter, you wouldn't hesitate if you could do it. But we struggle to ask and accept favors from people. I'm happy Amelia convinced everyone to be open to today. I think it's going to go a long way toward connecting the people of MacKellar Cove even more."

Anna smiled. "You're a truly wonderful person. Thank you."

I smiled and squeezed her hand. "Thank you."

"And Amelia, thank you for helping make this all possible," Anna said.

Amelia shook her head. "I didn't do much besides talk to people. My son and his friends deserve most of the credit."

"They do," I agreed. "James really took this idea and ran with it. And it's amazing."

"Well, I'm going to go back and help get things started. Are you coming?" Amelia asked us.

We all nodded and walked toward the front. One weird, connected family of sorts.

I'D SEEN glimpses of James through the day but hadn't managed to have a conversation with him. I wondered if he was avoiding me. He looked busy, but was that just so he didn't have to talk to me?

I groaned at myself and grabbed a plate of food. Piper waved me over and invited me to sit with her and the people she was speaking to. She introduced them all and pointed to one of the buildings.

"The Smiths live in that building. They were telling me how much they appreciate all this," Piper said.

I smiled at them. "That's so great to hear. Hopefully this can become a more regular thing."

"We would love that. So many people here can't seem to get their heads above water. We've lived here for five years. Every time we feel like we're making some progress, things change and we're right back to where we started," Mrs. Smith said. "It's disheartening."

"Hi, everyone."

I turned to the voice and smiled at Elizabeth Joseph, the reporter.

"Elizabeth, hi. How are you? Would you like to join us?"

She nodded and took a seat. "Hi. I'm Elizabeth Joseph. I work for the Thousand Islands Times. How is everyone?"

"Good, Ms. Joseph. Thank you for being here," Piper said.

"I'm happy to be," Elizabeth said. "This event is big news. And wow, is it amazing. Just the smell of the food as I drove up made me want to come, but knowing how many people are here and how many ways there are to help the community...it's pretty great what is happening."

I nodded. "It is. I think it's been a huge success. The Smiths live in the neighborhood and were just talking about how we hope this can be something we do every few months."

"That would be great," Elizabeth said. "Do you mind if I ask you a few questions?"

"Not at all," Mrs. Smith said.

"Thank you. Were you involved in planning the event?"

Mrs. Smith shook her head.

"Did you offer to help or were you just told about the event?"

"We were told. It was supposed to be a way for people to give back, and we don't have much to give. I was saying before you walked up that we've lived here for years and every time we think we're getting ahead, something happens," Mrs. Smith said.

"To me, this event does as much to show people they aren't alone as it does to feed and entertain you for a few hours. I think it's great, and I'm so grateful to Ms. Mayer for inviting me to attend today. Do you know Ms. Mayer? Had you met before today?" Elizabeth asked.

Mrs. Smith shook her head and I waved. "She's talking about me. But no, we didn't know each other."

"Oh, I'm sorry. I assumed since you were sitting together," Elizabeth said.

I smiled. "I joined my friend, Piper, and we all started talking."

"I'm so sorry," Elizabeth said. "Maybe I should talk to some people about the event in general and we can catch up in a little while."

I nodded. "Sounds great. Thank you."

Elizabeth stood and walked into a group of people. She immediately started talking to them, laughing and smiling. I didn't have that much ease with people.

"I apologize for that," Mrs. Smith said.

I shook my head. "There's nothing to apologize for. Elizabeth contacted me a few days ago about an interview about my business. I mentioned coming out here and doing a story about the event and meeting other local business people and making a few new connections. She writes a column that highlights local business owners."

"Oh, well, Charlie owns his own business," Mrs. Smith said, patting her husband on the chest.

"Yeah? Well, we should have her interview you also. She's looking for people to speak to. I think it's a relatively new column."

Mr. Smith nodded. "That would be great. Might help business a little and get us ahead finally."

"That's what we're hoping to do here. Get people a little ahead," I said.

"I think you're going to do exactly that today. Thank you."

We finished eating and went to talk to people. I wanted to put faces to the people in town. I didn't know a lot of them, which was strange since I felt like I knew most people in town. It just proved how small I'd let my circle get.

I finally spotted James and waved to him. He was talking to someone and waved back. I wasn't going to push it and turned to find someone else to speak to when I came face-to-face with Elizabeth.

"Hi! Are you meeting a lot of people?" I asked.

"So many. This is a great opportunity for me. Thank you so much for inviting me out here."

"I'm happy you came. It's a great event. Everyone worked really hard to make it happen."

"How did you get involved in all this?"

I chuckled. "Well, a few different ways. Mostly because the man I'm seeing is one of the people who is in charge of the whole thing. He used to live here and wanted to give back to the neighborhood. His mom still lives here."

"Who is that?"

"James Rucker. He's a police officer. His mom is the director of the community center."

"Where you volunteer?"

I nodded. "Yes, but I didn't know she was the director until after I started volunteering there. And we weren't seeing each other then."

"Life in a small town, right?"

"Exactly."

"So, tell me more about your jewelry business. I see you have goodies for everyone to take home. I've been on your website and I have your new app. You seem to be a really good businesswoman. How do you make it all work? How did you make all this happen while still working?"

"I have a lot of help," I admitted.

"I thought you worked alone?"

I nodded. "I do, but this was not a solo project. Lots of people came together to make this happen. My work is my own, but this project was a group effort."

"Okay, I'm with you. Tell me what you do at the community center?"

"I love it there. I've been filming videos lately to help other people make their own jewelry, but I was told that there was nothing for kids. I've started creating videos for kids, and testing out projects at the community center so I can reach a new market. Kids are crazy creative and always want to try something different. They experiment in ways that adults don't. I give them instructions and some of them don't listen to everything and come up with their own designs for things. It's fascinating to watch them."

"Do you like working with kids or adults better?"

"Honestly, I prefer to work alone. I enjoy teaching and filming videos, but it's time consuming. Creating is an outlet for me. It allows me to express myself in ways I can't otherwise. Teaching keeps me in a box because I can't change things on the fly, and I can't just go with it. I have to stick to the script, so to speak."

"And here? Did you stick to the script here or did it all just sort of come together on the fly?"

I chuckled. "I think a little of both. James had the idea to do something and it just kept going. Food and repairs and games and prizes. Publicity to get the word out. We had people talking it up to the neighborhood so the residents would come out. The people who live here are proud and they don't like to accept charity. They want to do things on their own. To sit back and take something isn't in their nature, so we had to work on convincing some of them to attend."

"I can understand that," Elizabeth said. "I think we all have some trouble with that. Back to your jewelry…Do you come up with all your own designs?"

I bobbed my head side-to-side. "Mostly. Not all. I definitely look online for inspiration and the latest trends. I try to make all my pieces on of a kind so people know what they're getting is truly unique."

"Do you accept request? If someone sees a design but wants it in a different color, do you do that?"

"It depends on my schedule. I stock pieces at Island Designs, like you saw. That looks great on you, by the way."

"Thank you," Elizabeth said, clutching her necklace. "I get so many compliments on it."

"It suits you. And pieces like that, I try to make sure Olive has some variety in colors and styles. Making custom pieces is something I can do, but I like to let me mind wander and the pieces to come to me."

"How do you come up with ideas? Do you have a certain place you work?"

"Catherine Park is a favorite of mine. Karissa and I will go out there every so often and sit and watch the water. It's so great to be there."

"Is this your big interview?" James asked, his tone angry. "You're supposed to be talking about the event and helping promote what we're doing, but you're using it to get publicity for your own business? What the hell, Trinity?"

I looked from him to Elizabeth and back before he stormed off, leaving me wondering why he was so angry.

23

JAMES

I stalked across the complex and tried to figure out what she was trying to say. She told me she got publicity for the event, but the parts of the conversation I overheard sounded like Trinity was building up her business instead of helping the people we were there to serve.

Just like everyone else I knew, she was using the situation to her advantage. Taking what could have been great for the people we were there to see and making it something that would help her alone.

I was so angry that I just left. I knew I wouldn't be good to anyone while I was still there and so pissed off, so I got in my truck and drove away.

I slammed into my house. The door rattled against the wall before bouncing back. The blast of it shook through me.

Breath huffed out of me in angry pants. I couldn't remember the last time I felt like that. The last time I trusted someone so completely and watched as they shredded that trust.

Never again. I was done. I was done with women and trusting people and thinking anyone out there was good. I was right about her from the moment I laid eyes on her. I thought she was a criminal, and while I might have been wrong about that, she wasn't a good person.

I stalked into the kitchen and grabbed a beer. The cap twisted off too easily in my hand and half the bottle was empty before I even thought about it.

Everything reminded me of her. Everything around me felt like her. She'd infiltrated my world and made herself a part of it. She was in so deep I wasn't sure I could function without her.

But I would. We'd only been together a few weeks. I'd lived more than thirty-nine years without her. I would survive again.

I finished the beer and dropped it into the recycling, delighting in the smash of the bottle against the bottom. I grabbed another beer and let the anger and betrayal fill me before I launched it against the far wall.

The bottle exploded, beer and glass spraying all over the wall and floor. I stood there for a minute, heaving and trying to decide if I wanted to drink the other two in my fridge or smash them.

"One of each," I said to absolutely no one.

I twisted the cap off one beer and chugged it. When it was gone, a faint buzz settled into my body. I tossed the other bottle in my hand then grabbed the neck and threw it like an axe against the wall.

"That wall needed some color," I said, walking out of the kitchen. The mess would still be there tomorrow.

I went to my room and stripped off my clothes and the sheets and carried all of it to the laundry room. It all went in the washer, eliminating her scent from my home. She'd never be there again, and it was time to erase her.

Someone knocked on my door, but I ignored it. The knocking got louder, followed by the buzz of my phone.

I slammed the washer closed and started it then went to the shower. I turned the water as hot as it would go and stepped in, putting my head under the stream to drown out the sound of whoever was trying to get in touch with me.

I scrubbed my body clean and closed my eyes and groaned at the memory of Trinity using my body wash.

I shouldn't have smashed those two beers. I wondered if Hudson would deliver me a bottle of something. Anything.

I shook my head and finished my shower. I got dressed and paced my house. Whoever was trying to get in touch with me gave up, so all I heard was peace and quiet.

It was all I was going to get, and I was okay with that. I didn't need anything or anyone. Ever again.

I BARELY SLEPT that night on my crisp sheets without Trinity in my bed. I hated her for stealing so many things from me.

She called multiple times overnight and sent me messages asking to talk so she could explain. I had no idea how she was going to explain, but it didn't matter. I wasn't interested in hearing it.

Masterson was at work before I was. He raised an eyebrow when I walked in but didn't say a word. It was our last day together, and it hadn't come quickly enough for me. No partner, no girlfriend, and no place to myself. Maybe Colin would let me pitch a tent somewhere on his property and disappear for a few weeks. I had vacation time coming. It was a good time to get the fuck out of town.

Before I second guessed the choice, I sent Captain Reynolds an email asking for three weeks off, effective the following day.

"Rucker!" he shouted almost immediately. "Get your ass in here."

I locked my computer and made my way to his office, closing the door behind me and taking a seat in his guest chair.

"Three weeks?"

I nodded. "Yes, sir. I have that much time saved up, another week from the rollover, and since it's almost October, I figured I'd better use some of it."

"This have anything to do with you and your girlfriend calling it quits?"

"Does it matter?"

He held my gaze for a minute then shook his head. "Doesn't appear as though it does."

"So, can I have the time?"

He nodded. "Yep. But you need to work today. It's Masterson's last day with you."

"Yes, sir," I said, standing. "Thank you."

He nodded again. "Don't do anything stupid while you're gone."

I huffed a laugh. "No more stupid than when I'm here."

I walked out of his office and glared at my coworkers staring at me. I went back to my desk and sat down for a minute before nodding to Masterson and walking out with him.

We were on patrol again today for our last day together, but he was driving. I needed a day without having to make decisions or think, so it worked for me.

"What crawled up your ass today?" he asked as we drove through town.

"You."

He snorted. "I'm guessing that means girl trouble. Did she finally realize you're not worth the effort?"

"Fuck you," I spat.

He chuckled and I debated tasing him but figured that wasn't a great idea when he was driving. Or probably any time, but it was seriously tempting. To wipe the smug look off his face...

Maybe it was too tempting.

"I read some of the interview your girl did. She's pretty great," Masterson said.

I huffed a laugh and focused on the world outside the window. It was much more interesting than whatever Masterson wanted to say.

"She's hot, too," Masterson continued. "If you two are done, I'm thinking about asking her out. She could show me around town, or at least around her place."

I reached over and punched him in the arm. Hard. I wanted to do more than that.

The asshole laughed and pulled over. He calmly turned off the car and got out. I watched him as he walked around the front of the vehicle and stood on the sidewalk.

"You gonna take a shot at me when I can hit you back?" he asked.

He didn't have to ask me twice. I scrambled out of the car swinging, ready to bloody his nose or face or some other part of him. I didn't care as long as my fist connected with his body.

He sidestepped my first swing and caught me with a kidney punch. I reeled, the pain sharp and direct. I righted myself and faced him again. He stood there like he was waiting for someone, not a care in the damn world.

I swung again. I connected with his shoulder but he took advantage and socked me in the stomach. I doubled over, but I wasn't done. I reared back up with an uppercut that surprised him and resulted in a loud crack.

He stumbled backward, holding his mouth. But the shit-head wasn't smiling anymore, so I was happy.

He came at me, tackling me and shoving me against the side of the SUV. My head hit the doorframe and my back slammed against the handle. I fought back, shoving at him and punching his ribs as best as I could.

"What the hell are you two doing?" I heard above the roar in my ears. "Stop it, James. Knock it off!"

Her shouting broke us apart, but we still glared at each other.

"What is wrong with you two? Cops fighting on the street in the middle of town is not a good look. You both should know better."

I finally looked at her and registered that it was Blake yelling at us. Masterson pulled over in front of Cracked and she ran out to stop our fight. The windows were plastered with diners enjoying their breakfast with the show Masterson and I put on.

"Sorry, Blake," I said.

"I'm calling Trinity," she replied, pulling out her phone. "She'll talk some sense into you."

"Don't," I said firmly.

She looked at me sharply, clearly understanding my one word to mean exactly what I intended it to mean. We were done, and Trinity did not need to be involved in anything I was doing. Ever again.

I turned from Blake and got back in the SUV. Masterson followed my lead. I blocked the view of me through the window with my arm and grimaced at the pain seeping through the fog of adrenaline. Three weeks of vacation couldn't come soon enough.

Masterson drove off and we cruised around in silence. Tension radiated off him, both of us pissed off and ready to keep swinging.

"What the hell is your issue with me?" Masterson finally asked.

"I don't want a partner," I grumbled.

He laughed. "And you think I wanted to be paired with you? It's a job. You do what you're told."

"Why did you move here?" I demanded.

"I needed a change."

"Do you know anyone in the area?"

"What does that have to do with anything?" he asked.

"Why did you come here?"

"Is this about me or your girlfriend?"

"I told you I don't want to talk about her," I growled.

"Yeah, except you decided the same thing about both of us. That we aren't worth it. We don't measure up to your invisible standards of what a person should be like, so we're just cut out. What the hell is the matter with you?"

"Stay out of it. This is our last day together. After this, we won't have to worry about spending time together or getting into each other's business. Let's just get through the next few hours and go our separate ways," I said.

He shook his head and laughed.

It didn't matter. I didn't need him. Or anyone else. I was done.

WHEN MY SHIFT ENDED, I went straight home and packed a bag. I decided calling Colin was a bad idea because Elise would know where I was, and it would get back to everyone else. So I packed up my camping gear, booked a site online, and drove down to Cedar Point State Park.

I was about to turn off my phone but hesitated for a minute. I sent quick texts to my mom and Hudson that I was going to be off the grid for a few weeks and not to worry. I turned my phone off before either of them responded and left it in the glove box of my truck. I grabbed my tent and pack and set up my camp.

The peace and quiet of the woods was welcome for the first few days. No one knew where I was and I could fish and walk and not think about anything. Except I couldn't stop thinking about everything. And every time I did, I got more and more upset.

I let my guard down with Trinity, and she took advantage of that. She wormed her way into my life and made it impossible for me to go on without her.

The hardest part was I wanted her with me. I wanted her to show up and explain and say she was sorry. I wanted to see her and hold her and love her.

But I couldn't. I couldn't trust her if she was going to use an opportunity to highlight her own business. She told me she had a reporter who was interested in doing a story about the event. Someone who would really shed some light on the way people lived. Someone who could help in a way I was never helped.

No one organized an event like that when I lived there. No one tried to give back. No one cared enough about my neighborhood.

But I wasn't any better. I wanted to believe I was because I got a bunch of people together and fed the neighborhood, but I wasn't. I walked away and didn't look back until someone from there inserted themselves into my world. I separated them and told myself I was better. I refused to visit my own mother.

I was worse than everyone else because I knew what it was like to live in Oak Hill and I still pretended they didn't exist.

There was a part of me that wanted to rush back to MacKellar Cove, but nothing had changed. Not really. It didn't matter that I wasn't any better, I still couldn't trust her. And I definitely couldn't trust myself around her.

I went for a long hike and made it back to my campsite as

the sun was setting. I settled into my chair and watched as the fire I started flickered. I roasted hot dogs and opened a can of spaghetti and wished I was with Trinity.

When I was done with my dinner, I went to my truck and got my phone. I turned it on and ignored all the missed messages and searched for the article.

Local Community Comes Together

I scanned through the article, devouring everything the reporter wrote. Hudson gave me credit for the idea and wanting to get everyone together. Ramsey mentioned an underserved part of the town full of people who had great ideas but didn't have the opportunity to turn them into reality and how he wanted to help make that happen. Colin said he didn't know the neighborhood existed until the event and was looking forward to inviting people out to his farm to explore the woods and enjoy the fresh air.

And then there was Trinity. Who said none of it would have happened without my mom's support for bringing the neighborhood together and my leadership to make it happen. She gushed about how much we were giving back and how good it felt to do something. The reporter asked about her work at the community center and she said she got as much from working with the kids as they did from learning a new skill. She talked about moving to MacKellar Cove a year ago and not being sure it was the right decision for her but knowing after the event that it was a town she was proud to be a part of, and one she hoped she could help more in the future.

"Dammit," I breathed as I finished the article. Everything she said was positive and good. She made Oak Hill sound like a place she would be happy to live. She made me want to live there.

But mostly she made me wish I'd stopped instead of jumped to conclusions about her. Again.

I looked around the campsite and knew I couldn't stay there. I had to talk to Trinity. I had to apologize. I had to tell her I was wrong, again, and ask her to forgive me.

I only hoped it wasn't too late. I'd already wasted too much time being upset at her over what turned out to be nothing.

I packed up my truck and was about to drive away when I thought about calling her. I didn't like the idea of talking and driving, but I also didn't want to wait thirty minutes until I got back to MacKellar Cove.

Her phone rang and rang, but she didn't answer. I told myself she just didn't hear it and checked my messages. The first was from my mom asking what happened to me at the party and if I was okay. The next was from Trinity, crying and asking where I was. That hurt. I had one from Masterson apologizing for the fight. And the last one was from Hudson, telling me I needed to get to O'Kelley's if I still had two braincells to rub together.

24

TRINITY

I sat at a table in the corner by myself, watching the world exist around me. I didn't want to participate. Participating was what got me there. Participating was what made me think things were good. I was a fool.

It'd been almost a week since the party, and I hadn't heard from James. The rumor was he left. I didn't know where he went, but he was gone. Run out of his own town by me.

No one came out and said that last part, but the looks I got told me that's what everyone thought. It was all my fault.

So, I hid in the corner and drank. I sat there and pretended I was a part of something I no longer was because I only had one option. I had to move.

He finally did it. Officer James Rucker finally ran me out of town. And not because he was so horrible and cruel, but because he thought I was.

I still didn't know what I did that upset him so much. I tried to replay the whole thing in my mind, but I was lost. It didn't matter, though. By the time he got back to town, I was going to be gone.

Someone walked over and I hid my gaze behind my glass,

hoping they would pass by me without speaking. It had happened enough that I was sure it would again, but no such luck. Piper took the seat across from me and waited until I set my glass down.

"You can't keep doing this to yourself," Piper said firmly. "No man is worth this self destruction."

"I destroyed him. I deserve it. I never should have gotten involved with him. He's loved in this town, and I'm the pariah."

"No one thinks that," Piper said gently.

I glared at her, but she didn't flinch.

"Do you think you're going to scare me off? Because I've worked here long enough to have faced every version of terrifying. And sorry, Trinity, but you're not any of them. I called Karissa and Finley. They're on their way to get you."

"No," I said, shaking my head. I groaned. It hurt. "I wish you hadn't done that."

"Why? They're your friends, and you need friends right now."

"No, I don't. I need to enjoy my last night in town so I can hold on to memories when I'm gone."

"Last night? What are you talking about?"

"I'm talking about moving. I guess this is goodbye, Piper. It's been nice knowing you, but I'm leaving tomorrow. My bags are packed, and I'm ready to go. Like the song. Except I'm leaving in my car, not on a jet plane." I snorted at my own joke.

"You can't leave," Piper said, panic in her voice. "You can't. Why would you leave?"

"Because this is his town. He's the one who should keep it. I ran him off, but I'll be gone when he comes back so he can stay. I need to go." I got up from my seat and the room swayed. Nope, that was just me.

I stumbled to the front door and put my hand on the

frame to help me open it. The cold evening air blasted me, but the feel of it was better than everything else I was feeling.

I made my way home slowly, thankful that the sidewalk was well lit. Ha, just like me. I glanced at my car, parked in the same spot I used that first day I moved to town. How fitting that I would start and end my life in MacKellar Cove in the same place. A parked car full of my life. How sad.

The stairs were a lot harder than the sidewalk, but I knew if I didn't hurry, I would run into Karissa and Finley, so I kept moving. I made it to my floor without seeing either of them and got inside alone.

I was safe. I could hide in here and pretend I wasn't home and no one would bother me. And in the morning, I could vanish and they'd never know where I went. None of them had my mom's phone number, or knew where she and Grandma lived, so I could just go and hide and hope their lives were better without me.

No, it wasn't hope. They would be. I knew they would be. Especially James.

I flopped down on my couch and wanted to cry, but I still had a few things to pack up. I looked around my empty home and sighed. It was a fun dream for a little while.

I must have fallen asleep because I woke up to someone pounding on my door. I ignored it, pretending I wasn't home, but the person was relentless. My neighbors started shouting for the person to stop, and I knew I had to let Karissa and Finley in.

I opened the door without checking the peephole and immediately tried to close it on them. It wasn't just Karissa and Finley, but James was there, too.

"Let me in," he demanded.

"No," I shouted back, trying to close the door. His foot was in the way, but I wasn't above slamming it on him so he'd move.

"Dammit, Trinity, let me in."

I shook my head and fought back my tears. "Please just go. I'm sorry I'm not already gone. I'm leaving in the morning so you never have to see me again. I didn't know you were coming back tonight. I'm sorry, James. I'm so sorry."

All the fight faded from me, and I sank into a puddle on the floor. He pushed my door open and started barking orders to Karissa and Finley.

"Get her a washcloth. She needs water, or coffee. And unpack her damn car," he said.

I shook my head. "No, don't. Please just leave me alone. I'm going. I'm not going to force you to give up your town. This is all my fault, and I'm going to make it right for you."

"You're not going anywhere," he growled. "Not without me. If you want to leave, we'll go together, but you love it here. And I love you, so I'm not going anywhere."

I choked out a sob and laughed. "This is not a funny joke. You saying you love me. That's just cruel. I know I hurt you, but I didn't expect you to be mean. I can't drive tonight because I've been drinking, but I'll be gone in less than twelve hours. Just go away, James."

I pushed myself to my feet and walked away. My body wanted to give out, but I needed to put distance between us.

The door closed quietly behind me, and I collapsed onto the couch. Alone again. Safe.

The tears came and I couldn't stop them this time. A sob ripped from my chest and I burrowed into the side of the couch.

Then he lifted me onto his lap and held me. I fought him at first, but he wouldn't let go. He whispered, "I love you," over and over again in my ear as he held me and let me cry all over him.

As my sobs slowed and my tears dried up, James held me

tighter. He didn't stop talking to me, telling me he loved me and he was sorry. I wanted to say something, but I wasn't sure what to say.

"Are you okay?" he finally asked.

I shook my head. "I'm sorry I hurt you. I didn't mean to. And I am leaving tomorrow. I don't know why you're here, but I'm not going to force you to move away."

"Didn't you hear what I said? I love you, Trinity. That wasn't a line, and it wasn't a joke. I love you. I want to be with you. I want you in my life, forever if you're willing. You can move out of here, but if you do, you're moving in with me. You're not leaving town without me. So, wherever you want to go, I'm in. Because I. Love. You."

I shook my head again. "You were so mad at me. And you left."

He brushed the hair back from my face and took a breath. "I know. And I shouldn't have. When I overheard you and the reporter, it sounded like you were promoting your business. That you got someone to do a story about the party and then used it to your advantage to help yourself."

I shook my head but he squeezed my thigh.

"I know now that isn't what you did. I jumped to conclusions. Again. But I know you. I've seen who you are. I don't let people in. And I fell hard for you. I loved you, and it scared the hell out of me, so I saw what I wanted to see and believed what I wanted to believe."

"How do I know this isn't going to happen again? That you aren't going to push me away again because you get scared?"

He shook his head. "You don't. I don't know either. Loving you is the most frustrating, aggravating, amazing, wonderful thing that has ever happened to me. I can't imagine my life without you in it. Hudson sent me a text that I needed to get back here, and when he told me you told

Piper you're leaving town, I felt like I'd been gutted. I don't want to even think about my life without you in it, Trinity. And I know I'm going to screw up, a lot, but I want you there calling me on it."

"If this is going to work, you can't run off. I need to know what's going through your head."

"Understood," he said.

"If you need space, that's okay, but you can't disappear on me. I don't do well with that."

"I'm sorry about that."

"And if I say something that makes you mad, I need you to tell me."

"Got it," he said. Then he leaned close and kissed my neck.

"You have to be willing to talk to me instead of everyone else."

"Absolutely." He licked my throat.

"And trust me."

"Always." He nipped at my jaw.

"And love me."

"Already do." He suckled on the pulse point behind my ear.

"And let me love you."

He smiled against my skin. "I'd really like that to happen."

"I already do," I admitted.

"Thank God," he breathed. "Can I take you to bed yet? I've missed holding you."

"That's all you've missed?"

He shook his head. "I've missed everything about you. I hated myself for it when I wanted to hate you, but I love you too much to hate you."

"I guess that's good?"

He chuckled. "Just trying to do what you asked and talk to you and trust you. I love you, Trinity."

"I love you, James."

He groaned. "It took you long enough to say it."

I laughed. "I actually said it a few weeks ago, but you were asleep and didn't hear me."

He shook his head. "I missed a lot. Never again. Now it's time for bed."

I squealed when he stood and picked me up and carried me to my room. Like we were meant to be. Together.

I WOKE up the next morning with a headache and a faint memory of the night before. It all felt like a dream, but when I tried to move, a James sized lump held me in place.

I smiled against my pillow and realized if he was there, then everything else happened, too. Yelling at Piper, Karissa, and Finley. I owed all of them apologies.

James stirred behind me and pulled me closer to him. He kissed my shoulder and nuzzled against my neck. "Best way to wake up."

I held onto his hand and enjoyed the feel of his body against mine. "I was not very nice to everyone yesterday."

He took a breath and kissed my neck. "They'll understand. I wasn't either. For the last week."

"I just hope they forgive me," I said softly. If they didn't, I wasn't sure what I was going to do. My friends were amazing people, but they didn't owe me anything. Especially when I was nasty like I was.

"I'm sure they will. Let's get up and go see them so you can feel better."

I nodded, grateful that he understood how important my friendships were to me.

We showered and dressed and had breakfast. Our first

stop was to Karissa and Finley's although I was sure Finley wouldn't be there.

Karissa opened the door right after I knocked. James asked if I wanted him to go with me, but I needed to apologize on my own.

"I'm closing this door again if you're here to say goodbye. I'm not going to listen to you," Karissa said.

"I'm here to apologize."

"For what?"

"For being a bitch yesterday."

Karissa snorted and shook her head. "Oh, please. I've been much worse than that. You were drunk and hurt. But I really thought he was going to make everything better. I'm sorry, Trinity."

I shook my head and smiled. "He did, but I owed you an apology."

"Wait, you and James are good? You're not leaving and you're together?"

I nodded, unable to keep my grin from growing.

"Well, damn, you should have led with that. Tell me everything."

I told her about the talk James and I had and him staying the night. She was thrilled for me and not at all upset. It made me feel better when I walked outside and headed for Book Boyfriends Unlimited to talk to Finley.

She was behind the counter talking to a customer when I walked in. She looked over with a grin, but it faltered when she saw it was me. She was going to be a harder sell.

Once her customer was gone, I walked up to the counter. "Got anything about a woman who's a crappy friend to the people who cared about her for over a year and throws it all away over a man?"

"We're standing in a romance book store. I have a lot of those."

"How does it turn out in the end?"

"The friends forgive her, because that's what friends do, and she gets the guy, because romance is made for happy endings."

"Well, one out of two isn't bad," I said.

"Oh, Trinity, I'm sorry things with James didn't work out."

I shook my head. "No, that's the one that did. I was talking about us. I am so sorry for what I said and did last night. I wasn't being fair."

Finley laughed. "You were hurting, and you were lashing out. I've been there. It sucks to have your heart broken. But did you say things are good?"

I nodded.

"Well, damn. Good for you. I'm happy for you guys. You both deserve it."

"Thank you. You do, too."

She snorted. "I'll find my happily ever after one day."

A customer walked in, so we chatted for another minute then I went to find Piper. She wasn't at O'Kelley's, but I thanked Hudson for calling James. He was his usual gruff self and said he was happy things worked out.

I found Piper on a bench on the Riverwalk on my way home. She was staring out at the water again, looking how I felt the night before.

"Hey," I said, sitting next to her.

"Trinity. You're still here?"

I nodded. "Turns out I'll be sticking around a while. And I have you to thank for that."

She shook her head. "I didn't do anything."

"You did. You called Finley and Karissa, and you told Hudson who told James that I was leaving. I hoped he would stop me, but I never imagined he actually would."

She smiled. "I'm glad it all worked out."

"Me, too. But I'm sorry for how I treated you yesterday. You didn't deserve to be yelled at or spoken to like I did. I am sorry."

Piper chuckled. "Oh, please. That's the least of my worries. Most people are much worse when they've been drinking."

I laughed with her. "I'm sorry about that, too."

She shook her head. "It's okay. I love my job. Talking to people and seeing new people. It's the best job ever."

"Well, I'm glad I didn't run you off."

She snorted. "Not gonna happen."

"Hey, are you okay?"

She nodded. "I'm good. Just enjoying the sunshine. And you brought a little more since I know things are good with you and James now."

"Thanks."

She grinned. "Maybe one day we'll all find men like James for ourselves."

I nodded. "You will. I'm sure of it."

She chuckled. "Girls' night out Sunday? Hudson changed my schedule so I can be there if that's okay."

"Of course. That's awesome."

She nodded. "I thought the same thing. Do you think it would be okay if I brought a friend? She's great."

"Absolutely. You don't have to ask. We're not a secret club or anything."

"No, but it is at Finley's store after hours, so I wasn't sure if she was careful about who's in there. If it's not okay, I'll let my friend know."

I shook my head. "No. Finley's never said anything about that. I'm sure it's fine. We'll see you then. Both of you."

Piper nodded. "Sounds good. It's time for my shift, but I'm glad things are good with James."

I smiled. "Me, too."

I walked the rest of the way home and was surprised to find James in my condo. He left when I did and said he was going home to drop off his stuff. I didn't know he was coming back. Or how he got in.

"A little B&E from the cop?" I asked.

He shrugged. "Not exactly. I convinced Richie to let me in."

"Seriously?" I asked, a bit shocked that my landlord would open my condo for someone without my approval.

James nodded. "We're friends. And he knows you and I are in love. But he did tell me I should use my own key next time."

"He gave you a key?"

James shook his head. "No, but I'm hoping you will. I have one for you."

"This feels very domestic," I said as he wrapped his arms around me.

"It feels right," he said.

I nodded. "I never expected it, but yeah, it definitely does."

"I love you, Trinity."

"I love you, James."

EPILOGUE

PIPER

"*P*iper, come sit!" Blake shouted over the noise of the crowd.

I turned back and smiled at her. It was insane. It should have been my night off, but I felt bad leaving Hudson without the extra help. I held up a finger for Blake to wait and went in search of Hudson.

He was behind the bar like always, serving drinks as fast as he could. Tony, the other bartender, was right beside him, doing the same.

I pushed my way to the front of the line and asked, "Do you want me to help?"

Hudson looked up long enough to see who was talking to him and shook his head. "We'll be okay."

A crash behind him had us both looking to where Nikki, the new server, stood over a mess. Plates and glasses were shattered on the ground with food and drinks flowing around her feet. The tray I assume she was once holding with all the food was on top of the mess.

Hudson hung his head and groaned.

"I'll clean up," I told him. "You fire Nikki."

He nodded and turned away from the bar. By the time I made it around the end, he was leading Nikki to his office. Her lower lip was trembling. She knew what was coming.

I grabbed the tray from the top of the pile and propped it up against the cabinet. The bar mop was close, but with the shards of glass and ceramic on the floor, I knew that wasn't a good idea. I went to the back and grabbed the broom and industrial dustpan and set to work.

By the time Hudson came back, without Nikki, I had most of the mess in the trash. I'd also told Steven to put a rush on remaking the food and to let me know when it was ready and where it needed to go.

"You're a lifesaver," Hudson said as he helped me clean up the last of the mess. "You're supposed to be off tonight. What are you doing here?"

"I guess I'm part of the in crowd now." I nodded to the group of them. Hudson was friends with all of them, which was why they always drank at O'Kelley's, but my induction was new. And fragile in my mind.

"You always were," Hudson said with a strange look. "Did you think you weren't?"

I shrugged. "I don't really know most of them well."

He snorted. "You do realize that's a two way street, right? You can't get to know people if you don't try to talk to them. Open up a little."

"I'm just a private person. I talk but it's weird to talk to say too much. Making friends as an adult is not easy."

"You're friends with me," Hudson argued.

"You're like a brother. Annoying and weird."

"You clearly haven't had a conversation with any of the guys over there. That could describe all of them."

I laughed.

"Is there another reason you don't want to hang out with them? Did something happen?"

I shook my head. "No, of course not. I would have told you."

"You promise?"

I nodded. "Absolutely. I just have trouble getting to know new people, especially when they all have history."

"So bring your own armor. Invite Sofia to go with you."

I nodded. He knew me too well. "She came last weekend to girls' night."

"And?"

I huffed a sigh. "It was fine."

"Where is she tonight?"

"I don't need her to do everything with me," I said.

He gave me a look that said I was nuts. "You don't want to go over there without support, but when I ask about your support, you act like I'm being ridiculous. Just go sit down."

"But you need the help."

Hudson looked around the bar to where things had quieted down. The other servers had already delivered the food Nikki dropped, and everything else. Tony had all the drinks filled. It was almost quiet.

"Come on," Hudson said. "I'll go with you."

I laughed at him and nodded. He really was like a brother. And he knew me well.

Hudson carried a pitcher of beer to the table and set it in the center before turning a chair around and sitting in it. He nodded to the chair on the other side, between Blake and James. I smiled at him and rolled my eyes, but took the seat.

"Piper, you finally joined us!" Finley said. "We were wondering if he was ever going to let you take a break."

Hudson shook his head. "She wasn't even supposed to be working tonight. She was trying to help because I had to fire Nikki."

"Aw, sorry to hear that. She seemed nice," Trinity said. She leaned against James, his arm around her shoulders. He whispered something in her ear that had her turning her head up to smile at him.

I wanted something like that. A guy who would whisper in my ear and make me smile. Someone who would admit when he was wrong and beg me to take him back. Oh, hell, just someone who would keep me warm at night through the long MacKellar Cove winter would be nice.

"She was nice," Hudson said. "But she sucked at serving food and drinks. I hate firing people."

"Part of the job," Ramsey said.

"The worst part. But that one is a lifesaver." Hudson jerked his head toward me. "I wouldn't make half of this work if it weren't for her."

"You two should date," Finley said.

Hudson and I locked eyes and broke out laughing. "He's like a brother to me. Seriously. There have never been any moments charged with sexual tension or lingering looks. Plus, I prefer men who make me laugh. This one's too stiff."

"Some women like that," Ian teased.

I rolled my eyes. "I like that kind of stiff, but he doesn't relax."

"True," Hudson agreed. "And I'm just not ready to date anyone. This one's great, but it's like you two dating." He pointed to Finley and Ian.

The siblings scowled at each other and shuddered.

I laughed. "I think finding the right person takes a little bit of luck and the right timing. And it takes some of us longer than others to find that combination."

"And until we do, it's a lot of fun to explore the possibilities," Finley said with a smirk. "Like that guy at the table on the other side of the bar. He's seriously checking you out, Piper."

I turned to where she pointed and saw a cute guy watching me. He lifted his glass. I smiled at him. He was familiar but not someone I knew. He had definitely been in before, though.

"You should go talk to him," Trinity said. "See if the timing and luck is right."

I looked around the table at all of them watching me. "I can not go talk to him with all of you staring at me."

"Well, I need to go back to work," Hudson said and got up.

"We're not paying attention," Finley insisted. "But he's totally still watching you. Go talk to him."

I huffed and stood. He was really cute. I added a little sway to my wide hips as I walked across the bar to where he sat. He was by himself at a table for three or four, but the bar was crowded.

I smiled as I approached, and he grinned back.

"Hey," I said when I got closer.

"Hey, thank you. I wasn't sure how long your break lasted. I was hoping you would come over when you were done. I don't want to lose the table but I need a refill. Jack and Coke."

He handed me his glass, and I just stood there.

"I don't know who my server is. I think she left. Dark blonde hair, black shirt. I can't remember her name, but she hasn't been back over in a while. Can you get my drink or do I need to wait for her?"

I smiled. "I'll get it. Not a problem."

I refilled his drink and set it on the table with a loud clunk. I turned to walk away and he said, "Can I give you my order? I'm meeting someone here, and I wanted to order some food and a drink for her before she arrives."

I turned back to him and pasted on a big smile. "Actually, no. I can't take your order. I'm off tonight. Those are my friends over there, and I was trying to enjoy my night. You can flag down someone else and get your order taken, or you can go up to the bar."

"But I don't want to lose the table."

I shrugged. "Sorry, I can't help you."

I walked away with a roll of my eyes and a pissed off stomp. That was why I hadn't had a date in forever. Because I couldn't read a guy if it killed me.

"What happened?" Trinity asked when I sat back down. She looked so happy that I almost felt bad admitting it.

"He thought I was working. He wanted a refill."

"Seriously?" Finley asked. "That was some serious eye contact for a refill."

"He's meeting someone. Before I left, he wanted me to get food and a drink for her, too."

Finley burst out laughing. "You and I need to stick together, Piper. That is totally something that would happen to me. Men are stupid."

"Hey!" the guys at the table said.

"And they're only good for one thing," Karissa added.

"Hey!"

"And there are toys that help with that," Laura snickered.

"Oh, jeez."

"Stick with us, Piper. Men like that guy are so not worth it," Finley said.

"Bad luck," Laura said.

"Crappy timing," Karissa added.

"But we're good. Single isn't the end of the world. I think it's pretty damn great. And that hottie over there is calling my name," Finley said. "Don't wait up!"

She moved off her stool and walked over to the guy. I watched as she leaned into him and flirted. It wasn't long before they were walking toward the back, whether out the back of O'Kelley's or to the bathrooms, but it was clear

Finley's attempt at flirtation was a lot more successful than mine.

"Wow," I breathed.

"Yeah, Fin has no fear. Maybe you should stick with her because Laura and I are pretty much out of luck when it comes to men," Karissa said.

"I think I fit better with you two," I said. "Maybe she can teach all of us how to flirt."

Karissa laughed. "She'd make a million bucks if she taught a class on flirting."

"I'd pay it," Laura said.

I laughed with Karissa. But flirting was only half my problem. Even if I could make them interested in something other than the drinks I served, my instincts about men were worse than horrible. It was easier to just not take chances. And it hurt a lot less.

THANK **you** for reading James and Trinity's story! I always love enemies to lovers books and watching things turn around for two people who think the other character is the last one they should be with. I hope you enjoyed the ups and downs they put us, and each other, through.

The next book in the series is Piper and Gavin's book. Gavin has no intention of staying in town once his aunt's inn is ready to sell, but Piper catches his attention. She hasn't trusted her instincts since she lost her boyfriend and job at the same time. But when Gavin invites Piper to a family dinner, and tells his aunt they're dating, she goes along with it. By the end of the night, his kisses feel far too real, and Piper isn't sure what's real and what's part of the game they're playing. Pick up His Curvy Gift today!

. . .

DID you love Trinity and James? They're moving in together! Subscribers get to join in the fun! Sign up now!

JAKE WAS Alyssa's first love, first boyfriend, first everything. She promised to come back after college, marry him, and build a life together. Fifteen years after she left, she finally returns, with three failed marriages behind her and a very angry ex in front of her. But she can't leave. Not if her cousins want to inherit their family's vineyard. Read Never A Bridesmaid, Always A Bride now!

ABOUT THE AUTHOR

USA TODAY Bestselling Author Mary E Thompson spent most of her childhood wishing she had a few less curves. She hid in the pages of books because her favorite characters never cared what size her clothes were. Now, neither does Mary, and she writes stories that celebrate women like her. Real women who have curves, chase dreams, and find love, because we should all be happy, no matter our dress size.

Mary spends her non-writing time with her husband and two kids, watching too much TV, cheering for her hometown football team (Go Bills!), and hiding chocolate from her family.

Visit https://MaryEThompson.com/ to sign up for Mary's newsletter, **Romancing the Curves**. Subscribers get free ebooks and other fun stuff, like exclusive, members only content and giveaways, plus are the first to know about new releases and sales!